CW01573524

c Wask

ERICA WAGNER's books include *Gravity*, *Seizure*, *Ariel's Gift* and *Chief Engineer*, winner of the Eccles Centre and Hay Festival Writer's Award. She is the editor of *First Light*, a celebration of the work of Alan Garner. She was made a Fellow of the Royal Society of Literature in 2023 and in 2025 was awarded a Public Humanities Fellowship by the School of Advanced Study, University of London.

www.ericawagner.co.uk.

Also by Erica Wagner

NOVELS

Seizure (2007)

SHORT STORIES

Gravity (1997)

NON-FICTION

Ariel's Gift: Ted Hughes, Sylvia Plath and the Story of Birthday Letters (2000)

Chief Engineer: The Man Who Built the Brooklyn Bridge (2017)

Mary and Mr Eliot: A Sort of Love Story (2022)

AS EDITOR

First Light: A Celebration of Alan Garner (2016)

Wash

A NOVEL

ERICA WAGNER

SALT

CROMER

PUBLISHED BY SALT PUBLISHING 2026

2 4 6 8 10 9 7 5 3 1

Copyright © Erica Wagner 2026

Erica Wagner has asserted her right under the Copyright, Designs and Patents Act 1988 to be identified as the author of this work.

This book is sold subject to the condition that it shall not, by way of trade or otherwise, be lent, resold, hired out, or otherwise circulated without the publisher's prior consent in any form of binding or cover other than that in which it is published and without a similar condition including this condition being imposed on the subsequent publisher.

This book is a work of fiction. Any references to historical events, real people or real places are used fictitiously. Other names, characters, places and events are products of the author's imagination, and any resemblance to actual events or places or persons, living or dead, is entirely coincidental.

First published in Great Britain in 2026 by
Salt Publishing Ltd
12 Norwich Road, Cromer NR27 0AX United Kingdom

www.saltpublishing.com

Salt Publishing Limited Reg. No. 5293401

A CIP catalogue record for this book is available from the British Library

ISBN 978 1 78463 401 8 (Paperback edition)
ISBN 978 1 78463 402 5 (Electronic edition)

Typeset in Neacademia by Salt Publishing

Printed and bound in Great Britain by Clays Ltd, Elcograf S.p.A

MIX
Paper | Supporting responsible forestry
FSC® C018072

WAR
EWR
EAW

Washington A. Roebling

By permission, Institute Archives and Special Collections, Rensselaer Polytechnic Institute, Troy, NY

What art was there, known to love or cunning, by which one pressed through into those secret chambers? What device for becoming, like waters poured into one jar, inextricably the same, one with the object one adored? . . . How, then, she had asked herself, did one know one thing or another thing about people, sealed as they were?

—Virginia Woolf, *To the Lighthouse*

Wash

DELAWARE & RARITAN. 1850.

'I especially remember one fakir by name of G. Melksham Bourne (a bankrupt picture dealer from N.Y.) — he came with letters — lectured on Water, hygiene, Phrenology etc. and captured my father body & soul —'
—WASHINGTON A. ROEBLING

✣ ✣ ✣ ✣ ✣

TRENTON. 1849.

IT WAS JUST a week ago that Bourne's son had worked up the nerve to go outside the house. He was ten, but small for his age; he had soft little hands, and big round green eyes which seemed older than the rest of him, a shock of pale hair, ill-fitting clothes which had been well-made but for someone else, that was clear enough. When the Bournes arrived — the Professor, his wife, and Peter — Washington had been instructed to carry their boxes and bags from the cart into the house. Little Peter Bourne had stood staring, clutching his mother's hand, while Washington wrestled their things across the threshold and up the stairs, into the room he'd had to vacate for these guests. Mrs Bourne and her son had hardly emerged since, except for meals — if you could call them that — but then, that morning, Peter had sidled into the light, blinking against the sunshine, holding the gatepost as if to keep himself upright.

Swan had arrived and was unloading his tools; Washington had gone out to help him.

— Looks like we've got some assistance today, Swan had said, nodding at Peter.

— I don't know, Washington said.

— Bourne's son? Swan asked, and Washington nodded. Want to lend a hand, boy? Swan called in the easy way he had. But Peter just kept looking at the pair of them, and Swan smiled amiably. You suit yourself, lad, he said, we'll sort ourselves out here. Won't we, Wash?

— The boat we came on had apple pie for dinner, the boy said then, as if it were an answer to Swan's question. The mention of pie made Washington's mouth water.

— Did it, now? Swan said. You're a lucky fellow, then. I do like a slice of apple pie.

Peter had not spoken again, but watched as they gathered their things, and followed as they went into the house to work, his face even paler than usual, as if the air beyond the door had sucked something out of him. Swan sawed, hammered, planed; Washington's father let Swan off his work at the mill to come here to the house. The place had been half-built when the Roeblings had arrived from Pennsylvania. Swan treated Washington like his second-in-command, so that he learned the names of tools, how to let a blade bite wood, how the scent of oak differed from that of pine. Peter stared. But every day after that he had ventured outside, a little farther every day, tracing a path to the fence and just beyond it.

And now, in the afternoons, he would follow Washington if his mother sent him on an errand — to collect an order of calico, or the boxes of figs Bourne's father had ordered. He was a silent shadow; but Washington did not wish to offer him the friendship it appeared he desired. Washington did not wish to risk what the sound of laughter in the house might provoke; he did not wish to hear the boy's confession or be enticed to give his own. Sometimes the boy would ask him this or that — what kind of a tree that was, or if he knew the name of the horse that drew a cart along the road. If Washington could answer, he would, but he would not go further than that. When they walked by the canal, the boy would read out the names of the boats they passed. Hearing the names spoken in Peter's clear, high voice made Washington wonder how they had been chosen, what sort of canal-man preferred Sally to Steady, Brunswick to Betty. It had never occurred to him to consider this before, but he kept these thoughts to himself.

See how far you can throw, Washington said. Out along the canal there was a pile of broken bricks on the towpath, ruddy brown and flat yellow with sharp, crumbling edges. He supposed a load had fallen off a wagon sometime, maybe even a wagon going to the mill. He liked the feel of the bricks in his fist, and the strength in his own arm as he pulled back his shoulder to hurl a chunk out across the water, the brick hitting the surface with a hollow gulp, the splash and swallow, a quick little rill of bubbles rising up and then disappearing. Sometimes he spoke under his breath when he threw, take *that*, take *that*, but now with Peter beside him he kept quiet, just throwing as hard as he could, as far as he could.

Go on, Washington said. This was five days after Peter Bourne had first ventured beyond the door of the house. Late morning. Washington had been sent out to the mill to collect some drawings of the new machinery there; his father, closeted with Bourne, still wished to know (of course he wished to know) what progress had been made. Now the drawings, rolled carefully and tied with black ribbon, sat in the dust at the side of the path; Washington had thrown his jacket over them so no stray breeze would blow them away. Once, he had lost some drawings this way. Take *that*, take *that*, his father had said as he raised the leather strap again and again and again.

The boy bent to pick up a piece of brick; he straightened and pushed his hair out of his eyes. His pallor made him look like an elf-child from a fairy book. An underhand throw, so the brick rose up and plopped down into the shallow water at the edge of the canal.

— You can do better than that, Washington said. Can't you?

— I don't know, the boy said. He turned his eyes to

Washington, his brows drawn together. Washington almost felt sorry for him, but scorn rose up over sorry and pushed it aside. Since Professor Bourne's arrival, Washington had never not been hungry. The emptiness in his stomach made for anger an easy home.

— Look, Washington said. Like this. He picked up another piece of brick and jammed it into the boy's palm, hard against the flesh, and then closed his own fist around it, swivelling to stand behind Peter and pull the boy's arm back with his own. Close to Peter like this he could smell him, the sourness of sweat and something sweet too, maybe from the neckerchief he wore, scented by his mother, a woman nearly as invisible as her son. A tickle of Peter's hair in his nose. Hauled his arm back so the boy gasped and then their two arms together flew out forward and released the brick so it landed out in the canal with a satisfying splash. Washington thought he'd hurt Peter's arm, but Peter was smiling, seeing how far the brick had gone, the ripple he'd made on the dark slick of water.

— Lookit that, the boy said. I can throw. Thanks, he said.

Washington had not been after thanks. He kicked at the pile of bricks and said nothing. Then he picked up another and took five or six steps back onto the green grass behind the towpath, almost as far as the old elm tree that marked the halfway point between home and the mill. He ran at the water, his arm drawn back, stopping short just at the very edge of the canal, the momentum of his run propelling the brick almost as far as the other shore, so the splash wet the bow of a shuttered barge docked there. Washington wiped his palms down his trouser legs, leaving streaks of red brick dust.

— Go on, he said to Peter. You try.

The boy seemed bolder now, walking quickly to the heap of broken bricks, choosing one that fit neatly in his hand. He marched right to the elm, its shadow darkening his face and hair, and then ran at the water, his feet in their city shoes kicking up puffs of dust. But at the edge of the canal he skidded, his foot slipping out beyond the path, and the brick went flying back towards the tree as he windmilled his arms, trying to keep his balance, his body pitched out over the water. Washington rushed forward, grabbed him by his wrist, yanked him back onto the path. They stood there for a moment, the sun on their heads, breathing hard, looking at each other. Washington thought Peter would be frightened, but his cheeks were pink and his eyes were shining.

— Better do it again, he said.

— Not now, Washington said. Time to get back. Father wants these things. He picked up his jacket and the drawings from the ground.

— What happens when you get all those bricks in the water? The boy said.

— Guess you get a dam in the canal.

— Really? The boy's eyes wide.

— Course not, ninny, Washington said. Can't just throw bricks in the water to get a dam.

— Oh, said the boy. How do you get a dam?

— Let's go, Washington said. Better hurry. Come on.

— *Wo ist Peter?* his mother asked, drying her hands on her apron. In the blue light of the room, her face was shadowed. The lamps had not yet been lit, and would not be until darkness crept right over the windowsills. His father measured the level of the oil in the lamps week to week; if too much oil was used, he would not pay for more, and then the darkness would be everywhere. Washington was laying the table, setting a spoon beside each bowl. Nothing else was needed now, neither forks nor knives, and so he left them nested in the drawer by the kitchen. He shrugged in answer to his mother's question, looked away, but she did not see, or acted as if she did not. She asked again.

— *Wo ist Peter?*

I don't know, he said in English, and now he met her eyes. Even this she did not understand. He would do this sometimes, push against her, her simplicity, her openness, because he knew he could, that there would be no price to pay. She shook her head, smiled, lifted her brow and her chin and he relented, repeating himself for her.

— *Das weiß ich nicht,* he said. *Ich dachte er ist bei seinem Vater.*

He had assumed the Bourne boy was with his father, upstairs. He was often up there, closed in the room his own father had given over to these visitors. Washington hadn't noticed the boy's absence; Bourne was a blusterer, but his wife and their boy were nearly silent, clinging to the edges of the rooms. Mrs Bourne was already seated at the table, her hands in her lap, her eyes on the china plate his mother had set before her. Washington couldn't decide whether she was too proud to help, or too afraid, but he suspected it was the latter.

His mother shook her head again and pointed upstairs — the room above was his father's study.

Professor Bourne and Papa are together, she said. They have been talking all afternoon. Yes, they had, he realized, and now he could hear it, the susurration of their voices on the other side of the wooden ceiling. Well, his mother said, call your sisters, tell them to bring the baby in.

The girls were outside, holding Charles's little hands and showing him how to walk on the patchy grass. Come on, he called, leaning out into the twilight, Mother says you are to come in now. As soon as he put his head out the door Elvira ran to him, throwing her weight against his leg and wrapping her arms around his waist. Yes, he said, that means you too, little Vi, we all have to suffer together.

— Suffer? she said, her blue eyes bright. She had never heard the word, he supposed, which amazed him. He reached down and lifted her up so he could hold her on his hip. She laughed, although he knew she didn't understand him at all, but she loved him, and that was enough. He carried her into the house.

— Sit, sit! his mother said, shooing her hands at her children, lifting Charles from Laura's arms, and setting him in the little pen, like a pen for an animal, Washington always thought, that Swan had built beside the kitchen. It had thick wooden slats and a rail too big for the child to see over, even when he pulled himself to stand. They all scrambled to find their places, Washington next to the empty seat at the head of the table, and opposite him another empty chair awaiting the presence of the Professor.

And now here he was, the Professor, his forceful tread on the stair, father following behind. Bourne was a tall, broad-shouldered man, taller than John Roebling, and the broad beard he wore over his chest made him seem even bigger. His father seemed narrow in comparison, almost slender. The Professor's hair was swept back from his forehead, dark with a silver streak that echoed the zealous gleam in his eye.

— Now then, now then! he boomed, clapping his hands together and rubbing them briskly. All gathered for another healthful repast! A healthful family is a happy family, that is my motto! Healthy, happy! Healthy, happy!

His gaze swerved around the room, resting on each of them in turn, though his own wife, Washington noted, still did not raise her eyes from the table, and his mother smiled anxiously when it was her turn. Washington sat as still as he might while the great man peered at him; the Professor liked to call him *a fine boy*, although he had not sought the Professor's high opinion. Behind the Professor his father moved quietly through the room, lighting the lamps, his own gaze unreadable. He settled himself at the head of the table, the Professor beside him. In front of his father was a burlap sack, the kind you might find in a barn, filled with animal fodder; next to it a covered dish from which no heat emanated. The autumn was coming, the nights drawing in, though it was not yet fully dark.

— Professor Bourne, said his father, will you do us the honor of serving tonight?

His father said this every night, as if he had never said it before; every night for the past week and more, since the Professor's arrival.

— Why thank you, Herr Roebling, I would be delighted, the Professor said.

He pronounced the title with a trilling *rrr*, though Washington knew that his father wanted nothing more than for the world to think him an American born and bred. Sometimes still he would overhear his father, when he thought he was alone, saying over and over the English words he found difficult, even his son's own name, *Washington, Washington*, the sound of it like a hiss, and Washington's blood would chill until he realized what his father was doing, that his presence was not required.

But his father did not correct the Professor. He did not say, *I am Mister Roebling to you.* He did not shout at the Professor, or pound his fist, or strike him, or sweep the crockery and cutlery off the table so his mother would have to scrabble on the floor to catch the broken shards. He did not do any of those things. He merely nodded and watched as the Professor reached for each of their plates in turn.

From the sack the Professor spooned a pile of sawdust, or that's what it looked like. Carefully he measured three spoonsful onto each plate; he then moistened the pile with a splash of water from a jug, placed by his elbow for the purpose. He uncovered the platter which Washington's mother had placed in the centre of the table; before the Professor's arrival, it might have held thin slices of the ham she cured, sweet and salty with a neat oily rime of fat around each leaf of the meat. There was never much of that ham — another effect of his father's stern economy — but Washington's mouth watered at the memory of it. Now the platter held a scattering of figs, brown as dead leaves, but for some, inadequately dried, which had gone green at their stems, the mold appearing to emit a kind of glow in the lamplight. On each plate passed to him the Professor deposited two figs, one on either side of the heap of wet brown dust.

He clapped his hands again, rubbed the palms together once more. Washington avoided looking at his father, settled at the table's head; he glanced at Elvira, next to him. The little girl was staring at the Professor, her mouth wide open; Washington knocked his knee against hers, blinked, and her lips smacked shut. All the children were accustomed to speaking without words. It was much the safest way.

— Peter? boomed Professor Bourne. Mrs Bourne kept her gaze resolutely on the table.

— Molly, said the Professor. Where's our fine boy?

Mrs Bourne — Molly, Washington thought to himself, for he had never heard her given name till now — shook her head, the gesture almost imperceptible.

From the corner of his eye, Washington could see his father lift the gold watch from the pocket in his waistcoat and glance down briefly at its face. His brows knit together for an instant; his mouth was pressed into a thin line.

Now the Professor smiled at Washington — or at least, his lips were turned in a smile, and the skin at the corners of his eyes fanned into little lines, but his regard was cold. Master Roebling, Bourne said. I thought you boys were at your studies.

— No, sir, Washington said.

Bourne still stared at him. He expected more of an answer, clearly.

— I thought he was with you, sir, he said. You and Father.

He saw his father's right hand twitch. It had been flat on the table; now it closed briefly into a fist, or nearly; his left hand, the damaged fingers curled into the palm, remained still. Washington recalled a snake he had once seen in the woods out beyond the edge of town, back home, as he still thought of Saxonburg; a great black rope of a thing, dark as pitch, lying in the litter beneath the trees, its tapering tail flicking, once, twice, before it was still again, waiting.

— Professor Bourne and I were correcting his manuscript, his father said, finally. His new text. "The Path to Health is the Path of the Spirit", it will be called. Professor Bourne and I were at work. You were told to watch the boy.

You were told to watch the boy. Washington felt the floor rock a little under his feet at the certainty of the pronouncement. There had been no such request. Next week he would be enrolled at the Trenton Academy, but for the last two weeks he had been allowed to help his mother with the new house, to hammer nails and saw wood with Swan, who would come by in the morning before heading for the mill. Swan would ask his mother where she would like a new shelf, or at what angle a draining rack for the dishes should go, and with the two of them to help her, Washington would see her spirit lighten. Thinking of this he felt ashamed at the way he had spoken to her not a quarter hour before, as if she were a lesser creature than he. Now she, like Mrs Bourne, sat very still, but her glance moved between Washington and her husband, first one, then the other, back again.

His father had not mentioned the boy to him. Peter. Washington opened his mouth. He shut it again, before the truth could betray him.

— Bring him to the table, his father said. Go and get him.

It was nearly dark when he reached the canal. The sun sinking below the horizon, and the moon rising, gibbous, not as clear as it had been back in Pennsylvania, where the only light came from the few lamps of their neighbors' houses, and just yards beyond Main Street the land remained as it had been for centuries, for millennia before, home only to wolves and bears and the red men whose land this had once been. *Wilden*, some of the neighbors called them, savages. His father never said that word, and shook his head when he heard others speak so, but Washington was too afraid to ask him what they meant, or why his father disagreed.

Here in Trenton there was plenty of light. Not only from the clean slip of the moon but from furnaces, forges, fine houses and well-lit theatres, the engines of coal-barges as they pushed through the slick water. It was never dark here, someone was always awake, a restless energy that made it hard for Washington to sleep, as if the city shook him by the shoulder or whispered in his ear, all the hours of the days and nights. He had learned that the sound he had at first thought to be a giant, snorting horse was really a passing train; a howling, high shriek like the wire mill's new steam whistle. By now, at least, he could walk outside without starting at nearly every sound, and so tonight he paced along the edge of the canal, peering at its gleaming, translucent surface.

Now the evening star was shining, bright beyond the halo of the moon. The sky was purpling, thickening, and Washington wished he taken his coat from its hook. Peter! he called. He stood straight, put his hands around his mouth. Peter! His voice rang in his head before vanishing into the trees. He listened for an answer but nothing came; there was only the lapping of water against the lip of the canal. On the other side, a boat was moored, but its windows were black and it was silent and still, a block of darkness against the city's glimmering light.

Years later he would recall the opalescent sheen of the water and below that something like quartz or moonstone, shining, he would have said, down below. It was only when he saw the boy's white hair, drifting like pondweed, that he understood what he saw.

He drew off his boots as quickly as he could, his fingers fighting the tight knots he had laced that morning, and threw off his loose, long-sleeved shirt. When he hit the water the cold made his chest contract, but he forced himself to draw the deepest lungful of air he could, pulling the chill dusk right down inside himself before diving to the canal's bed where Peter's body lay. It was hardly six feet, maybe just a little more, to the bottom — but of course he'd never thought to ask, no one had, whether the boy could swim.

He was spread-eagled down there, his arms and legs stretched out from his body; his collar floating loose and the white skin of his throat perfectly still, his green eyes open as if in surprise. Washington kept his own eyes open, wanting as much light as he could get as he fought to put his arms round the boy's shoulders, to pull him out of the mud and filth that lay beneath him, soft and thick against Washington's hands. But when he tried to pull Peter up to the surface, the boy's body stuck fast, and Washington gasped, or tried to, the awful green water filling his mouth and nose and making him kick up to the surface, gagging and choking, gasping for air.

Another breath, down again, prepared this time, grabbing one of Peter's arms in both his hands, gripping tightly just below the shoulder, soaked wool against his palms while he kicked as hard as he could, seeking some resistance against the water, which grew colder and colder by the minute. His chest burned as he held his breath. He thought he felt some movement but had to let go, breaking the surface once again, the air in his mouth the finest thing he'd ever tasted.

On his third descent the black silt released Peter's body. It took hours, or so it felt, to pull it to the surface, the dead weight uncooperative, resistant. He had to paddle through the water, gripping the boy's body by the wrist so it dragged below him, a sucking anchor.

He hardly knew how he got out of the canal. He cracked his chin on the stone edge of the path with the effort, and on his tongue foul water mingled with his own blood.

He laid Peter out on the towpath by the side of the canal and began to shiver uncontrollably. Shoeless, shirtless, his teeth knocked together as if his jaws were controlled by some distant puppeteer, the strings pulling his limbs as he juddered and shook. He gathered his discarded shirt, yanking it over his head, the white cloth a shroud clamped over his nose and mouth until he could pull his face through. He crushed his heels down into the soles of his boots, the dank water squelching out through the leather. His fingers were too weak now to do up his bootlaces at all.

And then he almost spoke to the boy on the ground beside him. Come on, let's go, hurry up, we're already late for supper, it's dark, we must go home. Through the clear, still air, the moon threw silver light all around; Peter's skin glowed with it, and his eyes stared upwards, fixed on the stars. The hazy band of the Milky Way was stretched across the sky, a path to follow out into the dark.

But Peter was gone. When Washington leaned over him, his knees unsteady, he could see that: a hollowness, an absence. Suddenly the bile rose in his throat and he nearly vomited all over the boy, only turning away so that his spew of swallowed canal water spattered on the grass instead. Briefly he was grateful that his stomach had been otherwise empty. He wiped his mouth with the back of his cold hand.

Well — he must get Peter home. He had no recollection of

how far he had come from the house or how long it had taken him to get there. At least it would be easier to carry the boy on dry ground than it had been to haul him from the depths. But for several minutes he struggled to find a way to take Peter's body into his arms. He was used to carrying his sisters, his baby brother; he had never bothered to consider that even when they struggled, or pretended to struggle, their living, breathing bodies worked with his own to make the effort mutual. Washington tried to think of all the work he'd done, the loads he'd carried, back in Pennsylvania, on the journey to this new place, even sometimes at the mill: furniture, bundles of clothes, raw wood, brick and stone. His father's leather valises piled in his arms, so high he could barely see over. Now he turned his face away to avoid the glassy blanks of Peter's eyes as he wrestled him up off the ground, staggering along the path, one arm grasping the boy's knees, the other his shoulders, freezing water running off both of them and soaking back into the earth. Water and mucus leaked from Peter's body, from his mouth and his nose, from the sockets of his eyes, the curled white shells of his ears. Warm at first, from what had once been Peter's living heat, cooler and cooler as time passed, as the darkness drew down around them.

Twice he had to lay Peter down on the ground so he could rest; the task of raising him up growing harder each time, until finally he was frightened that if he set him down once more he would not have the strength to lift him. By now, Washington was weeping; he was not aware that he wept, and would not remember his tears.

The lit windows of his father's house. The fence, the garden, the wooden door. Through the glass, as he approached, he saw his father and Bourne, their mouths moving, crumbs on Bourne's black beard, his father's back straight as an iron bar. Mrs Bourne's face, nearly as white and still as her son's. None of them knowing anything, this moment open and whole. He shifted the boy's weight in his arms so he could raise his hand to knock.

97 FERRY STREET

'I did not have proper food to keep up my nervous strength, and nobody cared for me — The work never stopped day and night —'

—WASHINGTON A. ROEBLING

✣ ✣ ✣ ✣ ✣

TROY. 1856.

PAST MIDNIGHT AGAIN, well past. He didn't know by how much, only that his candle was low, the wax puddling on the rough wood of his table, the wick guttering, throwing shadows on the wall, catching the frost on the window-glass as delicate feathers of light. The blankets from his bed bundled over his shoulders, he was almost tempted to warm his hands on the little candle-flame, like that poor clerk in the story by Mr Dickens —

When he blew on his hands he could see his breath. Last week's lecture, or one of them: *Reflections sur la puissance motrice du feu.* Carnot, a Frenchman, who had died not of cold but the cholera. The notes somewhere in a stack of papers by the dark iron grate, its mouth full of ash.

When he closed his eyes he could feel the room's dank chill against his eyelids.

Then there was a sound like rain against the window, though the night was brilliantly clear; when he had walked home in the dark from the Institute the Milky Way had swept a clear path across the sky.

Patter patter, patter patter. Silence, and then the skittering — pebbles, or sand. He rose from his chair, his legs stiff, and yanked open the sash; it was hardly colder outdoors than it was in this box-like room. Leaning out of the window, the night gripping his neck, he looked down, and took a moment to recognize the face tipped up at him.

— Andermann! What are you — ?

— Let me up, Andermann said, throwing a rough whisper towards the window. It's freezing down here!

— It's not much better up here, Wash said, but you had better —

Into the hallway and onto the landing, he crept down the uneven staircase as quick as he might, remembering to keep his hand off the banister, for it was cracked and splintering. The boards squealed at his every step, and he imagined his landlady, Mrs Beabout, her protuberant eyes snapping open at the sound. He had no wish to see her in her nightdress, nor any wish to be ejected from this place, bare and cold as it was. It had been hard enough to find somewhere to live on the meagre sum his father allowed.

Andermann's face was pale and bright in the brittle starlight. He had a good coat, buttoned up tight to his neck, sturdy boots with thick soles, leather gloves. A little knife of envy cut through Wash's alarm. But then the young man smiled, and he discovered how glad he was to find Andermann on his doorstep, even at this hour, even if Andermann was practically a stranger.

— Come on, come on, he whispered, and pulled Andermann over the threshold by his fine sleeve. Andermann had parcels in his arms, wrapped in paper, tied with twine. Here, Wash said, let me help you.

— No, replied Andermann, hugging the parcels close to his chest, speaking in the kind of whisper some boastful actor might use on stage to convey secrecy. A sound loud enough to wake the whole house; Washington barely resisted putting his hand over Anderman's mouth.

— Up you come then, quickly, Wash hissed. Quickly. You shouldn't be here. I should be asleep.

— But I knew you would not be, Andermann said, close to Wash's ear. He walked right behind as they moved up the stairs. A faint scent of alcohol on his breath, although he did not seem to be drunk. Wash could hear now that Andermann retained a little of the accent of his native Bavaria — he had been born there, it was said — or, at least, he clipped the ends of his words with the care of one who is still aware of making new sounds. His father was a metallurgist who had done well for himself, just as Wash's own father had.

— Ach, Andermann said when the door of Wash's room was closed behind them. Look at this. This will not do at all.

He set the parcels down on the narrow bed and put his hands on his hips, his dark eyes catching the candlelight, the expression on his face — it seemed to Wash, in the near-dark — caught between amusement and despair.

— You will fall ill if you live like this, Andermann said plainly. I do not wish for you to fall ill, so I cannot permit you to live like this.

The young man began to peel off his leather gloves and Wash felt the blood rise into his cheeks as he looked at his own poor quarters: the pinched, ill-sprung cot, the rough table, the cracked window-glass. Papers piled and strewn, no coat hanging on the door for Wash wore it, even to sleep, its elbows shining with wear. A trunk with a broken clasp, the leather stamped with the initials *J.A.R.*

— This will not do at all, Andermann said. And so this, this we will open first.

With bare hands he went for the string on one of the parcels he had carried for more than a mile and a half's walk from his own lodging. Quickly he undid the knot, allowing the brown paper to fall open. A squat, broad-shouldered bottle of brandy, its cream-coloured label printed in curlicues of black and red.

— Andermann, Wash said, you —

— must have a drink, yes! Andermann laughed. As must you, my dear Roebling. Just to warm us a little.

The bottle was sealed with wax. Andermann twisted the cork until the wax snapped, scattering fragments around their feet.

— *Prost!* Andermann said, putting the bottle to his lips. Hah! he exhaled, when the liquid had gone down his throat. Your turn.

Washington took the bottle from Andermann's hand, put his own mouth against its neck. He was not much used to drink, and the brandy tasted of fire, little else, and made him cough — but the illusion of warmth spread down his chest marvellously. He went to pass the bottle back to Andermann, but his friend refused it.

— No, he said. Look. There are further developments here.

Another parcel, the biggest one. Andermann bent to lift it onto the floor before attacking the knot, and when he had unloosed it sticks of kindling and split logs rolled towards the grate, scattering splinters over the floor.

— Andermann, Andermann — Washington tried again to speak. You must not —

But Andermann ignored him. I am sure you have a lucifer somewhere. Shall we get this fire going again?

— Andermann, Washington insisted. I cannot allow you to —

— stop you from freezing to death? I think I would be a very poor friend to you if I permitted such an unfortunate eventuality. We are scientists, man, not poets: no need for us to expire in a lonely garret! Go on: light the fire.

The grate was cold. He had an allowance for fuel each week and had calculated how much he could spend; he had made a table in the back of a notebook for food, candles, wood. It was not much. Most of the time he was able to discipline himself, not go beyond what was permitted, which meant no fires in the morning, ever. But the last two mornings there had been ice, not frost, on the inside of the window, and so, having woken before dawn with his face a frozen mask and his hands stiff and purple, he had knelt, shivering, and built a fire to warm the room just a little, a little, before he had to wash and dress and walk through the frigid muddy streets to lectures. But the price to pay was no heat for the evening's work, nothing until he crawled back between the coarse sheets and rough blankets of his bed.

Scraps of paper, kindling, logs. Little flames leapt up and licked against the iron and brick, the draughty chimney bringing quick life to the fire. He reached his hands out towards the warmth, and there was Andermann's hand on his shoulder, his friend crouching beside him, face lit ruddy by the flames.

— Better already, Andermann said. Now, look what else we have.

There were thick slices of a white loaf, spread with sweet butter and stuffed with salty, juicy ham. There were bright red apples, and there was a small, round, dense-looking cake.

— There are raisins in the cake, Andermann said. And figs. Our cook makes them — she sends one a week! I can hardly eat it all myself. And in any case, supper is always better shared, don't you think?

Washington felt as if he had been struck dumb. He nodded, and simply watched as Andermann — still in his coat, for in truth the fire had not yet had much effect — went to the rickety table and began, with care, to transfer Wash's lecture notes and books to the foot of the bed. The food he shifted to the table, using the brown paper as a cloth, and then tugged the whole set-up closer to the fire.

— Only one chair? Andermann asked. Roebling, you really must learn to conduct yourself as a host! This will not do! Grinning broadly as he said it.

— There is one in the hall, by the stair, I think, Washington said, finding his voice. A half-broken chair with a frayed cane seat, which he supposed no one could be bothered to discard. The back had been cracked off at the top, leaving the dowels to splay like fingers. He opened the door and yanked it in quickly.

Well, said Andermann, it has a seat at least. Come, come — and he pulled his watch from his waistcoat pocket so the chain glittered in the firelight. One o'clock, he said. This is when gentlemen take a light supper after a night at the gaming tables. What young blades we are, Roebling, hey?

He shrugged off his coat and threw it down on the bed, beside Washington's papers and books; his white sleeves billowed free, buttoned tight around his strong wrists.

— Roebling, he said. Go on then. Sit.

He put his hand again on Washington's shoulder; despite the bitter cold, despite the walk he'd had from his lodgings, Andermann's palm was warm, and he let it rest there, perhaps for five seconds, the space of two breaths, in and then out — before pressing down, so Washington buckled down into the chair, like a marionette whose strings had been cut. Only now did Washington allow himself to laugh, his astonishment set free.

— Food? asked Anderman.

— O yes —

Wash's hands were grimy, marking the soft white bread as he bit and swallowed. He hardly knew how hungry he was until he began to eat. There was a slick of mustard on the meat, its heat flaring up his nose, vivid as the brandy. He could have eaten the whole thing in three bites but forced himself to slow down: to prolong the pleasure, but also, yes, so as not to embarrass himself in front of Andermann; to show himself a kind of greedy animal, wolfing his food.

Andermann was not eating, he was watching; his own food on his lap, resting on a piece of the brown paper wrapping.

In Washington's lap now there were crumbs, nothing else.

Andermann held out his own sandwich to Washington. Here, he said. Go on.

— Oh no, I couldn't. Really, Andermann. It's just that — well, I hadn't eaten in a little while. Not since — breakfast.

The morning seemed years ago. Washington had no idea whether he'd eaten any breakfast at all. Most probably he had not.

Andermann picked up the brandy bottle and took a swig before passing it to Washington who did the same — now as if it were something he did every night, drink brandy by a cheerful fire. The alcohol's warmth moved up the back of his neck and around his ears. The fire had taken now, too, and was licking up towards the chimney, damp wood crackling cheerfully.

— What a mysterious fellow you are, Roebling, Andermann said.

Washington had no idea what this meant. He could not think of anything else to do but say so.

— Mystery. I do not think that has anything to do with me, Andermann. Truly, you are mistaken.

— First, Andermann replied, shall we dispense with formalities? Please, you must call me Max. Maximilian, that's the whole show, but it's rather excessive, I think.

— As is Washington, then. Indeed. Wash will do for me.

Andermann — Max — put out his hand. I'm delighted to *meet* you, my dear Wash, he grinned.

Washington took Max's hand, and they shook, and agreed they should have another toast in honor of this more intimate acquaintance. Although it was the middle of the night, Washington felt the exhaustion that oppressed him day and night flow out of him like water draining from a sink; the food, the warmth, the drink worked an astonishing transformation. And the company of Andermann, to whom he'd barely spoken until now, even after all this while in Troy. But he always had a ready smile, Washington had observed that, and a confidence in himself that he envied. Sometimes they sat next to each other in the interminable lectures to which they were subjected, day after day here at Rensselaer; Washington had noticed that often Andermann would put his pen down, not take notes at all, and catching Washington's look would roll his eyes as if to say, *This is the most arrant nonsense, is it not?*

— How did you know where I live? Wash asked. If they were friends now, he might speak plain.

— I saw you walk home one night, Max said. I followed you, that's the truth. I saw you headed out this way and I —

— You — what?

— If we are being frank, Wash, I thought you must be on some dastardly errand to come this way. Perhaps he is meeting a woman of the town! I said to myself. What could bring him out in this direction? I wondered who she might be, what raffish escapade you had planned. Under that stern exterior there yet beats a hot heart, I thought! And then I saw — well, I saw that these were your lodgings.

Washington felt the heat rise in his face; it was shame now, not brandy, that brought it there.

— Yes, he said rather stiffly. As you see. Well. I am grateful to you, Andermann. Max.

— O, now! This is no good, this is no good! Andermann exclaimed. He reached out to clasp both Washington's hands in his. He was taller than Washington by an inch or so, broader, never mind better fed and altogether more glossy. As Max held on tight, Wash felt he was in close proximity to a Macassar-scented bear.

— I did not mean to cause you embarrassment, Max said. It was quite wrong of me. I am always endeavouring to be a humorous fellow, you know; my father says this will be my undoing! But the truth is, dear Wash, I was startled to see where you lived — and it made me consider that I have often thought you looked, let us say, a little undernourished. I remark upon these things because I have a feeling in my breast — a deep feeling, a true feeling — that we will be friends, real friends, and friends must speak honestly to each other, must they not?

— Yes, Wash said, as best he could. There was something stuck in his throat, or so it seemed. And you are a humorous fellow, Andermann. Max. And I am glad of this visit, this — feast. I should never have expected such a thing. *Danke.*

Du bist willkommen — although we are Americans, Washington, and must speak as such. You with such a name, too! But forgive me, I cannot help myself — you must not fly into a rage and throw me from your quarters — your father... I know who your father is, so. We all do.

— Yes. You all do.

— He is —

— He is?

A spark of something in his chest. He looked away from Andermann, who had begun what he wished Washington to finish. Into Washington's mind came unbidden — no, set there by his classmate, sitting in fine clothes by the fire he had made — the image of his father, pressing coins, not very many of them, into his hand at the Troy depot, nearly shouting over the hiss and roar of the trains as they shunted along the tracks, the two of them standing still as a soot-smudged river of men, women, pinched-looking children, flowed around them. You will make your way now, Washington, his father had said. You are a Roebling. You will rise to that now, do you understand, boy?

And then a memory of home, of his mother, white-faced, the sweat-stains under her arms, the blue beneath her eyes, standing by the pony and trap. That *woman*, his father's woman, twisting her handkerchief as she stood apart from them all, waiting for John Roebling to whisper in her ear.

— He is *who he is*, Andermann said when he could stand the silence no longer. Washington would not give him the gift of breaking that silence, whatever gifts he had himself been given tonight. Niagara, Andermann said. The wire business.

— I think you mean to say that you believe my father to be a wealthy man, Andermann.

— O now. Now you *will* throw me out on my ear. I fear truly that you will.

Andermann's voice trembled and his eyes shone. He was afraid. In that moment, Washington saw that. His father was the man who did not forgive. *You are a Roebling.* But he, Washington, would not be that man.

— No, Andermann. Max. I will not. I am sorry. Sorry to speak coldly to you. Perhaps it is the chill of my surroundings which brings it on. Though you have begun to warm them — he hesitated — with this fire, I mean.

He tried a smile, and Andermann, Max, returned it.

— What can I tell you, friend? My father is indeed a wealthy man. He is indeed the man who bridged Niagara, and much else besides; the very chasms tremble at his approach! As you say, everyone knows. He wears a fine coat, as you do, and a silk hat, and if he were to choose to smoke a cigar or take a drink of brandy he would smoke and drink only the very best. Yet here I am, in this place, as you see. I am to shift for myself, more or less. It will make a man of me, my father says.

Andermann gazed at him a little while after he spoke; in the distance, a dog barked, and a cart ran over a cobbled street, the noise carrying easily in the still air. Then he turned his face to the fire, so that his pale smooth cheeks glowed and his eyes became shadowed pits in their sockets.

— I was six when we came to this country, Andermann said at last. It's strange how sometimes you don't know how much you actually recall, and how much you recall what others have said, the stories repeated over and again, like an old legend. I *think* I remember the journey to Le Havre, days in a jolting cart and my own complaints, my mother's lap not making the miles any more comfortable. Twisting in her arms and crying, and wanting to get away. And then she died on the ship. Just like that.

— I'm sorry, Washington said again, because it was the only thing to say.

— It was many years ago, now. What did she look like? I don't know, anymore. My father says that my hair waves as hers did, although it is dark like his; that is not much to go on, however. He turned to Washington and smiled. Look, he said. I am trying to make you pity me. How reprehensible.

— No it isn't. Reprehensible, I mean. I don't pity you, Max. I don't think you want me to, not really. But it's too bad you don't have a mother. Mine is kind to me, when she is allowed to be.

— My father is kind, Max said. I think he has always been afraid he might lose me, too. I tell him I am strong enough! But he does not believe me. He knows me better than I would like to think, perhaps. But your father is a tough old goat, hey?

— That hardly begins to cover it, Wash said.

— But I can help you, Andermann said. There was a peculiar urgency in his tone. He reached out, briefly, as if he would take Washington's hands again, but then he held back, and let his own hands drop into his lap, where they lay as if they did not belong to him. I have so much, he went on. I am fortunate. I can share with you. I can — look after you.

No one had ever said these words to Washington in his life. It was almost as if they were in another language. Of course, his mother — when she could — her arms around him and her chin on top of his head — but nothing between them was spoken. How could anything be spoken between them, in that house?

— I do not want charity, Max. His voice was rougher than he meant it to be.

— It is not charity, Andermann said, shaking his head. Charity! How can there be charity between friends, true friends? *Charity* is for widows and orphans — of course, I am glad the widows and orphans should have it, but I don't speak of charity. I do not even speak of gifts. I speak of — the companionate division of amity, Roebling. Wash, as you said I might call you. You would do the very same for me, I know, were our positions reversed. It is not even something to consider — charity, or a debt of any kind.

— 'The companionate division of amity'! That is quite a mouthful, Max.

— As soon as we arrived in America — as soon as he could afford it — my father bought a copy of Mr Webster's dictionary. Two volumes. We would sit by the fire and read aloud to each other, he from one volume, I from the other. I like to collect them — words — in the same way I think you like to collect stones.

— Minerals, Wash said. Although I suppose I must allow that 'stones' is not incorrect. He saw the light in Max's eye. I have noticed that you do not find our lectures in geology to your taste.

— I was not aware that you had noticed me at all, Wash. I am glad — honored — that you have, even if it was to see me sleeping through Dr Loudon's droning!

Both of them were laughing now; Washington could feel the warmth all through him. The fire had been burning long enough that the frost had gone from the windows; later he would find little puddles of damp on the splintered sill. Max sliced the fruitcake with an ivory-handled clasp knife he drew from his pocket; they ate three pieces each in pleasant silence, and finished the bottle of brandy — or rather, Max did, and then went to lean back in his chair, forgetting that it had no back.

— Max!

Andermann tumbled to the floor, the chair now entirely collapsed, and lay on his back, laughing. Washington went to him to pull him upright, bracing Max's legs against his own so that when at last Max stood they were hip to hip and breast to breast, and when Washington went to let go of Max's hands he found he could not, for they were held bone-tight.

The brandy on Max's breath puffed into Washington's

nose and mouth. Even in the dim light Wash could see that Max's dark irises were speckled with gold; could see that he had missed a spot on his jaw when shaving. Max swayed a little, even closer in, and then bent his neck, so that his cheek rested on Washington's shoulder.

— I think I should help you downstairs, Wash said. His words went right into the snail of Max's ear, he was that close.

— Yes, Max mumbled. I suppose you should. I am sorry for — and he hesitated — I am sorry for your chair. I think it is broken beyond repair, now. Though it was quite fractured from the outset of our little gathering, I think.

— It was, Washington said. Do not concern yourself. Though in truth he was not certain how he would explain the breakage. The chair was nothing more than a scatter of wooden rods and little planks, now. Well, he must cross that bridge when he came to it. Now he must get Max to the front door.

His friend seemed to sober up somewhat in the colder air of the hall. Washington had wrestled Max back into his coat and tied his scarf — wool and silk, finely patterned — under his chin.

— You are good to me, Max said, as they walked arm in arm down the stairs. Max managed to keep his footsteps light, and his voice to a (loud) whisper. You are too good.

— Hush now, Washington said. You are the one who has been good to me. Thank you. Thank you, Max. You have raised my spirits.

They were at the door now.

— You must hurry home, Washington said. Lectures at nine o'clock tomorrow. I will see you there, yes?

— O, Max said. O. Lectures. Yes. I shall see you there at any rate, shan't I?

— As I just said, Wash replied. Of course you shall.

Washington was not quite certain why he stepped away from Max at that moment — but he did — and so Max turned the key in the lock to let himself out, pushed against the door, his back to Washington. He was mumbling something, but Washington could not hear what it was. And then Max stepped outside, and shut the door behind him, so that Washington, now realizing that he was trembling, quickly locked the door again and bolted up the stairs and into his little room.

The fire was still blazing. It had not been a dream, then. There was the brown paper wrapping, discarded on the floor; there was the half-eaten cake, raisins gleaming plump in the flickering light. The empty brandy bottle. Apples, untouched. The broken chair.

Exhaustion came over him then like a blow to the back of the head. He managed to put the firescreen in front of the grate and blow out his candle before flinging himself down on his narrow bed — where he found Andermann's leather gloves, open-palmed in an empty shrug, left on the scratchy wool of his blankets. In the thin silver moonlight, he brought them close to his face, ran his fingers over the fine stitching of the seams. They seemed hardly worn at all, and they had a soft woollen lining.

He sniffed at them. Rose-water — and ink — cherry-wood — and something elusive and human that must simply be Max, the print of him, settled there into the lining. They were beautiful, the gloves. He slipped them over his hands and found they were a perfect fit. He crawled under the blankets — he had not even taken off his boots — and then the blackness came, and he knew nothing else.

PHOTOGRAPH

'There is only one friend whose spirit I want to communicate with — You have his picture with mine —'
—WASHINGTON A. ROEBLING

✣ ✣ ✣ ✣ ✣

TRENTON. 1864.

EDDIE POKED HIS head round the parlor door; luckily they had heard the creak of his steps on the floorboards. Wash pulled away from her, and she from him, so they sat together modestly on the settee.

— Mother says, supper soon.

— I thought Jo was fixing supper, Wash said.

— Mother said she wanted to make it special, Eddie replied. You know, for — and he turned round wide eyes to Emily, who showed her pearly teeth in a smile, making his brother blush.

— I can help, Emily said. Let me.

— No, no, Wash said. She wouldn't let you anyhow, dear. But I wish she would let Jo. Go on, Eddie, tell her we'll be along presently.

Eddie hung on the doorknob for another moment, his dark eyes still fixed on Em.

— Go on!

The door slammed in his aftermath. Emily laughed, but stopped when she heard Wash's sigh. She turned to him, and put her hand, small and strong, over his.

— Will you —

— I will, she said, and leaned in close, and put her mouth on his mouth, letting her lips rest there, lightly, so that he pressed against her to bring her closer, wrapping his arm around her waist.

— Look how we fit, he said. Like two pieces of a puzzle. It is a puzzle that you love me, Em.

— Isn't it just! she said, and touched the tip of his nose. When she was amused, the corners of her eyes made little spider lines that caused him to consider how she would look when she was old, and once he nearly told her that — imagining she might be pleased, thinking of their future together. Now, somehow, he was glad he had not remarked on this. Learning about a girl was like learning a language. It was slow; it was easy to make foolish errors.

— But I do love you, that's the truth, she said, her face now serious. My brother says you will be made a major soon.

— And that is why you love me? he teased. Why don't you just go for a full colonel then, right away? I am sure we can find you one.

— O Wash . . . ! she said. You will hardly let a person admire you.

— You know I am always rather cautious about how much there is in me to admire.

She was quiet for a moment. Soft curls were spilling out from the pins she used to hold up her hair; the curls feathered against the white skin of her neck and swirled behind her delicate ears.

— Well, she said, as it happens, I *do* have a bone to pick with you.

Briefly he thought he would jest about fearing he would be a skeleton picked clean — but when he opened his mouth to speak that was the sight he saw in his mind's eye: all those boys, their rumpled clothes flung about like so much laundry, their flesh pulled away from the bones of their legs, arms, ribs, the gray bowls of their skulls.

— Wash! There is a promise you made to me which you have broken.

— I am sorry, my dear. Have I? I should not like to break a promise to you, not for all the world. *Private Harris, Will, he was called by his companions, propped up in the dip of a ditch — his left arm and left leg blasted away, and it was as if he were hardly aware of the loss. I'm not gonna go, sir, I'm not gonna go, am I? Sir? Sir?*

— You promised you would give me your picture to carry with me. You did. And I must have it.

— I sent you a picture, he replied, glad her urgent question had wiped the image of Will Harris from his head. The one I had taken when I joined.

— A picture I *like*, she said. You have your cap over your eyes. And you look so stern.

A group of them had gone to the picture studio when they had arrived in Washington — Keen, McKenzie, the three brothers Skirm. Two of them were twins, identical, and the other was barely a year older. They had stood in a line together, the Skirm boys, their arms around each other, their rifles and bayonets fiercely displayed. He was somehow quite certain they would all be dead now. The boys had brought their rifles with them, but there was a haystack of guns available to be used as props, along with a linen-cupboard full of flags. The photographer was called Dupree, a Frenchman with elaborate whiskers.

— I have another I can give you, Wash said. I think I can find it. After supper, we'll go to look.

TROY. 1856.

Max had promised a surprise. He had come bounding up the stairs — Mrs Beabout would let him in now, for he had charmed her with wholly undeserved compliments and even with a little porcelain shepherdess now proudly displayed in the dilapidated parlor — bearing fresh bread rolls in a paper bag which he set amid the piled paper of Wash's table.

— For later, he said, in case you want them. But right now we are going out.

He had simply flung himself into the room, falling spreadeagled on the bed so that its frame and legs groaned and complained.

— No, said Wash, we are not going out. Look, he said, I have all this to get through. His work was all in disorder; the stifling heat had kept him up most of the night.

— Your trouble, Max said, is that you do not get enough exercise. Look at me! He bolted upright and flung his arms wide. He was in his shirtsleeves only, the linen itself gone soft with his perspiration, and there was a high color in his cheeks. I myself have already been training with Professor Von Thun this morning; he is schooling me in the manly arts!

— Our German professor who calls himself a swordsman?

— You are such a cynic, Roebling. Our exercises were most invigorating. He has quite the style with the sabre. I do believe you might enjoy it, Wash.

— I wonder. I have had rather too much experience with these self-styled German professors, you know. In any case, surely it's far too hot to be flailing about with a blade. I may take up my work and find a shady tree to sit beneath. I may even have a snooze.

— No snoozing this morning, sirrah. As I said: you are coming with me.

— For pity's sake.

— Yes, for pity's sake. I am taking pity upon you, dear Wash, and extracting you from this ghastly hot-box. No, do not pick up your jacket or tie — why on earth would you want those on such a day? If we need costumes we shall find them at our destination.

— Costumes? Destination?

— Hush. Max stood, stepped towards Wash, reached out and put two fingers against Washington's lips. Bacon, beeswax, leather, sweat. You keep quiet now. Come with me.

TRENTON. 1864.

He had not let on at the dinner table — not even by a glance — how startled he continued to be at his father's conviviality in Emily's presence. She was placed at his right hand, and he served her himself, spooning veal and dumpling stew onto her plate until she exclaimed, O my dear Mr Roebling, that is quite enough, I do thank you! And it was perfectly clear that she was, well, *charmed* by his father, and it was almost possible for Washington to understand why a person might fall under his spell. Yet did Emily not notice how silent his brothers and sisters were when she and John Roebling fell into an animated discussion regarding the virtues of Mozart's compositions? More than once, Emily lifted her napkin to her face to hide her apparently delighted laughter; his father's gray gaze sparked when it lighted on his fiancée.

Washington watched all this from the foot of the table, sitting by his mother's side in the moments she wasn't jumping up and down to serve them, despite the fact his father let them have a girl now to help, but she was a poor little thing, skinny and abashed and clumsy: she dropped a ladle after the soup had been served. To see John Roebling keep his temper in this moment was a wonder.

— Emily is a lovely girl, his mother had said, leaning in to whisper to him. *Enzlich!*

— O Mother!

— What? I thought I would have you on my hands for life!

It was rare that she smiled; it pleased him so to see it. He leaned into her so their shoulders touched. I am so glad you are fond of her.

— Your father and I both, she said. At least something has come of this terrible war.

— Annie Thaler has married, you know, Elvira interjected.

— Has she, dear sister? You presume I am interested in such news?

Emily heard the word 'married' from down her end of the table. Who did you say is getting married? Shall we have a double wedding, Wash?

— Dearest, Washington said. You mishear. It is some — local talk, that is all. No one you know.

— Annie Thaler, Elvira said, her face a picture of innocence, to Emily. The daughter of one of our neighbors. I thought my brother would like to know, is all.

Emily understood at once what Elvira had intended, of course she did. Washington felt heat rise to his cheeks. Anton Thaler, Annie's father, had been hired as a manager at the mill when they had moved to Trenton; Annie was the oldest in a family of five girls, with blonde hair falling down her back straight as a stream. For a little while, in the years before the war, Washington had been rendered quite speechless in her company.

— Her husband is a clergyman, Elvira said. I hear he is very tall and handsome.

— A tall handsome clergyman is quite a catch, Emily said, smiling at Elvira. I imagine Miss Annie Thaler left behind several disappointed suitors.

— Ladies, John Roebling said, you know my opinion of gossip. I do not believe this is suitable conversation for our table. We do not wish our guest — soon to be a member of this family, I am delighted to say — to lower her opinion of us.

O Mr Roebling, Emily said, you must never fear that. And I do apologize for my contribution to the — gossip.

Now she was blushing, Washington saw. His heart moved toward her, at least, that is what it felt like, his heart disarrayed by a mix of adoration and shame, by a desire also to protect her from what she might see of their father's temper if he was too much tested by some behavior of which he did not approve.

— Let us have our pudding, his mother said, rescuing the situation. Rice pudding made with cream. Your sisters were of great help in the kitchen, my dear, they worked hard in honor of your homecoming, and your engagement.

He saw that his mother must have been beautiful, once. It startled him that the thought had never occurred to him, not until he saw her gazing at Emily, who smiled uncertainly, for she spoke no German, and could not understand what his mother said.

— A pudding for us, dearest Em, he said to her. Made specially. With cream!

— *Und Muskatnuss.*

— Nutmeg, too, Washington said. You see? You bring spice to my life. You can't argue with that, now.

TROY. 1856.

Max led him along Second Street, past the little Seminary Park and the court house; as they walked north, across Congress Street, the buildings they passed became just that much more pleasant, well-built and solid, heading towards grandeur. In the sunshine it was almost possible to forget his sullen little cage of a room, although even now, well before noon, the heat was oppressive, and it was only mid-May. Max whistled as they walked; he had a fine whistle, melodic and strong.

— Pretty, Wash said. I've not heard that before.

— 'How Can I Leave Thee?' Max said. '*Ach wie ist's möglich*'. Saying this, he slipped his hand under Washington's elbow, so they walked arm-in-arm. My father sent me the music, he said. You could learn it on your fiddle. You are too taken with that Herr Mozart. You require a bit of the common touch, Wash.

He gave Washington's elbow a squeeze. They walked in step now, easily, left and right, left and right, keeping close to the shade the occasional awning offered. Max's whistle had faded to a little tuneless rhythm that matched their pace. If Ferd had made this kind of breathy noise beside his ear, Wash would have hushed him; strange how what was annoying in a brother could be endearing in a friend.

— Here we are, Max said. They were nearly at Albany Street and Washington Square. Ornate black-and-gold lettering on a glass-fronted door read *Rivers & Francis: Daguerreans & Photographers: Portrait & Memorial.*

— What is this, dear Max?

— Max, his hand on the doorbell, turned to him, smiling.

What does it look like, dear Wash? We shall have our portrait taken. A keepsake to commemorate — you know, the two of us.

— Really, Wash said. I do not need a copper plate to tell me —

The next words would not quite come. Yet with Max he could speak freely; he sometimes felt as if there was nothing they might not say. Washington listened more than he spoke, true; he loved Max's garrulousness, his easy, vivid way with language and his sharp observations of their fellow students, their professors. He was perceptive and irreverent, both; Washington had never encountered anything like it. He had remarked on it, once, shyly, in the early days of their acquaintance. They had been sitting by the fire in Max's rooms, eating slices of meat pie and drinking hock.

— I suppose I have got in the habit of openness, Max had said. My father and I — we only had each other. And, being very young when we arrived here in America, I picked up the lingo a bit quicker than he did; I would help him out with his speaking and reading. So sometimes it was as if I was the father, you know. And he would practice his talking by telling me anything and everything, whatever it was that troubled him, in his business or in his life. He still does.

Washington had seen the thick letters Max received, their pages scattered through Max's (often disorderly) lecture notes.

— And of course, Max had said, we talk about my mother. Father does, I mean.

— I would take you home to meet my mother, Wash had said, except that it's just possible you would have to meet my father too, and I should like to spare you that.

— I wouldn't mind, Max had said. There had been eagerness in his voice. You would have an ally, if I were there with you. And to meet your brothers and sisters — and Mr Swan — I would like that very much. And to see the mill.

— The mill! Wash had said. Anyone would think you were angling for a job.

— O Wash! You know I am not!

Washington had been joking, of course he had, but he had begun to notice this particular quality just beneath the surface of Max's good cheer; something febrile. He took slights easily, or what he imagined were slights: his ruddy skin would pale and a shadow would appear around his eyes. This was not the first time Washington had had to reassure him in this way.

— Max, Wash had said that night, laying down his slice of pie. Its sweet jelly shone in the firelight. Honestly.

— I am sorry, Max said. I am being —

— Max, Washington had said. You are being Max.

— O, I suppose I am, Max had said, and then he had smiled, and laid his hand on Washington's knee, just briefly, before picking up his glass and taking a long draw of the pale wine.

— You know, Washington had said, sometimes I joke because . . . the truth is, Max, I do envy you sometimes. Not for all this — he gestured around Max's pleasant warm room with its Turkey carpet and well-sealed windows, the wine and food — but your . . . ease, I do not how to express it.

Washington had not been looking at Max as he spoke, but at the fire, glowing, licking.

— Your ease in the world — and for what you say just now about how you are able to speak to your father and the manner in which he speaks to you. I hope I might get to meet him someday. My father and I — Washington allowed himself to hold Max's gaze. He felt no pressure, but an open space into which his words might enter. Well, Max, once you spoke of Niagara, my father's work there. I was with him, then, though I was only a boy. He had caught his hand in a rope machine, a foolish accident, caused by his excess of zeal, no doubt — he could not write. He needed a scribe, and determined I should serve that purpose. I have never been so talked at or exhausted in all my life, even here. Harangued day and night, what he expected of me each day, what he expected of me in the future, to follow in his illustrious footsteps — Washington could taste metal in his mouth, it came with his words: iron and blood. Inescapable as the great rushing falls themselves. I escaped, one day, to see the great feat — you know, Blondin crossing the falls on his wire. I have never had such a beating as I did when I returned from that escapade.

Washington had never spoken to anyone in this way before. Of what he felt, of what he wanted, of what there was and was not. Of what he had suffered and what might be to come. For a while Max had said nothing. Wash had looked up from the fire, met Max's eyes, and for a moment — though it had seemed more than that, and less than that, all at once — they had just observed each other.

— My father does not beat me, Max had said finally. He never has. But I do not tell him everything, Wash. There are things which I cannot tell him. You must understand that.

Washington was not certain that he did understand. But he had nodded, because that had seemed kind. That had seemed right.

— Things which I don't tell him, Max went on, but which I . . . which I would hope to tell you, Wash. One day, anyway.

— Yes, Wash had said. One day, Max. Whenever it pleases you.

— Do not envy me, dear Wash. Promise me you will not.

That promise had been made many months ago, and yet Washington recalled it now, standing in the broiling sunshine outside the embellished door of the photographers' studio. Max pressed the bell and they heard it sounding above, and then footsteps on the stairs, clattering, so fast that Washington feared that the clatterer might fall in his haste; he wondered if whoever was coming to greet them feared losing custom to impatience. Although come to that — it was Sunday. What custom could have been expected?

And then the door was pulled open. Before them stood a youngish man — looking almost as if he could be a fellow

Rensselaerean, not least because he had the disheveled aspect of an overworked student. He was slight and narrow-shouldered, standing erect in his dark clothes; his shirt-collar was stained with sweat, but the neck that emerged from it was clean. Neatly-trimmed whiskers around his half-smiling mouth, a tidy nose, clear green eyes.

— Mr Andermann, the young man said, how very good to see you again. Welcome. And I am delighted to meet — Mr Roebling, isn't it? They shook hands briefly; the young man's nails were dark with grime, but in truth they were not much grimier than Washington's own perennially ink-stained digits. Please, please, he said, do come in, come upstairs.

He spoke with an accent that Washington could not place, an upswept, looping sound.

— Do I have the pleasure of meeting Mr Rivers or Mr Francis? Washington asked.

— You meet us both at once, I confess. I am Francis Rivers, sole proprietor.

— It sounds more businesslike, you see, Max said. Rivers & Francis. Francis & Rivers. A clever notion, don't you think, Wash?

— Mr Andermann flatters me, Rivers said. I aspire to a business partner, of that I can assure you.

— Surely you are in need of one if you must do business on a day of rest, Washington said.

Max winked, at Rivers or at himself, Washington could not quite tell. I have informed Mr Rivers of the demands of our beloved Institute; he consented to open for us specially, he said. At this Rivers nodded graciously and stepped aside to let them in.

The stairs were narrow and shabby, not much better than those in Wash's lodgings. But light poured down upon them as they climbed, and at the top they stepped clear out into a long, wide room: the whole top floor of the building, it appeared, and a great section of the roof had been replaced with glass planes. The blazing sun, careening off the whitewashed walls, was wholly dazzling.

— My God, Wash said. It's roasting.

— Yes, said Rivers. The price of the light, I fear. You shall have to cultivate your cool expressions.

Rivers had the same kind of easy charm that Max did; both of them seemed hardly troubled by the heat, though Rivers, he supposed, would be accustomed to it. The two of them, Max and Francis Rivers, laughed together as if they were well acquainted. Wash could hardly help but join in.

— Will you have costumes? Rivers asked. There was a rack of raggedy fancy-dress in the corner of the room: moth-eaten fur (fur! In this heat!), stained taffeta, threadbare silk hats, a rusty sabre or two.

— No, no, Max said. We are friends and brothers, Wash and I. We have no wish to disguise the fact.

Rivers had his sleeves rolled up now. His forearms were very white, striated with the kind of fine muscle that comes from the constant use of the delicate skills of the hand. He gestured to a chaise covered in mauve sateen, which was the most respectable piece of furniture in the room. It faced the wooden box of the photographic machine, its single eye staring outward. The camera was of highly polished, light-colored wood and was fixed on a sturdy metal tripod.

— Come, Max said, let us arrange ourselves, dearest Wash.

Rivers stood with his arms folded, near his apparatus, as they settled down carefully on the settee. Or rather, Wash settled himself carefully — Max dropped straight down and threw his arm around Wash's neck. Without thinking, Wash reached up, took Max's hand where it rested upon his own collarbone and set his other hand on Max's knee.

— Gentlemen, are you ready? You are settled, so? You look a fine pair, if I may say so. Very fine.

He moved quickly round the chaise, lifting away from the

wall as he did so two light metal stands. At the top of each stand was a slender open jaw. These Rivers set behind them, clamping their skulls in the frames. Little soft pads — but not too soft — jammed behind Washington's ears; the feeling, as Rivers tightened some screw to hold the contraption fast, was like the onset of a headache.

— The least pleasant part of the operation, Rivers said. But you will thank me. It will hold you steady for the exposure.

— I am always glad to be held steady, Max said. For that I generally rely on my friend here, but it is excellent to know that other methods are available.

Rivers gave a bark of a laugh.

— You are not from these parts, I think, Washington said.

— No, Rivers said. I am not. He had stepped back from them, was observing them closely, and then, coming nearer, with light hands began to straighten and adjust their collars and cuffs, his touch as sure as that of any tailor. Newcastle-upon-Tyne, Rivers said, or thereabouts. England. It was to go down the mines to the dark or come up to find the light. I chose the light, as you see.

— A happy tale, Max said.

— Not always. But not so bad now. I was lucky, Rivers went on. I found work with a gentleman in Albany; he had no children and left me the business when he died.

— Men make their own luck, it's said, Max remarked.

— So it's said, Rivers answered, and that may or may not be true. A cold little smile flickered about his mouth. Right then! He straightened, brightened. Are you gentleman ready for immortality?

TRENTON. 1864.

They repaired to the parlor after supper.

— Washington Augustus, his father said as he settled himself into the wing-back chair that bore the imprint of the back of his head. The fabric of its arms was worn where he rested his hands, but unevenly so: the damaged fingers of his left hand curled permanently into his palm. You have brought your violin?

— Yes, Father, he said, and I have brought home some new tunes. There is quite a mix of music in the camps. I will play, he continued, but if you will pardon me and my bride-to-be for just a few moments; I made a promise to her I mean to keep.

— A promise to a lady is not lightly given, John Roebling said. Go on, he said. We shall attend your return.

Emily looked at him a little quizzically. Little Eddie stood gawping.

— Close your mouth, brother, Washington said. We won't be a moment. Come my dear, he said, holding out his hand. She took it and he led her up the stair, past his father's office — he avoided even glancing inside; just passing the door made his breath come short. He had not told Emily any of that: the way his father would make him take the strap down from the wall with his own hands. Why should he tell her? He would protect her from all the ills the world could bring. He would keep her safe.

The room he shared with Ferdinand was just as he had left it. Ferdy was off for the weekend with the Millers, his mother had said; life went on, apparently, as if there were no war being fought at all.

— Which one is yours? Emily asked, her gaze set on the two neatly made beds.

— By the window, he told her. There could be a draft in winter, but he liked the light; liked to be able to look at the Moon when she hung in a square of glass, laced around with clouds. Liked to see the blossom of a thundercloud, or the quick stain of dawn. He would lie in his narrow bed and have, at least, an idea of a horizon, a universe beyond the mill and the endless reels of wire. He had never thought that universe would be so soaked in blood.

Emily sat down on the bed, his bed, and ran her hands lightly over the coverlet. Then she picked up her neat little feet and lay down, stretched full-length, her head where his head would be that night, her body where his body would lie.

— O Em!

— Come on, she said. Her cheeks were flushed, the color creeping down her white throat to the collar of her dress. It was a blue gingham, practical and pretty. He recognized it, had seen her wear it before. That was part of what love was, he was coming to know: being able to recognize a dress.

— Someone will come up, Wash said. Eddie. My *father*.

— No they won't, she smiled. We said we'd be right back down. And we will.

He sat down slowly, carefully, cautious of the bed frame, his hip by her hip, folded her hands in his, bent down swiftly and kissed her on her soft mouth. Her lips opened and a thread of molten wire drew out inside him, from his chest, to the small of his back, down to — so he pulled away from her quickly and reached up to smooth her hair, dark threads unspooling against the linen of his pillow.

— Your picture, he said. Let's find it. Careful how you get up. The bed — creaks. As he spoke the heat roared up into his face. He watched her rise from the bed. There would come a time when he would see this, morning after morning. To see her swing her feet down to the floor, put her palms flat on the mattress to push herself to stand, that would be the most ordinary thing in the world. *Good morning, Mrs Roebling*, he would say. How remarkable.

— So, where is it then? she asked. Show me.

— Here. He and Ferd shared a desk pushed up against the wall; the drawers on the left were his own, the ones on the right, his brother's. He had never opened his brother's drawers, and he was sure that his brother had never opened his. Whatever conflict there could be between them, there was nevertheless always an unspoken accord that privacy, in this house, was a valuable commodity and therefore to be respected. He opened the smallest drawer, in which were stumps of pencils, a coil of twine, and a small, sturdy wooden box, and pulled out a portrait of himself, three inches by four, or thereabouts.

— Look at you! she said.

— This was a while ago, he said. Right when I started at Troy.

— Your hair, she said. So long! You look quite poetic.

— I didn't feel poetic, he said. I felt — scared.

— What were you scared of?

— O, Em, he said. I don't know. Everything. Working morning till night. Six days a week, seven, really. I thought my head would explode. I knew I mustn't fail. A lot of us did, though. A lot of us did.

Her clear brow knit itself into a frown; she put her hand on his arm.

— It's strange, she said. When I was at school, you know, I always thought we didn't work hard enough. Perhaps that sounds foolish, to you.

— No, he said. I'd like to hear more about your school days. I like to think of you writing out phrases in French. *Est-ce je peux avoir une tasse de thé, Mademoiselle?*

— Well, we did more than that, you know, she said. We never

spent enough time in the laboratory, to my mind. Or at our telescopes. Saturn looks like a jewel through a fine telescope. Miss Partridge had a very fine telescope, and on the darkest nights we would sit out for hours, if she allowed it; she made the most delicious cocoa to warm us.

— Not much cocoa up at Rensselaer, he said. But we did have a good telescope or two. You are quite right about Saturn. He is almost as lovely as you are, dearest, on a clear night.

— What else have you got in there? she asked. His planetary compliment left her unmoved; she had seen that there was something else in the box, a frame encased in stained embossed leather, closed with a delicate brass clip. She drew it out, turned it over, examined it, but the light was bad. There were two sets of letters, initials, stamped into the leather on the back of the case; it did not appear that she had noticed this. He felt his chest constrict. He stood very still, right next to her, her shoulder in its good plain wartime dress beside his wool-clad arm.

How long had it been since he had seen —

Eight years —

The rich black cap of his hair, those shining eyes —

In the photograph, his chin tilted up, his mouth closed, as if there were words on his tongue about to be spoken —

And one arm thrown around Wash's neck, their shoulders touching: Wash had reached up, taken Max's hand where it rested on his collarbone; had set his other hand on Max's knee. Their legs were crossed, a matching pair, left over right. The photographer had steadied their skulls with clamps and a clock had ticked as the seconds of the exposure passed.

— Well, she said, look at you and your friend. Who is this, Wash?

How lightly she spoke. As if there were nothing in it. As if the answer were simple.

— O, he said, over the tightness in his throat. Max, he said, that's Max. Max Andermann. We were students together in Troy.

— Handsome gentleman! she said.

— I suppose so, yes, he replied, mustering a smile. Surely you are not supposed to remark upon the beauty of other fellows when you are in my company, Emmie.

— I have to keep you just a *bit* jealous, darling Wash, don't I? Or you'll take me quite for granted.

— Washington Augustus!

His father's voice, at the bottom of the stairs.

— Washington Augustus! We were promised some music, as I recall!

For a fraction of a second he wished himself in a tent, in Maryland, in Virginia, in that time between battles when the horror became, at least briefly, unimaginable, distant: when there was a fire, a cigar, dry clothing, the sound of someone frailing a banjo just over yonder. He wished himself, in any case, to be not here, not now, caught between Emily and his father and the memory of Max.

— I like that picture, she said. You look happy. Bold, she said.

— Not sorrowful and timorous, as you usually find me?

— Wash, you will tease me to death!

To *death*. Perhaps you could love a person to death, or rather, not love them. He half-expected to hear Max's firm tread on the floorboards, see him stride through the door, bend down low to kiss Emily's hand.

— Will you let me have it, then? she asked. I like to think of you, in the company of your friend, content. With Max.

— Go on then, he said. You take it. I am sure he would like you to have it too.

The words came out of his mouth before he could stop them.

— Washington! *Du musst jetzt wirklich nach unten kommen!*

— Come, he said. We really must. You have your picture now, at any rate. He took her hand to lead her back down: she held his gift delicately, by its edges, in her other hand. He stepped ahead, so she walked behind him down the stairs; he could not see her face, but only hear her voice, when she asked —

— What became of him? Of Max?

He nearly stumbled; let his hand rest on the banister a moment, did not turn his head to look at her. He could say Max had been killed in the war. He could say he had gone out to Colorado Territory after gold. He could say anything at all.

And then there was his father, waiting for them, the set of his brow relaxing when he saw the pair of them descend.

— At last, John Roebling said. Your fiancée and I were discussing Mozart at supper. Have you been practicing your Turkish concerto?

— There is not too much call for Mozart in camp, Father, but I will see what I can manage. Perhaps you'll sing for us, too, dear?

— Certainly, Emily said. "Love's Chidings", perhaps! She squeezed his fingers with her own, and as she did time stacked up inside of him like logs in a fence: his childhood, Troy, the war, his future an unseen path stretching out beyond blood-soaked ground. We must wait to marry, he had said to Emily the last time they had met. We must wait, because —

— Don't, she had replied in a quiet voice. Don't speak of it. You will invite it.

Now he saw her slip the photograph into the pocket he knew hid in the folds of her skirt; now her hand was empty, as if Max had disappeared in a magic trick.

— Come on, dearest Wash, Emily said. Time to play.

TROY. 1856.

The street outside, when they returned to it, was cooler and less dazzling than Rivers' sweltering studio had been. Sweat streamed through Max's dark hair; Washington could smell him — smell them both, as they flapped cloth away from their bodies in an effort to move the still air that threatened to stifle them.

— Well, Washington said, that was an adventure, Max. You are always full of surprises.

— He is a charming fellow too, is he not? Max asked, his wet face beaming. His accent! So unusual! I had never encountered the like before. He told me that when he first arrived on these shores he was as hard to comprehend as any Dutchman!

— How did you meet?

— Oh, said Max, we were introduced.

A little silence came — Max was usually more forthcoming — before Washington said:

— So. I must get back to my books.

Max looked down at him — for the most part Washington would forget that Max had a good three inches on him, but there were times when his friend could, it seemed, bring this height to bear, as he did just now.

O no, Max said. Not yet. You are *dazed* with the heat, dear Wash. Wasn't it intolerable in there? I must admit I had no notion that immortalization would entail suffocation! Here, he said, you are coming with me.

And with that he clasped Washington's left hand in his right paw, yanked on his arm and began to run.

— Max!

Max let go his hand then, but Washington was following now, the pair of them running in the windless heat, past the Sunday-shuttered storefronts, through the empty cobbled streets. A woman in apron and cap tipped a bucket of soapy water out of her narrow door as they passed, but gave no indication of having seen them; they might as well have been spirits invisible.

Dock Street petered out towards the water's edge. There were still places in Troy where the city felt raw and unfinished. There was a rough landing where the little skiff ferry went across to the works and lumberyard on weekdays. It was by pilings, where mud, sand and stones worn smooth by the water's unrelenting flow, and it sloped down to the broad expanse of the Hudson, flat as a silver plate in the sunlight. Max began to unbutton his shirt.

— Race you to Starbuck's, Max said, jerking his chin at the low buildings hunkered on the island halfway across the river's span: a stove works, heaped round with pallets of pig iron and tumbles of slag.

— So you are a swimmer as well as a swordsman, then? We'll see about that, Washington said, his reticence at this whole adventure vanished, melted away by his own sweat and a longing to plunge into the water. Now they were racing to undress: boots, socks, linen, trousers, shirts; so there, his bare feet planted on the bank, was Max, the whole of him, broad and white and glistening. And Washington was taken completely unaware when Max threw the roped cords of his arms about him, under his ribs, under his knees, lifted him and —

— Hey! The blue sky tilted up into his vision, the white disk of the blinding sun. Hey!

The water closed over Washington's head, the freezing green swallowed him. He took some in, oily, rank, a river of industry and commerce, and when he broke the surface he saw that Max was already swimming out hard towards the farther shore and a stretch of clear sand some yards away from the island's warehouses and huddled brick offices. But Washington could see too that Max was as prodigal in his swimming as he was in so much else: his arms windmilling, legs flailing, churning the water with more flap than a paddle-steamer at full tilt.

It was Steubgens who had taught Wash to swim, with his own sons, at Thorn Creek in Saxonburg. His father would have thrown him in the water and let him sink or save himself, but Steubgens had stripped himself down to his drawers and led them into the stream before astonishing them all — Washington must have been about seven, the Steubgens boys either side of him in age — by slipping into the swift flow and swimming back and forth as sleek as a trout. He had held them all by the waist, one at a time, teaching them how to kick neat and firm, how to turn their heads aside to gulp the air while their arms lifted and pulled.

— *Nicht spritzen! Ganz ruhig.* The fish should not even know you are among them, Herr Steubgens had said, and Washington had been his most adept pupil. The stream at Thorn Creek was a wild haven, his own private water cure. Beneath the stream's surface, his eyes wide to the weeds and smoothed stones, the air from his lungs a patterning halo around his head. When he had first arrived in Troy, the autumn cold had already begun to bite, but no matter: he had soon swum the wide Hudson from bank to bank.

Only another moment passed before Washington slipped by Max, cutting cleanly through the river, fat drops of water from his friend's frantic splashing spattering his shoulders. Max started in the water, tipped upright as Washington cruised along, and now it was his turn to cry Hey! before throwing himself forward again in a vain attempt to regain the lead.

But it was no good. Max was still swimming — if you could call it that — when Washington stepped out of the water and up onto the quiet stretch they had spotted from the far bank. Naked, Washington peered up towards the stoveworks, hoping that no clerk was diligent enough to row himself over on a Sunday. The place seemed — thankfully — silent and deserted.

He picked his way up towards a patch of thin grass, peering among the river stones for stray nails and the like. A case of lockjaw would be poor reward for this morning's outing. The high sun quickly dried him, the heat now prickling pleasantly after the water's chill. Behind him Max's splashing drew closer; he began to be able to hear grunting breaths. When he sat, the ground was rough and tufty under his thighs; he drew his legs up and wrapped his arms around his knees, waiting, while the river water dripped through his hair and down his neck.

So here was Max, scrambling up the bank, back rounded, knees scraping the gravel before he straightened, stood, the wet streaming down the pale length of him, his powerful shoulders, the little softness around his middle, his muscled legs.

— Are you not a man of mysteries, Roebling! Max exclaimed, panting, flinging himself down by Washington's side, so close their arms nearly touched, did touch, before a thin gap of air entered between again — I felt certain I would best you across! You have been keeping secrets from me, friend — surely you must swim to Starbuck's each and every day. You are positively piscine, dear Wash. I am quite astonished. There is no end to your talents, it seems.

— I'm not sure there is so much to it, Washington said. There was a pleasant creek at home, a good place to run off to when things got stiff.

— A creek — in Trenton?

— No, no, before that. Saxonburg, when I was just a boy. It was easier to escape there. And, you know, my father is not entirely wrong — though it pains me to say it — water has a healing way — just not in the manner upon which he so vehemently insists.

— I must admit, Max said, you do look quite revived by our aqueous escapade.

— Well, Washington said, I do feel so. By our whole adventure. You are a tonic, Andermann. Truly you are.

The sun was hot now; their skin was fully dried, the river scent rising off them: a scent of the power of the great stream as it spilled down from the Adirondacks. On the farther shore the sabbath city lay, whatever bustle and noise there was stilled by distance and the rush of the flowing water. Heat blurred the rising hills beyond Rensselaer up towards the cemetery, green on green towards the lick of the horizon. The whole weight of his life back there: the piled books and scattered papers, ink and pens, measurements, calibrations and re-calibrations; his head an open pit into which facts and equations were endlessly shovelled, into which all the stuff of the brutal and material world was poured, ceaselessly, ceaselessly. But here was the riverbank to hold him, the furnaces of the works behind them cooled and silent, the river's tide lapping quietly against the shore like a cat at a saucer of milk.

As if his whole life were suspended beyond him, or above him, hung away just out of reach so that there was only this little island, this day, Max, who now shifted his weight so their shoulders touched again, skin to skin, and when Washington turned to say something of the light the river the island the works the shore, Max turned too and kissed him, nothing Washington had ever felt before, the firm swift press of a mouth on his mouth, a hot wire around his heart. Max pulled back, his dark eyes lit, and then rose quickly, grass and gravel on his thighs and buttocks, ran back down to the water and dove straight in.

PRETTY WINK

WASHINGTON, D.C. FEBRUARY, 1864.

— '*THE LADIES' DRESSING room is a sacred precinct,*' Wash read. He was lying on his back on his cot, the little cloth-bound book held over his head. '*A sacred precinct into which no gentleman should ever presume to look; to enter it would be an outrage never to be overlooked or forgotten.*'

— I don't imagine we'll get anywhere near the ladies' dressing room, Paine said. I reckon that's an outrage you need not fear, my friend. He dipped a hog-bristle brush in blacking and rubbed vigorously at his boot.

— Well, I don't know about that, Wash said. He closed the little book, reached down beneath his cot and pulled out one of the sheets scattered there. He had rough sketches of the hall he'd nearly finished constructing — if you could call it that — of barely-seasoned timber roofed with paper and tar. Look, Will, he said, we have a map!

Paine smiled, kept at his polishing, his stockinged feet flat on the floor.

— That's as may be. Still, fair enough to say my skills are more in the reconnaissance line. I never was much of a dancer.

— Never too old to learn, Wash said. He sat up, letting his penciled sketch fall back to the floor and rifled through the pages of his book. He waved it in Paine's direction. Mr Hillgrove will come to your aid. This really is a capital volume. A *Complete Practical Guide to the Art of Dancing*. A bargain at 75 cents, I say.

— That's how you're spending your pay, is it? Paine asked with a wry look. Will your father be surprised to discover that his eldest son has embarked upon a career as a dancing master?

— People will need plenty of amusement when this war ends, Wash said. If it ever ends. They may not care for bridges and railroads anymore.

Paine observed the shine of his boots, was still not quite satisfied and kept polishing.

Wash sighed and brushed at his dress coat, which he had laid out on the end of his cot.

— Your buttons look plenty bright, Paine said.

— It's not my buttons I'm concerned about, Wash said. His demeanor adjusted itself; he frowned. I never feel I have the hang of those kind of conversations one is meant to have —

He trailed off.

— With the ladies?

— Just so.

— You'll find a way, Paine said. In any case — you have sisters. You must know how to talk to them.

— I feel that may be part of the trouble!

Paine laughed. He set his boots on the floor and tucked his brushes into a sturdy wooden box with his initials, WHP, burnt into the lid.

Just then there was a knock at the flimsy wooden door; a skinny corporal in a battered cap poked his head round before either man could say *come in* or *go away.*

— Captain Paine?

— Corporal?

— Sorry, Captain. Howe wants you.

— Right now?

— Well, Wash said, do you think he'd have sent this fine young man if whatever it was could wait? Right-Now-Howe, you know he's that way.

— Something about your report, sir.

Paine sighed. Go along, he said to the corporal. You tell him I'm on my way. He looked at Washington. I expect you to be a full dancing master when I get back, he said. He pulled his boots on, settled his hat on his head and followed the corporal out. The door slapped shut, its thin slats rattling.

Wash lay back on his cot and stared at the rough ceiling of the bunk. His stomach growled. There had been some sort of stew earlier, made with vinegar — 'Brazilian stew', the mess sergeant had said. Washington had thought it best not to venture into that particular jungle; the stuff stank. He'd walked off — his hunger keen now, he still wasn't sorry he'd turned it down. Both he and Paine, and Henderson, LaPierre, Pike, a whole crew, had got the shits last week from some noxious concoction served up in the mess. The memory of crouching over a gully with his britches round his ankles and a fist in his gut kept his ravening at bay.

He half-sat to light his candle. Hillgrove had slipped to the floor; he picked up the little book again and lay back to read. '*Never forget that ladies are to be first cared for, to have the best seats, the places of distinction, and are entitled in all cases to your courteous protection.*' He shifted on the cot, scratched at his knee and considered offering his courteous protection to some girl or another. A yellow-haired girl, maybe, like Annie Thaler back home. Once she had let him hold her skein of red yarn while she wound it into a ball for knitting; sitting in the glow of the Thalers' parlor — Mrs Thaler beside the fire with her embroidery — Washington had watched Annie's quick neat hand spool round and round the growing red ball, bright as a hot little sun. Something in the movement of her arm had stirred him — he could not begin to explain why — and he had been quite transfixed. His own hands, holding the skein taut, had trembled, and when all the yarn had been swallowed by the ball, and she had smiled at him and thanked him — well, he hardly knew how he would rise from his chair. '*In ascending a staircase with ladies, go at their side or before them,*' he read. Yes, he thought, he could see the reason for that. He considered how Annie Thaler's slender waist would look, just ahead of him on a staircase, as he followed her to go —

A knock on the door again, another head poking in without waiting for any answer.

— Hey Roebling, Anson said. Lookit you, like a lonesome pine cut down in a wood. Come out? He stepped inside. Washington could smell the drink on him. Anson was a Virginia man, too proud of himself for defying loyalty to his state — *that cocksucker Lee*, Anson would say. He turned his head back over his shoulder. Roebling, he said. G'wan, said the voice outside. Make him come. Have a laugh. The owner of the second voice appeared. Grady, an Irishman. Captain Anson, Captain Grady. In truth, Washington didn't like either of them. But his boredom, his restlessness, his hunger made him sit up. The boredom and the rest of it was somehow made worse by the alarm of the days just past on the Rapidan; as long as the war dragged on he would never become accustomed, he thought, to this violent flux between tedium and terror.

Anson pulled out a flask from his coat, took a long swig, held it out to Washington.

— Bourbon, he said. Kentucky.

Washington took the flask, warm from Anson's body and sticky, too. Some browning fluid clung to the metal and he wondered, as he put the neck to his lips, where the bourbon had come from and whether that brown stuff was blood. The alcohol flared up his nose, went hot down his throat.

— Where's your friend Paine? Anson had a way of making everything he said sound like he was about to hit you.

— Called off, Wash said. Howe wanted him.

— A real prig, he is. Glad he ain't here.

— Widower, they say, Grady interjected. *Widderer*, it sounded like. He spat. A speck of tobacco juice landed on Washington's muddy boot. Keeps the fond image of his beloved wife sacred to his mem'ry.

Grady was a skilled gunner; his thick red forearms were covered in powder burns.

— The memory of her sacred cunt! Anson barked.

— Leave that, Wash said. The captain's a fine man.

— O now don't you prig up too, Anson said. Come on. Time to refill this beauty. He shook the flask. Maybe get a little more besides. You look like your spine needs a little shaking, Roebling. Too much time with that Bible-thumping pal of yours.

Washington realized he'd risen — seemed to have put Mr Hillgrove down — and realized too he'd taken his coat and put it on. He allowed Anson to shove him out the door, Grady behind, and then they were on the path that wound through the wooden barrack buildings. Dusk was coming over the camp; smoke rose from fires and from the chimneys of the rough buildings and tents that stretched away from the city in row after row. Tin pans clattered and meat sizzled; the smell of bacon frying made Washington's mouth water. His mind lightened a little, and the company of Anson and Grady began to seem more acceptable. The raw air bit sharp; they pulled their coats tight, walked quick along the rough slick road. Anson and Grady hastened on and Washington followed.

BROOKLYN. NOVEMBER, 1875.

Her hand was cool on his brow. The lightest and briefest touch: the backs of her slender fingers, the care she took that the sapphire she wore did not graze his skin. The room was close, the air thick, but he could not bear a draft now: a whisper of winter, the bitter air beyond the window glass, even a breath from the landing through the opened door would cut him like a knife.

— Surely that's enough for today, she said. Liza has the supper ready. You must say goodnight to John.

— What I must do is to write to Henry Murphy, before he dismisses all my good men. He set down his pen. His hand trembled like an old man's and he laid his palm flat on the desk to still it.

— Dismisses? Surely not.

Her tone was a little sharp; he did not like the contradiction.

— Puts them on half pay, then, he allowed. The result will be the same.

— Yet the action itself is not, she said. It is as well to be precise about such matters, I believe. She moved away from where he sat and, standing by the fireplace, struck a light, illuminating the gas-jets that framed the mantlepiece. With his back to her he could hear her light tread, imagine the sharp flick of her wrist; she would have to lift herself onto her toes — just — to make the quick flame. He had been working by the light of the desk-lamp only.

— More light, she said. You complain of your eyes, yet you are not a cat or an owl that can see in the dark.

Her hands on his shoulders now. He reached up to take them in his own.

— Lucky for you, he said. I might scratch, if I were a cat. A cat will scratch when he is vexed.

— O husband, she said. You do scratch. Even without any claws. She bent to kiss the top of his head, reaching up to draw the hair back from his forehead as she did so, the gesture like a scent caught and then recalled, a breath of an older, easier time. The blood pulsed in his temples: his headaches were so regular now he was aware more of their absence than their presence. Yet still he turned to her, and when he did she kissed him again, the bone of his cheek below his eye, where the soot of the caisson fire had left a speckled constellation of marks upon his skin. She smiled and then took the letter up from his desk, lifting it to the light.

— Let us see what you have written to Mr Murphy then, she said.

WASHINGTON, D.C. FEBRUARY, 1864.

The place was called *Pretty Wink*: there was a painted wooden sign above the fanlight, almost discreet. It was one in a whole street of such places, their windows blazing, laughter and piano music, fiddle music, spilling out into the thoroughfare. He understood, of course, as soon as they approached the door what his companions intended; understood even better when in the gaudily-papered hallway of the place they were greeted by a woman with the black hair and olive skin of a Spaniard, her eye teeth shining in the lamplight, her cheeks and lips thickly rouged. At the neck of her deep red gown she wore a ruby and diamond brooch nearly the size of a baby's fist. She kissed Anson on the cheek as if they were old acquaintances, and then turned to embrace Washington, her red mouth planted on the unshaved bristles by his jaw, her breath, ripe with sugar and brandy, in his ear.

— Welcome, she said. We are always glad of new company here. I am Madam Sophia, she said. Sophia means *wisdom*. Would you be wise, my dear young captain? She ran her hand lightly over the officer's insignia on his jacket, slipping her fingers under the lapel of his coat to do so, her rings — more rubies, yellow stones that might have been diamonds too — catching the light. From behind her stepped a girl, dark-haired, dark-eyed too, and also dressed in red, but her gown was unbuttoned to the waist, her chemise unlaced, her breasts entirely bare, their dark nipples swaying. Before Washington could move or speak she had pressed herself against him, reaching around his ribs with one hand, pulling at his buttons — the buttons of his shirt — with the other.

— Leave me be, he said. And then: No.

— Your voice says one thing, but I bet your prick says another, Anson laughed. No harm in a quick dip, Roebling. Lighten your goddam mood.

The girl pulled herself in closer and so he pushed at her, more roughly than he had intended, gripping her so that he could feel the bones of her wrist in the clasp of his hand. She was thrown off balance. There was the sharp intake of her breath as she fell then upon Anson who caught her in his outstretched arm, his grimed fingers on the taut skin just above her breast.

— Hey, Roebling, Anson said, his eye steady, a rifleman taking aim. No way to treat a lady.

— I see no *lady* here, Washington said. It was out of his mouth before he could stop it. The madam — Madam Sophia — darted forward like a snake; her palm was hot and moist against his cheek when she slapped him, hard, so his face burned.

— You are in our house at my pleasure, she said. For that matter, I see no *gentleman* here, she said. She looked him up and down, her mouth a purse of scorn, two quick score lines between the dark arches of her brows. Her temper aged her; revealed the cost of her life, he thought. His own lack of charity warmed him queerly. Anson stood with the dark-haired girl in his arm, and she did not move from his grasp, allowing his fingers to travel to her nipple. Anson was grinning now, cupping her flesh like a man who weighs sugar or flour.

Grady pulled a clasp-knife from his pocket and began to pare his nails, his eyes on the floor where muck and melting snow pooled, his mouth caught up in some half-smile. Anson rocked back on his heels and grinned.

— No ma'am, he said, no gentleman. A boy only, I believe, so I reckon you need not fear.

And so Washington balled his fist and pulled his arm back, the wool skirt of his coat swirling at his hips as he twisted and swung, the dull crack at Anson's jaw, the softness of his skin there because his mouth was a little open still to speak, flesh pushing in past the teeth but hard bone too, bringing blood to his knuckles. Anson and the girl reeled back together and, still caught up, fell to the ground. Anson never would have expected he'd strike, Wash knew, bright bile in his throat, the petticoats of the whore up past her thighs as she tumbled, a flash of her dark fur only making his blood run hotter.

— You whey-faced fuck, Anson said, ignoring the whore now, clambering up, a spray of blood on his bottom lip, shouldering himself on Grady's arm. Grady's bright knife, Washington now saw, was directed towards the region of his own midriff. Sweat ran down under his collar. He rocked back on his heels, wondering whether he would have time to pull his coat off and wrap it around his arm — once, in the yard of the mill, he had seen a man do this, when two Hessians had come to blows over some nonsense and one had yanked a knife from his boot. John Roebling had dismissed them both on the spot; perhaps they had killed each other outside the gates.

Grady's expression did not change, the stolid planes of his face unmoving. His eyes, Washington now observed, were a cold glass-green, small, deep-set in his skull. They remained fixed on Washington's face as he swung his knife-arm up hot and quick — no time to remove his coat now — Washington yanked away in the nick, only to find himself in the brawny arms of the piano-player, held tight as a lover, enveloped in a liquorous stink of unwashed linen and rancid hair-grease.

— You fuckers, the piano-player said. You gonna quit this. We ain't the kinda place be sawdusting the floor for blood. Plenty cunt here for all if you act decent.

He loosed Washington from his embrace. The dark-haired girl had got to her feet, pulled at her dress, half-trying to cover herself; Anson held tight to her waist. The madam, Sophia, had not moved in the scuffle, standing her ground, her dark eyes narrowed. She moved close to him again; her manner was no longer ingratiating.

— Are you then, she said, a boy, who does not know how to behave himself in company?

She was well-spoken, Washington heard now; this fact had passed his attention at the door. A depth to her gaze he had not perceived — his breath still came hard, his heartbeat pulsing in his throat.

— No ma'am, he said. I am not. A boy.

— No indeed you are not, she said, and gave a brief dry smile. She reached to place a hand on his chest, straightening his shirt, smoothing it with her palm. You are, rather, an officer in the Army of the Potomac. General Meade's great army, soon to be victorious, we may be sure, over its Confederate foe. You have seen much bloodshed, of that I am sure; I cannot imagine you wish to see any more tonight. Tonight is your respite, my dear. We have no wish to offend, here. We have, I can assure you, whatever meets your taste.

A final pat on his breastbone. His breathing a little easier. Anson's eyes still on him — he had yet to wipe the blood from his face — and Grady's too, their own violence and scorn held in check by the presence of this woman. She looked like a general, he thought, a real one.

— Look, she said. She gestured towards the back of the parlor — or what had been once simply the parlor of this house but was now lively with men in and out of uniform, stretched back in chairs, their feet carelessly on tables, their voices careening off the walls. The brawl had not made a dent in their socializing. There was a long table towards the back of the broad room cluttered with jugs and bottles of every description; a slender black-skinned man with a shining gold hoop through one ear and a bright red satin waistcoat guarded the stash. She caught his eye, it appeared, gestured, he nodded, swiping at the table with a rag. Do you find yourself a drink, she said. Mr Elijah will take care of you. Go on. She gave a little tap to his shoulder now, before turning to Anson and Grady. Captain Anson, she said, we must tend to your wound, so nobly sustained in battle. Won't you follow me upstairs? Captain Grady, will you join us too?

Washington moved towards the bar. He tried to walk easily, as if he were accustomed to such places, but his spine was stiff, his tread jerky. He curled and uncurled his hand; the blood on his knuckle beginning to darken and crust over. The last time he had struck someone — well, that would have been Ferd, he was certain, and a long time ago. Violence had not been sanctioned in the Roebling house, unless of course it was committed by one person in particular; that was a different story.

The bar-tender set down his rag as Washington approached.

— Whiskey?

— All right, Washington said. Fine.

The bar-tender unstoppered a bottle, poured the tawny liquid into a glass with an elegant twist of his wrist and pushed it across the table. He badly wanted the drink now. His hand shook when he touched the glass.

— Madam Sophia stands you that one, the bar-tender said. Next one's on you. His voice was warm, with a laugh tucked inside.

— Perhaps you'll buy that one for me, said a voice beside him. Seeing as you've had the one for free. The speaker hardly reached his shoulder; her blonde curls fell in ringlets about her neck. Her eyes were a powdery blue; her clear skin was unrouged and the collar of her pink sateen dress was high. He observed the hollow of her neck in the fabric's soft shadow. Go on, Elijah, she said. I'll have a sangaree. I'm sure this gentleman's good for it. Aren't you, sir? She looked at him directly; her gaze was clear and fair. He did not deny it. He watched as the bar-tender mixed liquids together, grated sugar; everything was available freely in this place, that much was clear.

— That'll be two bits.

— Extortion, Washington said.

— His special recipe, said the young woman. Much finer than your whiskey. Whiskey's too rough for me.

— Does the trick, though, he said, and threw the stuff down his neck. In a moment he would feel looser, easier, and just the knowing of that brought some of the easy looseness right away. The bar-tender winked, poured another glass, and Washington drank that one down too. Of course, the girl was not what she seemed — he was not a fool — but he could almost convince himself that she was like a girl you might meet in a place that was not a place like this. She was not like Madam Sophia — and she seemed unlike the others, too, the ones he could see laughing and flirting at tables, along the walls, all at the edge of his eye. He fumbled in his pocket for coins, set them on the bar.

— And another, for that second whiskey of yourn.

Another coin, then. It hardly mattered.

BROOKLYN. DECEMBER, 1875.

— Read it back to me, he said.

— The letter regarding the link contract.

— Yes, he said. Yes.

Seated at his desk, she leaned forward into the light. It was a dark and brutal day; rain pattered steadily against the cold window glass, the sky a close lid overhead. He had moved to the chaise, lying back with his hand over his eyes. A sort of scrim over his vision, everything either too dull or too bright, the flame of the lamps intolerable, everything beyond their light muddy and indistinct. The pain in his jaw was worse today, knifing right up towards his skull, crawling around his neck like a noose.

— 'In consideration, finally, are two firms: Mr Carnegie's Keystone Bridge Company, of Pittsburgh, Pennsylvania; and the Passaic Rolling Mill Company of Paterson, New Jersey. You have had reports, prepared by Col. Paine and Mr Collingwood, of the products of each, and to my mind the results are quite clear.' She looked up from the page. I think it might be better if you wrote simply, 'clear' instead of 'quite clear', she said.

— Why is that?

— *Quite clear* implies that there might be some doubt, she said.

— No it does not, he said. It implies exactly the opposite.

— Yes, she said. It does. The very fact that you wish to stress the clarity of the matter indicates this. It is better to say, 'You have reports, prepared by Col. Paine and Mr Collingwood, of the products of each, and the results are clear.'

— Leaving, he said, *my mind* out of it too, then.

— Well, she said, yes.

— Perhaps because you feel there is some doubt, as you say, in Mr Murphy's mind regarding the soundness of my own.

She put the letter down — he could hear the rustle of the paper as she set it on the desk — and folded her hands in her lap. He uncovered his eyes and looked at her, attempting to avoid the lamp's glare — impossible. She was regarding him evenly.

— I did not say that, she said. I gave no indication that I felt so.

— No, he said, I know you did not say it. You *implied* it.

She looked away from him — then down at her hands — and then turned to pick up the letter again, the white skin of her neck, the curls of her gathered hair catching the lamplight.

— You may write what you wish, Colonel, she said. Of course.

— Very well then, he said. 'You have reports, prepared by Col. Paine and Mr Collingwood, of the products of each, and the results are clear.' She smiled, took up her pencil and scratched out the words now surplus to requirements.

— Read on? She asked. He nodded. 'It is necessary that the size of the link head should be as small as possible consistent with the uniform strength of the bar,' she read.

— Murphy will follow, he asked, the way in which I have described the anchor bars above, do you think?

— I believe so, she said. It is clear enough to me.

— Good. Carry on.

— 'The only head which fulfils this requirement in my opinion is that manufactured by the Keystone Bridge Company. The Passaic Rolling Mill has never made anything like this,' she read. 'I will stress that I do not think the East River Bridge is the proper kind of a structure to be experimented on. Lastly, I desire to say that if the rule is to be invariably adhered to of giving all contracts for supplies to the lowest bidders irrespective of all other considerations, I hereby absolve myself from all responsibility connected with the successful carrying on of the work.'

She put the letter down again, walked over to the window and stood with her back to him.

— I believe there is something you wish to say, he said. Blood roared at his temples.

— You must think carefully, she said.

— As I always do.

— Do you? About what you truly desire?

— My desires are neither here nor there. There is the work. He sat up. It cost him to do so. He felt the carpet beneath his stockinged feet. He steadied himself with his palms on the chaise. Its fabric was worn now; he recalled that she had ordered it from Paris, all those years ago. A *méridienne*, she had told him it was called, just the thing for taking a little rest in the middle of the day. It is not expensive, she had said, not for what it is. It *was* expensive. But, he reflected, he had got his money's worth. He rested on it all day now, and the head-rest was greasy from the print of his skull.

— I think you imagine, she said, that there is only one answer that Mr Murphy — that the Trustees — will give. Regarding your proposed absolution, I mean.

— It is not my business to imagine, he said.

She shook her head. That, you know, is nonsense. Without your imagination there would be — will be — no bridge. We must ensure, however, that the scope of your imagination ranges beyond the structure alone.

He laughed. We?

It took her three steps to reach the chaise from her place at the window. She sat down close beside him; the greeny-gold fabric of her tea-gown spread itself a little over the gray wool of his trouser leg and he felt the line of her thigh press against his own. She took his hand in hers. It made him start and then relax; the intimacy had become unfamiliar — and yet it was so familiar, too. Her palm was warm and soft and dry.

— Now, she said, you must listen to me.

WASHINGTON, D.C. FEBRUARY, 1864.

The bar-tender pushed the glass he had mixed for the girl — the young woman — towards her; she reached out her small hand, her close-trimmed nails like little pink sea-shells, and lifted it to her lips.

— To your taste, Miss Violet?

— You always know what I like, Elijah.

Washington watched her swallow. She set her eyes on him again.

— So, she said. You have heard I am Violet. She said it softly, in the southern way: *Vye*-let. Will you tell me your name? There is no one to introduce us, I fear; we must do the honors ourselves.

— Washington, he said. I am pleased to meet you, Miss Violet. She held out her hand and he brought it to his mouth, holding his lips against her skin for just longer — he knew — than was strictly necessary or proper.

— I imagine you are weary of remarks regarding the coincidence with the locale, she said. She made no effort to remove her hand from his.

— Your intuition matches your beauty, he said, to his own great surprise. Her uptilted chin gave him some sort of license. In any case, he continued, my name is an infernal mouthful; I'd be as glad to be rid of it as I would be out of this infernal place. He realized, in saying this, that he did not, in fact, quite mean it. In any case, he said, my friends call me Wash.

— And you would have me be your friend? I am glad of that, she answered. And while I take your point about locales, infernal or otherwise, I myself would not be sorry if you'd linger with us just a little while longer before you flee. Are you still chilled from the damp outdoors, or will you remove your coat?

He hardly knew he was still wearing it; he shrugged it off and threw it over the back of a nearby chair. He was nicely warmed now: by exertion, by anger, by whiskey. He stood before her in his shirtsleeves and loosened his collar. She raised her drink, and they clinked, glass against glass, though his was empty now.

— Will you have another?

— Better not, he said, though he wished for one.

— Here, she said. Try mine. Slips down quiet as anything.

He saw that as she passed the glass to him she turned it, so his lips would touch where hers had been. The stuff was sweet and spicy; wine with a sharp undercurrent of spirit, the sugar masking its strength. She made the merest nod to the bar-tender and he swiftly made another, and Washington swiftly began to drink it, watching his companion as she licked her lips, sipped, kept her eyes fixed on his.

Having been pleased with what he considered his charm moments before, Washington discovered that what there was of it now deserted him: perhaps he was capable of a single clever remark and no more. She — Violet — *Vye*-let — would think him stupid and leave him here alone. It was strangely comforting to think this, for it allowed him to ignore the truth of the situation: that it was not in this young woman's interest to abandon him.

— I wonder, she said, whether you would like some little edibles to pair with your sangaree. Have you supped? Even if you have — her right cheek dimpled when she smiled — I have heard that army rations leave something to be desired.

— You could say that, Washington replied. I would not like to describe to you some of the treats a soldier is offered. Unless, he said, you have a taste for weevils and mold.

She wrinkled her nose adorably. You will do better here, she said. I believe we'll find a cold collation, certainly. Ham, pickles — there may be oysters, too, brought in from Chesapeake Bay. Does that strike your fancy?

— O yes, he said. His mouth watered at the thought. He could not recall when he had last seen a piece of ham that had not begun to glow rancid green, never mind an oyster. That would be fine indeed.

She reached out, taking his hand in hers. Her palm was warm and soft and dry. Come, she said. Follow me.

She walked ahead of him with a carefree saunter that cut through the clusters of red-eyed drinkers and their flushed consorts as if they were but spirits or shadows; her fingers ever kept lightly hold of his. At the stairs she turned and glanced at him.

— Mind, she said, that sixth step. You see it is splintered, the board lifts. I tore my blue gown there the other day and nearly took a tumble right down.

— I could repair that, he said quickly, if you wish. The wood of the tread was plain worn out but could be easily replaced. It would be the work of a moment. There was spare lumber left from the dance-hall, a whole pile of it that the men would surely steal for firewood before long.

— I should not like to think of you in peril here, he said, or of any more risk to your pretty frocks. How badly he desired to please her! The realization struck him like a blow.

— You are awfully gallant, Captain Wash-ing-ton, she said, drawing out the syllables of his name with a smile. Let's discuss your proposition while we refresh ourselves.

He watched her lift her foot in its buttoned brown calfskin boot over the troublesome stair; she held up her skirt to do so, and he glimpsed her stockings, their delicate weave with a fine rib woven in. Her hips switched gracefully as she rose before him; truly Mr Hillgrove had been correct regarding the indelicacy of following a woman up a staircase.

And then they were in a room. A room with a table, a settee, two chairs — but also a bed, its linen turned down in welcome. Washington had presumed that ham and oysters would be got in some public setting, an upstairs dining-room, perhaps — but no, here was a selection of delicacies, laid out on the little table: two plates, bone-handled knives and silver three-pronged forks, a bottle, two fine glasses. She walked immediately to the table and poured: something straw-colored, almost golden, and he gulped at it when she handed it to him. It was syrupy and rich, almost as sweet as the sangaree, and it coated the inside of his mouth.

The thought came to him that he had left his coat downstairs, thrown over the back of a chair — it might be stolen, but there was nothing in him that wished to retrieve it now. The girl, the woman, Violet, was looking up at him, holding her glass but not drinking from it. Something had changed in her — her face, her manner, he could not have named what it was — even the way she held herself, the quality of the light in her eyes. He was rooted where he stood.

— Well, she said, you know — we can eat afterward — You look as if there's something else you might fancy, Captain Wash-ing-ton. She laughed, moved towards him, quick as a cat, took his glass from him, her fingers brushing his. Standing on tiptoe she kissed his throat, just where his grubby collar had loosened, where the heat rose within him. Like swimming in a fast river, he lost the will to pull against the current and let himself be dragged along.

— Just a small matter, she said. I will need to see your money. Then, we can leave off thinking of such things. Five dollars. Madam Sophia provides all this — she waved at the repast — for General Warren's aide-de-camp.

— How does — he made himself say it — How does Madam Sophia know I am General Warren's aide-de-camp? He had thought himself anonymous, at least.

— O, there is very little that Madam Sophia doesn't know in this town, she said with a silvery laugh. You would do well to further your acquaintance with her, Captain Wash-ing-ton. I am sure she would forgive you for your earlier provocation. I for one am glad Antoinette was not to your liking. I believe you are the sort who likes a little mystery, do you not?

She was standing straight before him now, her slender form pressed right against him. Somehow he had not reckoned that she would know all that had passed when he had entered this place; but of course, she did. Everything must have been planned, or swiftly arranged with that gesture of the madam's hand. Violet reached into his jacket with the neat fingers of a pickpocket. In his notebook she found what she sought: his last bills. There were four of them; she dug for his remaining coins and slipped it all into some fold of her dress.

— There, she said. Now we need not think on that, dear Captain.

She took his hand again and placed it on the collar of her dress, where she led his fingers first to one button, and then the next, until he'd got the rhythm for himself and the pretty soft fabric parted, falling away like the petals of an opening flower. Under that, her chemise, laced; he pulled at the lightly-knotted bow and there were her breasts, high and white and small, her nipples the same shade as her mouth. He pulled himself hard against her now — wrapping her arms around his neck, she turned him as if in a dance — leading him, for he would be led — so the bed was there for them, her blonde ringlets making a halo around her head as she lay down, lay under him.

Now her fingers, reaching for the buttons below his belt — one was missing, he realized, he had meant to sew it on but had run out of thread and was going to ask Paine if he had any in his tidy box — but as her warm little hand worked its way towards him, he recalled not only the button but also his father's words, a long and vivid letter sent just a few weeks after he had joined the 6th New York. He recalled the sound of the rain on the canvas tent when he had unfolded it; a leak that dripped into a tin bucket. He had been expecting news of the mill; that had not been what the letter contained.

It was not, his father had written, that the urges of the body were to be distrusted or despised; carnal desire, John Roebling said, was natural, and a man's seed — Washington's eyes had opened wider and wider as he read by the light of a smoky oil-lamp — was one of the body's necessary essences, like the blood in the veins, the slime of the nose, the products of the bladder or bowels. Excreting the seed — Washington coughed, nearly spilling his cup of coffee — was one of the methods by which the corporeal self was kept *in balance*, and of course, his father continued, was necessary for procreation, for the generation of human life, the peopling of the world. Washington briefly imagined his father *peopling*, and the blood rushed to his cheek. He took a gulp of the cold and bitter coffee in his tin cup.

— Come, Violet said — her voice running alongside the recollection of his father's — there you are, dear Wash, you are a fine soldier, are you not?

Yes, a fine soldier, that's what John Roebling had hoped he would be. He had been, too, he told himself, his mouth to this strange girl's skin, the salt of it, a faint bitterness against his tongue from the scent she wore: honey, rosewood. He cupped his hand around the little hill of her breast and then — *However*, his father had continued, a soldier's life was a treacherous one, and not only thanks to shot and shell. Where there were soldiers' camps, so there were camp followers: women who could be bought for dollar bills and whiskey —

Dollar bills and whiskey, his last four dollars crumpled in the cloth of the dress he caught up in his hands to pull up now over her white thighs —

Washington had read the letter over and again until its folds and edges were threadbare; he had kept it tucked in his pocket-book until the pocket-book was lost in the retreat after Second Bull Run. Now, even as he pulled his own shirt open so his skin could touch this woman's skin, as he lost himself in her sky-blue mirthful eyes and smelled her breath, her sweat, and reached with his right hand to touch her, the slick wet between her legs, even as he did so, his father's closing admonitions returned to him nearly verbatim. John Roebling had recounted the story of a neighbor of his own parents, a man called Köhl, who had fought with Blücher's army against the Little Corporal. He had returned to Mühlhausen with a row of medals across his chest, which he would display at every opportunity. He had, however, also returned with syphilis, and gradually, as the years passed, his nose collapsed into the pit of his face, madness overtook him, and overtook too the *dear young woman* (Washington recalled that these were his father's words exactly), Johanna — the same name as Washington's own mother! — whom he had married upon his triumphant return from the battlefield.

This is the price of dissipation, his father had written. *A bitter price, and one not paid only by he whose weakness is his undoing.*

It was this letter which had kept Washington away from such places until this point, through the two years and more he had worn the blue coat — yet he must have known, tonight, where Anson and Grady were leading him, he must have allowed this weakness into himself, a crack in the mortar of his spirit, fractured by months of advance and retreat, by the green stink of suppuration, by his every plan being blown to smithereens by either explosives or incompetence.

It happened before he meant. She had put her hand on him, on his, to draw him into her, but he came off before he even touched her. It went through him like a fit; he groaned and clutched at her shoulder, his mouth on her soft neck. He whose weakness is his undoing.

She laughed, but not unkindly, the back of her hand stroking his face.

— O Captain Wash, she said, no matter, never fear. We shall have a bite to eat and try again in a moment; I think you have waited too long for this. Yet the evening stretches before us. She sat up, her gown falling right away from her shoulders, which were patterned with little freckles; now she crossed her legs like a girl in school, her skirts pulled right up around her hips; the hair at her cunt — the word put itself into his mind, he heard the voice of the piano-player who had wrestled him away from Anson — was darker than the hair on her head, but still blonde, sheened with her moisture and, he saw, the trail of his seed. She reached for his hand and put his fingers right to the heart of her.

— I am still ready for you, she said. Sweet as those oysters. Let's eat, and then you'll see your way true. We should have had a prowl around those platters when we came up — it never does to fuck hungry.

He couldn't look at her again; couldn't bear to see her face. He pushed back off the bed, fumbled with his buttons. At least he had not taken his boots off. Despite himself he was half-hard again, and he hated himself for it. He grabbed his hat and moved to the door. The ham and oysters lay sweating on their platters, his appetite was gone, all he wanted was to be out of this room, out of this place.

— Last chance, she said, my dear. Still time to change your mind. He heard her bright laugh as the door slammed behind him.

That sixth step nearly caught him as he fled; the raucous noise of the place assaulting his senses, the smell of drink with an undertow of piss and any other sort of vileness, the roars of coarse laughter, the brutal piano-player laying into his instrument as if he would beat it to death.

— Cut yourself a slice, soldier?

— Look at him, another voice, a woman's, Antoinette's; he

knew her name now, still by the door, her black hair all down around her shoulders, her breasts still bare. A bit of cuff for you and then you run away? She laughed. Where's the fun in that?

BROOKLYN. DECEMBER, 1875.

My health has become of late of so precarious a nature, that I find myself incapable — this word is crossed out — *less and less able to do any work of any kind. I am therefore reluctantly compelled to offer my resignation as Eng. of the East River Bridge. The hopes that time and rest would effect a change have been in vain, rest being simply impossible.*

He was sleeping. Or perhaps, he was not sleeping. He was, perhaps, wide awake. Was sitting up, perfectly alert, insistent. Knowing the course that needed to be taken. There was no choice now. Things had got — too bad. Unspeakable. He had no words for it. The pain stole all his words, wiped them away, only its terrifying presence, weight, filling him, blinding him, deafening him. All the others, Emily, the doctors, in some far distance, unable to reach him, unable to help. Queerly, sometimes, a vision of his father, standing very still at the end of the ferry rack, on the pilings, the boat pulling through the water, a white swell curling at its prow. A moment held in suspension, high above the pain.

He dictated the letter to her. The final paragraph of a letter about the awarding of contracts. The Keystone Bridge Company. The Passaic Rolling Mill. She took down his words as she had taken down so many thousands of others, the morning light, the afternoon light, the early evening light, the light of a candle or an oil-lamp, shining on her tousled hair. The tips of her fingers blackened with pencil-shavings. Her back aching but she will never complain, there is no room for her complaint. She writes and writes and writes.

My health has become of late of so precarious a nature, that I find myself incapable — this word is crossed out — *less and less able to do any work of any kind. I am therefore reluctantly compelled to offer my resignation as Eng. of the East River Bridge. The hopes that time and rest would effect a change have been in vain, rest being simply impossible.*

He was sleeping. Drugged, as he so often was these days, so often must be. It is the only thing that banishes the intractable pain. He has grown less fearful of the effects the drug might have. He denies his desire but knows she sees it all the same. His dry mouth, his sweating, the sheets soaked through. As he sleeps, her mouth shaping the questions: have you not given enough? She removes herself from the question. She was raised with the sacrifice of soldiers. But sometimes, she thinks, this, this is too much. For a while he was vomiting blood. There was still a stain on the Turkey carpet. She recalls the long walks she took — two years ago, now, the time has passed either very slowly or very fast, she cannot tell —

He did not dictate the letter. Or rather, the final paragraph of a letter regarding the awarding of contracts. She waited until he was asleep. It was an experiment, to see if she could enter into him, find his desire or release him from it, release them both. It could no longer be borne. She could no longer bear it. She did not know, then, the extent of her own resilience. She did not know what she would finally discover down at the riverfront, among the men, in the shadow of those great towers of stone, among the reels of shining coiled wire, shards of metal, wood shavings, hammers, anvils, buckets, mud, the reeking bodies of the men, their glistening skin, their hats, the stumps of cigars, broken clay pipes, the swinging clanging movement and music of the work. She had not yet clasped that in her hands. And so she wrote. An experiment. A trial.

My health has become of late of so precarious a nature, that I find myself incapable — this word is crossed out — *less and less able to do any work of any kind. I am therefore reluctantly compelled to offer my resignation as Eng. of the East River Bridge. The hopes that time and rest would effect a change have been in vain, rest being simply impossible.*

WASHINGTON, D.C. FEBRUARY, 1864.

The walk back to his quarters was much longer than the walk to the Pretty Wink, not least because he had — of course — left his coat behind. Five dollars down, a new coat to buy, aside from all the other humiliation — February mud clogged his boots and February wind poked its fingers into every seam of his clothing — how stupid, how stupid! to leave his coat. A thin moon hung in the sky, cold as a metal shard, and at one point in his journey he had half a thought that he would be walking this road forever, that there was no destination to reach, that he would forever feel these sharp stones pressing though the thin leather of his boot soles, the damp chill forever soaking through the wool and linen of his unwashed clothing, no end in sight to any of this.

A little light spilled out from the hut he shared with Paine, through the chinks between the rough split logs. He pushed through the door. Paine was sitting on his bed, his boots off once more, his hat hung on the back of a chair, writing with a pencil in his diary.

— Hey, Paine said. Look at you. Half-froze. You called away too? Left your coat in the General's tent?

Handed the lie, he took it. Yes, he said.

— Foolish in this weather, I'd say. You want a brew? There's some old coffee by the stove, just needs heating.

— No, Wash said. He stood by the warmth, reaching his stiff hands out. There would be a bruise on his knuckle where he'd caught Anson's jaw. The clot of blood was black now.

— So it was Warren wanted you? What was it?

Paine was orderly, thorough, perceptive. It was these qualities which had forged their bond and made their friendship valuable each to each — and valuable too to the army that made use of them. But now Paine's perspicacity seemed altogether too sharp. Washington dropped his hands to his sides; his injury was just the sort of thing Paine's quick eyes would catch.

— Just — some foolishness. Wash saw a little flinch at his friend's cheek; he had never spoken so of Warren before. I mean, about the dance. The hall. I think someone was getting at him — you know, the higher-ups always have higher-ups to beat them, I guess that's some consolation.

— Wonder who gets at old Abe! Paine laughed.

— Mrs Mary Lincoln, I bet, Wash said. He felt his shoulders relax a little; he had started to warm, too. What about Howe? A good time to change the subject.

— Howe can't read a map, that's the plain and simple truth. And he will not trust his lieutenants; he must have the man who drew the map explain to him what it shows.

Washington sat down on his own bed and drew off his boots. The action recalled to him the warmth of that chamber, the warmth of the girl, the way in which those moments were briefly sealed off into a separate universe of possibility, beyond obligation or virtue or his father's warnings or whatever else his life had in store, should he be permitted to survive this conflict.

— You look fair washed-out, Paine said, if you don't mind I say. Warren, you know — he can get the darkness about him sometimes. He admires you greatly. I have heard him say it.

— Well, thank you, Will, Wash said. He lay down on his cot. He was disinclined to undress.

— Did he tell you — well, I'm sure he did, Paine said. Who he was bringing to the ball.

Hard experience had taught Wash that the trick to lying was keeping things as simple as possible. Evade, don't fabricate. Deny rather than offer. No, he said to Paine. He did not.

— Rumor has it, said Paine, setting his diary and pencil aside before unbuttoning his collar and slipping off his shirt, that his sister is coming from Cold Spring. Shows that things must not be so bad if he feels it's safe for her to travel, anyhow.

— Yes, Wash said. I suppose it does. Washington had heard the general mention his sister on more than one occasion; he had been with him once when his commanding officer had made a brief diversion to acquire a length of calico to send home to Cold Spring for her.

— Blow the lamp? Paine asked.

— Sure, Wash said. He would be glad of the darkness. He pulled his blanket over his legs. Paine had drawn on a nightshirt, and now with his calves shining like soft moons, knelt by the side of his cot, his hands clasped, his head bent. He prayed nearly silently, but Washington could hear the whisper of his breath, sometimes the name of his little daughter and that of his late wife. Sometimes their generals or the president, a comrade who had been wounded or had died. Paine knit his fingers together hard and held his shoulders tight as if he were pulling on a rope that led to Heaven and could yank blessings right down. This was a blasphemous thought, of course. Disrespectful, at least.

Paine finished his supplications — if that's what they were — and pulled himself to his feet. He lifted the glass of his own lamp, blew the wick, and darkness closed its fist. Wash lay on his cot and let his eyes adjust to what began as black but then opened out into a pattern of shadow, the fires and lights of the camp through the oiled paper windows, the rough bark walls of their cabin, Paine's form perfectly still in his cot two feet away. He slept on his back with his arms crossed over his chest: he had trained himself to sleep that way, he had once told Washington, in case the Lord came to take him in the night. He would go as he would wish to be found.

Washington could see Paine's eyes were open; they shone

despite the dark. He would not have sensed the falsehood; that was, somehow, worse than suspicion. He lay listening to Paine's breath slowing and tried to slow his own. That girl's freckled shoulders, the alabaster skin at her wrist. The taste of wine in his mouth. He wished for sleep, but it would not come.

BEDROCK

In the summary we have given of the leading phenomena of unstratified and volcanic rocks, we have unavoidably been led in to theoretical speculation, and have seen that the most probable explanation of these phenomena is found in the hypothesis of the original fluidity of the entire material of the earth, caused by the presence of intense heat. From the fluid mass of metals, and metalloid bases of the earths, and alkalis, the first granitic crust appears to have been formed, by oxidation of these bases; and subsequently broken into fragments, disposed at unequal levels above and below the surface of the first formed seas.

— *Chapter VI, 'Primary Stratified Rocks',* Geology and Mineralogy, Considered with Reference to Natural Theology *by the Rev William Buckland, Vol 1, London, William Pickering, 1836*

✣ ✣ ✣ ✣ ✣

BROOKLYN. MAY 17, 1872.

HE PICKED THE stone up off his desk, held it in his hand. He sat as still as he could, reaching out slowly; the smallest movement pushed a burning ache through his joints. Today was a bad day. There were more bad days than good now. For a while he had kept track, in his pocket-book, of the fluctuations of his health, just, of course, as his father had once done. He had developed a little code, *h* for headache, *j* for joint pain, all the rest, underlining and annotating according to severity and location. He had supposed, when he had begun to do this, that it would make him feel better — no, that was not quite what he had supposed. That it would make him feel — in command of himself, perhaps. It had rather the opposite effect. So he had abandoned the practice. He had no time, now, for what was not useful.

On its face, a quadrangle: two inches across at its base, rather less at the top. He had not yet measured it precisely. Thickness, perhaps an inch and a half, very roughly. Dark gray, glitter of mica, the laminations of metamorphosis, the vast pressures of the Earth's heat, the Earth's time. It weighed a few ounces, no more. He closed his eyes — that was more comfortable, anyhow — and let it rest there in his palm, folding the fingers of his right hand around it. Its rough edges, its granular surface. His own sense of the ancient. Of what could bear the weight. Of what he had been looking for. It was this. It was this.

The stone warmed against his skin. Outside his window, spring sunshine, a scent of blossom perhaps — perhaps — just detectable past the usual street stinks. The curtains half-drawn; a yellow finger of light spilled through the glass and onto the carpet. Sometimes, when the pain called for true stillness, he would lie on his chaise and watch a warm bar of sunshine move across the carpet, first making the polished wooden legs of the desk gleam, then the music stand — how long since he had set a score on its frame? He could not recall — the fireguard, the papered wall. Closed in this room as he was, he could yet observe the Earth's rotation.

In a week's time he would be thirty-five years old. He could hear some noise from downstairs: the table being laid. He had heard Emily discussing the menu with the cook: bouillon, poached chicken — peas, he was sure he remembered a mention of peas.

Bland food, food for an invalid, often left untouched on the plate brought to his room. But today, he decided, he would go down for lunch.

BROOKLYN. DECEMBER 1, 1870.

They had finished supper; Liza was clearing the dishes, Emily unfolding the pages of the *Brooklyn Eagle*. Frost touched the window-glass, but in here it was warm and comfortable. This room had been dark and gloomy when they had taken the house, not that Washington had thought to care. After his father's death — in the room upstairs — Emily had persuaded him that some new paper and paint would be in order. She had settled on a vining pattern of green and cream for the dining room, and Washington had found that he enjoyed letting his eyes rest on its printed tendrils; the pale background was restful to the eye and caught the light of the lamps and candles nicely. She had been firm with the men who came to strip the old paneling and lay the paper: they were to do their work only in the hours when the chief engineer was away at the bridge office or out at the river site. It was as if it had all been done by invisible hands; he had admired the way she managed the task, though he had never told her so.

Now she held the newspaper out in front of her, scanning the fine print of the front page. Gracious, she said. Old Joe Hooker wants war with Canada.

— Not sure that qualifies as news, Washington said. Old Joe Hooker wants war with anyone. He looked across at her; her hair was down, her soft blue dress was loose around her body. She smiled at him and he found himself considering the shape of that body beneath the cloth. He noted he felt a little less tired than he had on many recent nights. Emily liked to read the papers. He did not share her taste. Rumors and lies, he told her. O now, she would say, don't speak ill of Mr Kinsella, at least. Mr Kinsella must sell his wares like the others, he would answer, and so we'll twist his pages for kindling to teach him a lesson.

Yet he would humor her. An evening such as this one, peaceful and companionable, was what he had hoped for in considering the prospect of marriage; it had taken something, at any rate, to convince his fiancée that his vision of matrimony was not aligned with his father's. Yet there had been few enough of these quiet times even before he had come to be in full charge of the work. Though it was not only the work which made their lives different from what he had imagined or expected. He had so desired her — everything about her — *desired*, meaning: wished for her proximity, wished to understand, wished to *see*. And yet, now they lived in each other's pockets — well. In the early days of their courtship it had been so plain to him whether she was content or no, for instance; now, to his intense puzzlement, this was no longer the case. But tonight her face was clear and smiling.

— Leave off Joe Hooker, he said. What other news?

She peered at the right-hand column. There are sixty-two millionaires in Philadelphia, she said. I wonder how they made the count.

— Said they'd raise the income tax and saw how many ran away, he said, and was glad to see her smile. You must tell your friend Miss — Perkins, is it? To head for the city of Brotherly Love and hunt herself out a rich one.

— Do not be unkind to Miss Perkins, Wash. She cannot help herself.

— And so you must help her, my dear. She is lucky to have you as a friend. I am only glad that I myself am already claimed so I may escape her advances. She is — forthright, is she not?

— You are too mean, she said, laughing, and then cocked her head. Liza, she called, there is someone at the door. Will you —

The peace at his heart sank away. No, he said, don't send her. He pushed back from the table and ran down the stairs.

— You need to come, Paine said. Standing on the stoop, his hat in his hand, winter drizzle spangling his whiskers in the light that spilled from the hall. Come now.

◊

> The caisson would apparently settle on a broken ridge of rock, running diagonally from one corner to the other, and having a moderate dip of perhaps five feet in the hundred toward the land; but falling off very suddenly toward the east corner in the number one chamber.
>
> — Pneumatic tower foundations of the East River suspension bridge, *Washington A. Roebling, New York, Averell & Peckett, 1873*

✣ ✣ ✣ ✣ ✣

BROOKLYN. MAY 16, 1872.

HE HAD BEEN asleep when Collingwood came to call. A sound sleep, because he had dreamt: dreamt of driving out through the woods, dawn, autumn, the morning star up over the horizon as wrapped in a blanket he sat next to Bernigau, who was singing, singing — blue mist threading through the branches of the trees, the black mule — Schitzi — picking her way along the path — less a dream than a vision, he knew. It was too clear for a dream; it was a bright recollection, a crystalline gift.

He woke, sweating. Two days before he had ventured back down into the caisson after an absence of more than a week. The hot thick air had nearly choked him, and he knew that the men were watching him as they stood together in the airlock, the deafening hiss of the compressors, his clothes soaked almost instantly with sweat, the wet heat, a coating of mud running up his boots. He stepped down into the chamber where Collingwood was waiting, his face lit by a white spray of light, men moving behind him in the shadows, in the streams of glare.

— Here, Collingwood said. Look at this.

It was an iron rod an inch in diameter, three feet long, the tip of it dented, battered and the other end flattened and bruised by repeated blows of a sledgehammer.

— We have dozens, Collingwood said. Well, a couple of dozen. He gestured out towards the chambers of the caisson, as if he could see right through the brick walls that ran from the iron-clad roof to the muddy floor. Beneath the soles of their boots grit shifted on the rough compact surface.

Greiner! Collingwood called. A workman appeared from out of the darkness as if he had been waiting in the wings of a theatre. He held in his hands a bundle of rods, a bouquet, and the chief engineer could see the muscles in his arms work to hold them, though his still face gave no indication of effort. He was tall and heavyset, with thick moustaches — spattered with yellow mud, as the whole of him was — that drooped past his jaw. His shirt was open to the waist, like a circus strongman's.

— How many's that?

— *Fünfzehn*, he said. He stared straight at the chief engineer, his chin jutting up. *In der Nacht und heute Morgen.*

A Swabian, Washington guessed. He had to strain to understand. They thought highly of themselves, those men. He recalled now that Collingwood had hired a gang of them, all together, thinking to please Col. Roebling; Col. Roebling had not been as delighted as his lieutenant had expected, despite being informed that they were good hard workers. Such groups were more likely to be discontented and cause trouble: this one looked a likely specimen.

— We speak English here, he said. He wondered if the man was looking for some sort of special treatment, with his clumsy Dutch. Show me. He stepped close to the workman, took first one rod and then another, held them up to the light. As soon as he had got down here his hands had become weak and pale; the blood pushed out of his fingers so they wrinkled like a drowned man's. He held each rod tight so Greiner would not see his wrist tremble. His breath came quick and he tried to slow it, to little avail.

— That one's mine, the workman said. His accent was thick and rough. Bent-like.

It was. The cold iron skewed at one end, the metal trapped between the blows of the hammer above and the solid surface below. Greiner would have felt his bones ring with the force of it.

— Sledge bounced right back at you, did it? Now they stood in the light Washington could see that one of the man's eyes was ringed with a dark bruise that ran across his cheekbone and into his dark hair.

— Off with you, Collingwood said. Leave those here.

The man simply opened his hands in a shrugging gesture and stepped swiftly back, shoving his fists into the pockets of his dun pants. The compressed air dulled all sound but still the discordant clatter of the rods against the packed ground pushed against the drums of their ears, and Collingwood and Washington both had to leap away to avoid being struck.

Washington looked across at Collingwood.

— Fighting, Collingwood said. He was nearly dismissed the other day. Then did all that driving. He's no worse than any of the others. And manages a six-hour shift. You know where we are now, Colonel. How deep. Gets to them.

— Gets to us all, Washington said. Still. I suppose my fighting days are behind me.

He knew he had misspoken as soon as the words came from his mouth; Collingwood's father, Washington knew, had insisted on a substitute for his son during the war — the family jewelry business would not tend to itself. The assistant engineer, with his neat-clipped whiskers and narrow clerk's face, stood impassive, saying nothing. Well — now was not the time for niceties, and the embarrassment would only be compounded by apology.

— Show me, Washington said, what you've hit. Sweat was pooling in the hollow of his back; the stifling air crawling down his throat. He dropped the rod he still held and set his palm against his thigh to keep off the shakes. He was glad when Collingwood turned his back to him and moved to a rough wooden bench set against one of the caisson's brick piers; on it was a rough wooden box. Collingwood pulled something from the box and held it out to Washington between finger and thumb. Washington reached out for it, but in that moment it was as if Collingwood's hand was at the end of a tunnel, black-walled, roasting, narrow, and Washington could not even crawl through the closing walls, the white mouth of light where Collingwood stood, finger and thumb, just there, out of reach, the workman with his bruised face, the clatter of the battered rod rattling in his skull.

And then. And then. A needle. The prick at his arm, the cool flood, rising.

BROOKLYN. DECEMBER 1, 1870.

The cobbled streets streaked with mud, snow, horse-shit as he ran with Paine down toward the river through the freezing air — he had not even stopped to take his coat and the wind cut hard through his linen. The portal of the lock flung open, and in they climbed to the iron chamber, which he had already come to find a stifling coffin, though he told no one, not even Paine, not even Emily, of these sensations and this dread. The windlass squealed as Buxton — a reliable man — twisted it to seal them inside. His gut dropped as he waited for the snap of the valve that would let in the compressed air from below; a keening screech as the pressure came and set clamps around his neck and head as it built. He could feel the tightening around his face, the bridge of his nose and throat, and saw Paine flinch a little too, which relieved him — somewhat —

There was a clang as the pressure equalized and the door at their feet dropped open of its own accord. Slick metal to climb down, the rungs slippery on his boot soles and palms, holding tight as he moved first one foot and then another, first one hand and then another; he had slipped, not many days before, and cracked his chin on a rung, biting his tongue, tasting the iron of his blood in his mouth. He stepped down into the sweltering chamber, here where there was neither day nor night, neither sun, stars or snow. The flaring calcium lamps threw brutal shadows all around.

At the southwestern corner of the caisson, close by one of the dividing frames that cut the structure into chambers, one of the men stood perched up on a brace, peering at the roof above. He was stripped to the waist, his torso streaked with mud, a filthy kerchief around his neck; he craned his neck upwards. At the edges of the chamber other workmen stood, eyes white in their dirty faces, hands in pockets, shifting from foot to foot. Overturned wheelbarrows, shovels scattered, buckets kicked over.

— He felt a draught, Paine said. Air sucked up into the roof. Called the foreman. Better look.

Washington stepped up on the brace.

— What's your name?

— Starling, the workman said.

— Show me what you see then, Mr Starling.

Fire on night of Dec 1 . . . Candle, pointing with cement. Bad place, would not be seen. Burnt appearance — living coals . . . no smoke — amount of water applied. . . . Above frame no chance to stop up leaks —

Steam no good — apparently out. Digging out water shaft — boring commenced — no fire at first, smell outside — danger of letting out air, settling of caisson — over night.

— Just here. He shifted so that Washington could stand in his place, reached his arm up at a joint in the pine beams of the roof and began to claw at a rough twist of rag that had been shoved up into the seam where two beams met.

— No cement here?

— No sir, not yet, the workman said, still pulling at the cloth that was jammed up hard above him. Washington stood breast to breast with Starling and reached up too, their fingers working together to yank at the cloth, which had been half plastered over with mud from the floor. It had begun to dry, spattering down, a mote of it fell in Washington's eye; he rubbed at his face with his sleeve, his vision blurring briefly, calling the memory of dizziness, sickness. He shook his head and let his shoulder rest against Starling's, so briefly —

— Foreman said to shove something up there, something wet, kill the draught, Starling said. Took my shirt.

— We'll find you another. There are bigger fish to fry right now. Wash had no idea what they would see. The last fire had been a little over a month ago: splintered wood and rubbish that had caught after one of the men dropped his candle. Still the men could not understand, it seemed, what fire meant down here in the compressed air: wood that would have been too damp to catch at the surface burst into flame like Lucifer himself had set it alight. There were fire extinguishers now in every chamber, buckets, hoses for steam. It was impossible perhaps to think of fire under the river. That was the problem. How to think of it, how to make them think.

The rag of cloth came away from the fist-size hole in the seam and both men, the chief engineer and Starling, jumped back: the butt end of the cloth was aflame.

— Fuck! The burning rag grazed the workman's arm; one of the men standing in the shadows ran forward with a bucket and threw water over the rag and both the men.

Now Washington turned his face up to the open hole in the seam. A sucking wind, a great in-breath — and then he saw it, a dark, orange glow, muscled and shifting, an animal movement of light. He put his hand up close to the beam; reaching up he nearly toppled, the workman reached to steady him but Washington pushed him away — No, he said — No. Bile in his throat. Above the charred opening in the seam a red maw, five or six feet long, roiling with heat that knocked him back sure as a blow from a fist.

Fire — several small Fires. Leaks in seams — a caulking of oakum catches easily — some easily put out — 5' wide and 6" burnt away —

— Who was working here? A tin box hammered in near the beam, the kind of thing some of the men used to hold food or drink. That yours?

— No sir. I just came on my shift, sir. They say there's a man called McDonald, sir. That's his. I never met him. Different shifts, sir. His face was pale in the flared white light, his expression flat.

— *Shit!*

— Col. Roebling? Paine said quietly. He turned to Starling. It's all right, he said. You did well.

— I won't be dismissed, sir?

— Don't be an ass, Washington said. Tell the foreman Col. Roebling said you are to get another dollar today. But before you tell him that, say we need fire extinguishers. As many as he can find.

◊

The first spurs of bedrock were encountered at a depth of 75 feet, under the shoe on the water-side. It would seem that the caisson had been scraping along a vertical wall of rock for the previous five feet at that spot.

— *Washington A. Roebling*, Pneumatic tower foundations of the East River suspension bridge, *New York, Averell & Peckett, 1873, p. 87*

✣ ✣ ✣ ✣ ✣

TROY. MAY 18, 1856.

MAX WOULD ALWAYS make a special point of sitting next to him in Dr Loudon's lectures. When Loudon would turn his back to face the chalkboard, Max would yawn and stretch, his mouth a great silent O, leaning his shoulder on Wash's own; when Loudon turned back to face them, he would scribble intently in his notebook, but when Wash glanced over he would see that what Max had written was gibberish, or worse, sometimes — filth.

— Max! he had hissed at him, once — maybe more than once — appalled. *Cock*, Max had written. *Balls. Cocking balls. Balling cocks.* Careful drawings on the margins of the page. Max was a fine draughtsman, in fact; the difficulty lay only in his choice of subject. Loudon's demeanor was, undoubtedly, dull: he was a small man, little more than five foot, with skin pale as lime-wash and tufts of white hair at the edges of his skull's dome. It would have been hard to state his age; it had been said that he had worked with Sedgwick in the north of England; it had been said that, despite his threadbare britches and thin-soled boots, he was rich: a gold strike in Georgia, decades ago. He had a kind of quiet authority, which appealed to Washington, a sympathy with the vast scope of time the Earth's history encompassed.

— Don't you see, he said to Max one evening, when they sat by the fire in the latter's fine room, we are like mayflies, to the Earth. All of human history, a blink! compared to the history of the rocks —

— I do see, Max said. I wish I didn't. It's either alarming or tedious; I don't favor either choice. Let me see what you are at?

Max was drinking hock, his feet stretched out to the grate; Washington was sitting at Max's table, a sheet of paper held flat with four books, one at each corner, stretched out before him. He had his drawing pencils, a little knife and a box of watercolors: Max had bought the paints for him ten days ago. Washington had given up his resistance to Max's gifts — O they are not *gifts*, Max would say — as refusal, or attempted refusal, seemed only make him more acutely aware that the bounty only flowed in one direction.

On the paper, Washington had sketched in a copy of Cuvier and Brongniart's geological section through Paris; he had already been at work on it for days. He had a piece of waxed cloth to carry it in; he would roll it carefully and tie it with a violet ribbon Elvira had sent him — he was the recipient of charity on every front. He was at work on finishing the creatures found in the layer of sediment described as *Paleotherien*: skeletons of the long-extinct animals of those vanished ages, creatures that had bestrode the world on a surface long-sunk; now he patiently cross-hatched the gypsum and marl.

— I am rather glad there are no such beasts in Paris now, Max said. He rested his hand on Wash's shoulder, bending low so their faces nearly touched.

— I suppose, Wash said, making neat, rhythmic strokes on the paper. An easy silence rested between them, the hiss and snap of the fire as a knot of wood caught and burned hot, a spatter of rain on the glass. Wash picked up his knife and sharpened his pencil. It was quiet enough that they could both hear the scrape as the blade peeled at the lead, the wood; he turned the slender cylinder in his fingers to bring it to a fine point.

— I should like to go to Paris, Max said.

— Mmm hmm.

— Fine ladies there.

— Better than antediluvian monsters, Wash said. *Ha, ha, ha,* went the pencil against the paper.

— Look at you. You take such care!

— If something is worth doing —

— Yes, yes, 'it is worth doing well', so I have heard you say, Mr Roebling, more times than I care to count. It's fortunate I am so fond of you; I should find you quite dull, otherwise.

Washington put down his pencil. The room was really very warm; Max liked a fire, whatever the season. He pulled at his collar, loosening the fabric around his throat.

— That's fair, Washington said.

— Your dullness — or my affection?

— It's not up to me to say.

They regarded each other for a moment before Washington turned back towards the table, the paper, his delicate lines, the wash of colors painted with a dainty brush. But look, dear Max, he said. Look how remarkable this is. Just give it your attention. Do you know, I have come to think that perhaps nothing is really dull if you turn your full attention to it.

Max threw back his head and groaned aloud.

— O no! His voice was fit for the stage. O no! They have got you! They have turned you to a Rensselaerean, full and proper!

— Stop it, Washington said. Max. Now, stop it. *Look*. He pulled out the chair on the other side of the table, swung it so it was placed beside him and stared at Max, who sat obediently. Now you see: here is the river Seine. The section is taken at the Pont de la Tournelle: it is an old stone bridge that runs across the river from the Left Bank to the Ile St-Louis. But all this — he let his finger drift over his drawing, not touching it, hovering just over the paper, Max's eye following the movement of his hand — is the Earth's most ancient history. Paris bustles all around, ladies in silk gowns and button boots strolling along the riverbank —

— You know how to catch my attention, said Max.

— Strolling with their parasols on the arms of fine gentlemen, yet just below the soles of their soft shoes are layers and layers of rock, built up over eons. Different rocks in different eras, formed in different ways. Animals die — animals that no longer walk the Earth — and are preserved in the rock. See them here — he gestured. This is called stratigraphy, the study of these layers and how they are formed. What they mean. What they tell us. We know how long they have lain there, what they are made from, whether freshwater or saltwater has flowed over them in ages past. Some rocks are good to found on, others are not. All this, just here, by the side of a river in a beautiful city. And as for beauty — the drawing itself — well, the original is beautiful, Max. I can't speak for my copy.

— There is beauty here, Max said, surely. He looked at the drawing, and then at Washington. There is beauty here indeed.

◊

All our observations respecting the past and present lead to the conclusion that the plan of creation is one – that the laws and forces which are now in operation have been the same from the beginning: therefore, the true method for an interpretation of the past, is by those laws and forces which govern the present.

— *Ebenezer Emmons,* American Geology, Containing a Statement of Principles of the Science with Full Illustrations of the Characteristic American Fossils, *Albany, New York: Gray, Sprague & Co., 1854, p. 2*

✣ ✣ ✣ ✣ ✣

BROOKLYN. MAY 18, 1872.

— IT WAS WORSE, she said, here, in Brooklyn.

— How can you say that?

— Because you did not know.

— I still do not know. All along, I have not known.

— You are too hard on yourself.

He said nothing. It was not six in the morning. She had heard him stirring and had come to find him; he had not heard her slippers on the stairs and the click of the door-latch to his office made him start when she entered without knocking. Nearly everything startled him now, the slightest noise or interruption thrumming on his nerves. Her hair fell down around her shoulders, its curls untamed; her face was soft with sleep, two spots of high color in her cheeks, a little crease by her mouth where she had settled against her pillow. But her gaze was intent. She sat on the chaise, beside him, where he had slept — or tried to sleep — the night before. Before many months had passed she would remove the chaise and install a simple bed. He was still in yesterday's clothes; a woolen blanket pooled at their feet on the floor, a pillow flung beside it.

— They are dying now, he said. Two, just these last weeks. Meyers. McKay. A German and an Irishman. Another Irishman, Reardon, is very ill. They do not hope for him.

He studied the pattern in the carpet, could feel her gaze upon him. Her hand reached out for his, and so they sat for a moment, just like that, together.

— So you see, it was not worse in Brooklyn. Half as deep. Less. One hundred feet to bedrock. *One hundred.*

— In Brooklyn, she said, I thought you would die. I thought I had lost you. After the fire. She squeezed his fingers. Their hands warmed, palm to palm.

— Yet I did not, he said. He leant into her shoulder. You are still burdened with me.

— O, she said.

He felt the little movements of her body, shifting ever so slightly against him. He called to his mind the night they had met, her lifted chin and slender neck with a pale blue ribbon tied about it, the candlelight glancing off her shining hair. Kate Chase's warm introduction, General Warren's confiding smile. I had thought it best not to warn you she was coming, the General had said. I thought advance intelligence might tie your tongue even tighter. How straight-backed she was, dancing, how she never looked at her feet, how bright her eyes were, how she talked and talked and talked and he had been happy simply to listen.

— Emmy.

— Yes, dear.

— You are —

— I am — what?

— You know, he said.

— Still, she said. Tell me. Tell me what I am.

He put his mouth close to her ear.

— You are my *broad-hipped beauty*, he said. You are my dear good girl. My Em. He turned his face to hers and their lips touched. The sweetness of her, a fresh stream spilling through his exhaustion and dismay.

— And you, she said, placing her neat bare hand on his chest, are as unwashed as a soldier. You are not in camp now, Colonel. Hicks Street is no palace, but we do have hot water available, you know.

He pulled back from her, blood rising in his face, but she leaned in, kissed him again. I don't mind, she said. You know I don't mind.

He reached up, tucked a curl of hair behind her ear.

— Your tolerance is my deliverance, he said. He reached to his waistcoat pocket, pulled out his watch, wound it. The day ticking forward.

— What shall you do? Her voice lost a little of its tenderness in the asking.

— About?

She frowned. About the work, she said, with some impatience. About the caisson. You are at — 78 feet, I think?

— Yes, he said. Just that. Well, 78 feet and six inches, since I know you are of an exacting mind.

She rose and stepped over towards the desk. This is what Collingwood brought yesterday, is it not? She lifted the stone, the dark gray gneiss, an irregular trapezoid, from where it sat by his papers, his open bottle of ink, the decanter of whiskey, knives, pencils, pens, a scatter of metal nibs, rules. With her left hand she drew back the curtains and the morning came right into the room, and had he been closer to the stone in her hand he would have seen the light glittering off the mica constellating across its surfaces. The day stabbed at him. He blinked, his eyes watering.

— Bedrock, she said.

— Yes, he said. But — irregular. The edge of the chamber scrapes right down along it, a thick layer — but beneath the chamber floor it comes in spurs. We are still making our way through sand. Very compacted sand, but sand all the same.

— You said that sand was strong enough to bend an iron bar.

— Yes. It is. And the bedrock itself, well — no action has smoothed it. It is in sharp, thin ridges. Look, he said — and she came back to sit beside him, holding the stone out before them. A little streak of dirt, a trace of that sand, now ran between her finger and thumb. This was cut from one of those spurs, but if you had been to see it *in situ* —

— I should like to go down, she said.

— I think I will ignore that remark.

— Why?

He imagined recounting this conversation to his father. Impossible.

— Emily. Do you wish to understand what is happening in the caisson?

— Yes.

— Then let us leave any other discussion to the side, he said. There is enough to trouble us here.

Her look steady. Trouble *me*, he had meant to say. But he had not.

— They are sharp, these spurs. This reveals there has been no movement of rock, or sand, or water for a very long time indeed.

Hundreds of thousands of years, perhaps. Perhaps longer. We can dig to bedrock, as we did on this side of the river, but how long that will take — it could be another year. And the men —

He shook his head. She handed him the stone, the fragment of bedrock. He turned it in his hand, over and again. She had often seen him do this, take some stone or mineral, hold it, play with it, aware or unaware of what he did, sometimes she did not know. A rough surface, the rasp of it, its vast antiquity, some comfort. Any stone picked up off the ground, he had told her once, ancient beyond understanding. And yet he did understand.

— What is the pressure now?

— Thirty-four pounds, he said.

— All this — she opened her hands, holding the close air in the room — is 15 pounds?

— Or thereabouts, he said. Close enough.

— How remarkable, she said, that the air is just like a sea that we swim in, although we do not know it.

— But you know, Em. You are a clever woman.

— Yes, she said. I am. She took the stone back from him, turned it in her own hand; he took it back again, like a child's game. Here in Brooklyn, at bedrock, the pressure was — ?

— Twenty-three pounds, he said. Will you close the curtains?

— It is good to see the daylight for a moment, she said. Just for a moment. Now it was she who reached out to him, running her hand through the hair at his temple, grown overlong, the backs of her fingers down his beard, his cheek, his jaw, finally cupping his chin in her palm. Will you take some breakfast?

— I have no appetite, he said.

— That was not my question.

— If the bread is fresh and soft, and there is a little of that soft cheese, the girl could bring it up, he said. And coffee.

— Dr Smith says you should not have coffee.

— I respect Dr Smith, he said, but so far he has not found a solution to what ails any of us. Dr Smith tends to the men and the men still die. It is not his fault, of course. But I will have my coffee this morning, despite Dr Smith's advice.

— Liza will only just be rising, she said. I will make your coffee for you. She rose, smoothed the fabric of her morning gown. Blue veins ran down the delicate underside of her arm, the rushing rivers of her heart.

Why did it come to him then, just then, in the moment that she drew herself to her feet? Something in her stance, the straight back of that dancing girl who stood now before him a woman? Red velvet slippers, planted so firmly on the floor, her white toes hidden inside — how could it be, that he was thinking of her little toes, and thinking of this task, all at once, and it was so clear to him, suddenly.

— I shall pull the curtains closed?

— No, he said. Leave them. Open.

— You are sure?

He took a breath, pulled it into himself as deeply as he could, let it out. The sea of air all around them.

— We will stop, he said. We will stop. He had said it now. No going back.

— Stop — stop what? she said. Wash?

He opened his hand. The stone, dark, gleaming.

— Good enough to found upon, he said. It must be. It *is*.

— Well, she said. That is that, then. You have made up your mind. She bent, and kissed him. I will bring your coffee, she said.

EMMA/EMILY

« Madame Bovary, quand elle fut dans la cuisine, s'approcha de la cheminée. Du bout de ses deux doigts, elle prit sa robe à la hauteur du genou, et, l'ayant ainsi remontée jusqu'aux chevilles, elle tendit à la flamme, par-dessus le gigot qui tournait, son pied chaussé d'une bottine noire. Le feu l'éclairait en entier, pénétrant d'une lumière crue la trame de sa robe, les pores égaux de sa peau blanche et même les paupières de ses yeux qu'elle clignait de temps à autre. Une grande couleur rouge passait sur elle, selon le souffle du vent qui venait par la porte entrouverte. »

BROOKLYN. MONDAY, SEPTEMBER 17, 1877. 11 AM.

THE BOOK — BOOKS, REALLY, the story split in two and bound in green leather — was tucked up on a high shelf in the back parlour, above his desk, above a shelf of minerals labelled in his neat hand. It was not hidden, not at all, for he kept all the novels here, poetry too, his *dissipations*, he said. Sometimes, if he was not too tired — though he almost always was — he would ask her to read to him. Pickwick diverted him, diverted them both, for that matter; Walter Scott pleased them both, too. She would like to go to the Highlands, she thought, it sounded a bold, wild place: pink heather and green moss spangled with drops of mist that sparked in the light of a sudden sun. Swirling tartans, a bright cutlass, a candle left burning in a window, the sign of a bandit or a lover.

— You are a romantic, he said.

— Perhaps I was, once, she answered. Perhaps you were too. There was a cold sweat on his brow. She leaned in close to him, feeling for the vein in his arm with light palpitations; Dr Smith had demonstrated the method, and she had been an apt pupil.

His whole body softened as the drug ran into him. He closed his eyes and she watched the lids tremble, his lashes a shadow against the pallor of the fragile skin beneath, stained nearly blue with weariness, dark as a bruise.

— We must be careful, she said.

— Of what? He did not open his eyes.

— You know perfectly well, she said. Of this. Slowly she began to disassemble the hypodermic. In the silence between them was the soft rasp of the metal threads turning as she unscrewed the hollow needle from the glass barrel of the syringe.

— I will have no lectures, thank you. His voice was low and even but she knew this tone.

— I will leave you to rest, she said. You may ring the bell if you require anything. Esther will answer your call.

He did not like Esther, of that she was well enough aware. Today was Monday: Liza's single day of freedom. Esther was Liza's cousin, and had been instructed by her young relative as to the quiet, the patience, that was required in this house. Col. Roebling had not accustomed himself to Esther; perhaps he never would. But there was nothing to be done. Her heart quickened. She wished to leave the room before he could speak again. How she had once longed for the sound of his voice! How she still did.

And yet. She glanced at the clock above the mantelpiece. She did not wish to appear in haste.

The volumes, battered at the spine, lay on the corner of his table. Whether he had seen her take them down, she did not know. The rough edges of the paper against her fingertips. She had begun to read it while he slept, lost in its pages while the sound of his breath, rising and falling, settled through the close air. Sometimes a pause between the in-breath and the out-breath, and she would look up, listen to her own heart beating. His breath again. Waking and sleeping, sometimes there was little difference. Now, the drug coursing into him, his eyes were closed, his breath even. She picked up the two books and bent to kiss his forehead. His skin damp on her lips.

The click of the closing door. Her own bedroom across the hallway; it had been theirs, but no longer. Solitude was what he required. What did she require? She turned away from the question, deposited the book on her dressing-table. Glanced at herself in the mirror. She kept her tread as soft as she could on the stairs.

It was bright fall now, the sun heading towards its zenith. She had not called for a carriage; the days and nights and nights and days and nights in her husband's closed room made her long to be out in the open, and here was a high blue day, the cloudless air sounding with the work by the river. What had once been a confused cacophony was now beginning to separate into threads of sound, each thread — each wire — with its own meaning and significance. It was like coming to understand a symphony, its structure and themes, hear the instruments speak to each other in call and response. Her husband the composer — the composer's presence not required for the performance. It was the conductor, rather, who led the music.

She let this image turn in her mind as she made her way along the narrow sidewalk, picking her way through a litter of fallen leaves, refuse and dung which rose, at intervals, past the level of the street. She lifted her plain skirt above her ankles and stepped as carefully as she could in her neat black boots. The boots were new, as was nearly everything else she wore. The shoemaker had been surprised at her request: This is very — coarse leather, miss, he had said. And the soles — they will be much lighter if we use a finer grain. I assure you, the stitching will hold, for a lady's boot —

— I believe I am the one making the purchase, she had said. The smell of the tannery in the crowded little shop; a place down in New York, not her usual man. She had cash to pay him. His nails were black and broken, even his gray whiskers were stained with his trade. But she had liked that he had called her 'miss'; this had made her smile, despite herself. Well, she thought, I have reached that age.

And so her boots were nailed at the sole; her dark worsted skirt tight-woven, sturdy brown. She had a jacket to match, and beneath it a bodice and a plain shirt of linen. Her hair she had pulled up tightly; she had used a dozen pins, at least, to catch her curls. She imagined she looked like a schoolmistress. That, at any rate, had been her approximate goal. She had been confident that her husband would not notice this new severity in her dress; she had been perfectly correct, of course, in her assumption.

At the corner of Hicks Street, she lifted her hand to knock at the door of the office, but found that it was open. She walked in, and up the wooden stair. The treads were narrow and worn; not much effort had been expended in making up the place and she had once thought that a coat of paint, at least, would be in order. Now she understood not only that this was the least of anyone's concerns, she also had come to see that — as with her robust attire — attention to appearance was not always what it seemed.

— Mrs Roebling.

Farrington was in the midst of removing his jacket. He shrugged it back onto his shoulders at the sight of her, pushing his arms back down into the sleeves. We were not expecting you. Looking at her directly, as not everyone here did.

— Good day, Mr Farrington. Please, she said, do not stand on ceremony on my account. The day is warming, I believe.

The jacket off again. Light wool, unpressed, a small stain at the collar, though she perceived him to be a fastidious man. The master mechanic had never mentioned a Mrs Farrington, and she — as yet — had never enquired.

— Progress is being made, as you see. He gestured to the table between them, where his wooden model of the bridge stood. Five feet — perhaps a little more — tower to tower, wooden anchorages stretching out behind each one, the table itself nearly the length of the room. She had marvelled when first she saw it, how perfect it was in every detail, how Farrington had carved the ash wood to mimic the surface of the stone, had steamed fine strips to curve up into the towers' arches. In her mind she now carried her husband's words, thousands of them, transmitted through her hand, the pencil sharpened and sharpened again, as she sat hour by hour taking down the letters and reports he could no longer write himself but which seemed to exist, fully formed, inside him. And then she would come here to the bridge office, and each time Farrington would demonstrate something new to her, gesture with his blunt fingers at his miniature construction. This was in the guise of demonstrating how useful this model was for the men, who came from every part of the world, whose English was often bad or non-existent, and who, for the most part, could not read. But as he spoke and moved, the words in her mind would join with what she saw before her, a bridge of understanding, and all parts of the structure took on a whole and singular life in her mind.

She pulled off her glove, reached the tip of her finger out to touch the fine wire now stretching from anchorage to anchorage, passing over miniature saddle plates fashioned, Farrington had told her, from tin. He had put one of them in her palm before settling it into place on the 'Brooklyn tower'. Like a child's toy, she had said, like something for John. Yet much more perfect than any toy. Beautiful, she had said. He had smiled and — perhaps — colored a little above his beard.

She bent more closely to inspect the model.

— How does this autumn weather affect the deflection of the strands? The sun is quite strong at midday.

— We manage well enough, said a voice behind her. How well-versed you are in the work, Mrs Roebling.

◊

« Elle aurait voulu vivre dans quelque vieux manoir, comme ces châtelaines au long corsage, qui, sous le trèfle des ogives, passaient leurs jours, le coude sur la pierre et le menton dans la main, à regarder venir du fond de la campagne un cavalier à plume blanche qui galope sur un cheval noir. »

✣ ✣ ✣ ✣ ✣

BROOKLYN. MONDAY, SEPTEMBER 17, 1877. 4 PM.

THE STORY SPLIT in two and bound in green leather.

Emily in her chamber, settled on the chaise which runs beneath the window on the river side of the house. He is sleeping, below. John with his governess, gluing together light strips of birch to fashion a boat: he likes to look from the window with a telescope to spy the riverboats, steam and sail, little skerries and great ferries. He is making a model of his own design; she thinks of it afloat beside Farrington's model of the bridge.

The covers are scuffed and roughened. Twenty years old. Washington orders books from Brentano's, so does she: the latest they have had is one of Trollope's, and *The Wreck of the Grosvenor.* Sea stories, she finds, are particularly distracting and sometimes, if he has the energy, they will fall to talking of their own voyages, the sights and sounds and smells. She wonders if he will ever be strong enough to sail again.

But these volumes are old, and printed on cheap paper. *Nous étions à l'Étude, quand le Proviseur entra, suivi d'un nouveau habillé en bourgeois et d'un garçon de classe qui portait un grand pupitre. Ceux qui dormaient se réveillèrent, et chacun se leva comme surpris dans son travail.* During the war, one of the Parrott girls had somehow acquired *Salammbô*; there had been a terrible fuss when the book was discovered being passed from hand to hand. The controversy (Mary Parrott's fiancé had broken off their engagement as a result) put her off Flaubert entirely.

She leafs through the book, turning pages back and forth. The binding crumbles a little more, green dust falls on the fabric of her skirt. The endpapers are foxed. In a neat hand, on the top right-hand corner of the book's first leaf, are initials: M. K. A. It is not her husband's hand. Well — they are not her husband's initials. M. K. A. She touches the ink, believes she can almost feel the way the pen has marked the paper, not only by its colour but with pressure, the imprint of the letters dug into the weave of the page.

For a fleeting moment she has the sensation of something just out of reach. A memory, or an understanding. An infinitesimal glimpse. But it goes and she does not call it back. Yet under her fingertips it is still held there, both within and beyond her awareness. A distant image, a shadowed face. She feels her own heart beat. She begins to read the book.

◊

« Elle ne savait pas si elle regrettait de lui avoir cédé, ou si elle ne souhaitait point, au contraire, le chérir davantage. L'humiliation de se sentir faible se tournait en une rancune que les voluptés tempéraient. Ce n'était pas de l'attachement, c'était comme une séduction permanente. Il la subjuguait. Elle en avait presque peur. »

BROOKLYN. MONDAY, SEPTEMBER 17, 1877. 11.30 AM.

SHE TURNED ON her heel to face him. His foxy, impassive face. Hooded eyes, bright blue, cornflower blue, although in the first days of their acquaintance she had thought them dark. That seemed queer to her, now. He wore no hat; his tawny hair was slicked back from his forehead and fell in little curls at the nape of his neck, behind his neat ears. There was something almost womanish about his face, although there was nothing womanish about him. His coat slung on a finger over his shoulder, patches of sweat beneath the arms of his fine linen shirt. The fat gold chain of his watch.

— I am a quick study, Mr Kingsley, she said. As you have

often remarked. One might imagine that our discourse would have passed beyond your wondering at me, sir.

— I sincerely hope our discourse never passes beyond that stage, Mrs Roebling, he said. For you are a wonder altogether. He smiled, but did not show his teeth, which she knew to be white and even, the eyeteeth strong and sharp. And you are, he said, an apparition. I did not expect you here today.

This, of course, was not true. He had asked to meet with her. *Come to the office just after noon,* said the note; Esther had handed it to her after breakfast. His hand was firm and bold. Rather like that of her late father-in-law. A certain hand, a sure hand. So many letters and notes addressed to her now, sometimes — sometimes — making no reference to Washington at all. It had unnerved her, once. No longer. Yet now: the introduction of subterfuge. She smoothed the fabric of her skirt.

— Ladies are unpredictable, she said. Isn't it so?

— I must allow you your opinion, Kingsley said. It would be churlish of me to argue. Though I venture if I had offered such, you might contest the point.

All this while Farrington stood quietly, his hands folded in front of him, observing the empty conversation pass like a ball tossed and caught and tossed again. Just then the door to the office slapped open and then slammed again behind, an entrance less cunning than Kingsley's, to be sure, but all the same it was as if this tall young man had appeared from thin air. She had not heard his tread on the stair, so intent had she been on the nothings exchanged with William Kingsley.

— Mr Farrington, said the young man, his voice swooping and guttural all at once. Mr Farrington —

— Please, Harry, said Farrington hastily, might this wait?

For the young man had not seen her standing there; and he was bare-chested, his torso glistening with sweat and the fine black filings that scraped away from the steel wire as it spun.

He turned, caught her eye. His mouth opened. Nothing came out of it.

— Harry, she said. I think you must be Mr Supple, of Liverpool.

His mouth still open: wider. A puddle of wet in the hollow of his throat. He had a tattoo on one forearm, a blurred anchor, swirled with rope, in muddy blue; on the other, initials, it looked like, unreadable. His wrists and hands much darker than the rest of him.

— Nod your head, Mr Supple, if you agree this is your name and point of origin, Kingsley said. And so Supple nodded.

— My husband speaks of you, she said. Col. Roebling. He has heard of your work in the wire from Mr Farrington here, and from Col. Paine. Washington had said that this young man had been a sailor; many of the men who worked up in the spinning had been sailors, used to height, to high winds, to rope work, but few were as skilled or bold as Harry Supple. The chief engineer says you are a veritable Blondin on the wires up there, she said.

She felt foolish as soon as it came out of her mouth. A *veritable Blondin.*

— I mean to say that my husband, Col. Roebling, and Col. Paine too, are grateful for your work. Your hard work.

He ducked his head. Ma'am, he said. I'm sure. Thank you. Please to thank the Colonel. We hope he is very well.

She knew they talked amongst themselves, the men. They heard the rumours, they wondered that they did not see the chief engineer. She nodded at Supple. Anything she might say would only add to the speculation; she had long learned to keep her own counsel. She felt Kingsley's eyes on her, his cool appraisal.

— He is well, Mr Supple, I thank you. I will give him your kind regards.

Color shot up the young man's face. He turned away from her, relieved to recall why he had come. Mr Farrington, sir, he said. It's the traveller. The way she's twisting. Smollet thinks he's found a way to smooth her. He'd be showing you. When you come.

— Directly, Farrington said. Thanks, Harry.

Another duck of his head and he vanished as he had appeared, swift and silent down the stairs, leaving his scent like a print on the air.

The sun settled in Kingsley's bright eyes. You came to enquire about the deflection of the strands, Mrs Roebling?

— No, she said. I came to let Mr Farrington know I would walk down to the works.

— Well then, Kingsley said, perhaps you will allow me to accompany you. As it happens, we had the same aim, you and I, in arriving here to speak to Mr Farrington.

She heard his *we*, his *you and I*. She would color as Supple had, if she was not careful.

— Well, Mr Kingsley, if it is indeed true that your intention was as mine, I will gladly accept your offer. I should not like, however, to disturb the course of your day.

— Mrs Roebling, he smiled, I do not believe such a thing would ever be possible. Please, he said, gesturing at the stair, you lead, and I will follow. Frank — he turned to Farrington — we will find each other on the Brooklyn shore, I am sure. I shall look out for you and . . . who was it?

— Smollet, Mr Kingsley, Farrington said, his expression neutral. A clever young fellow.

— We can't have too many of those, Kingsley said. Remember the days when they called us clever young fellows, eh? Now we must make do with being called clever old dogs.

His tread behind her on the shabby stairs. She was aware of her hand on the banister, the angle of her wrist, the little gap between the top of her glove and the edge of her sleeve, the skin exposed there. She was glad of the air when they stepped out onto the street, it cooled the blood in her cheeks and throat. She knew the way as well as he, and they walked in silence side by side toward the workyard at the anchorage. He had a brisk step, as did she, and let her legs lengthen to match his stride. It was queer, when she glanced at him: two lines in the middle of his forehead as if something troubled him, but the corners of his mouth upturned in what she would call a smile. He is a cunning man, Wash would say, and almost spit the words. Cunning was not a trait he admired.

And then Kingsley stopped, dead in his tracks, as if in recollection of something he had forgot. She almost skipped, catching herself ahead of him, pinching the swinging fabric of her skirt between finger and thumb as she turned to face him.

— Mr Kingsley?

— Mrs Roebling. A little detour, I think. A diversion. Very brief.

— Mr Kingsley. There is work to be done.

— Of course, madam. Neither you nor I would ever shrink from that. But the head is clearer on a full stomach, I've found. Please — and once again, he gestured, his arm leading her toward Henry Street, and she did not quarrel, but followed where he led.

◊

« – Tout à l'heure! – Sais-tu à quoi tu t'exposais? . . . N'as-tu rien vu, dans le coin, à gauche, sur la troisième tablette? Parle, réponds, articule quelque chose!

– Je ne . . . sais pas, balbutia le jeune garçon.

– Ah! tu ne sais pas! Eh bien, je sais, moi! Tu as vu une bouteille, en verre bleu, cachetée avec de la cire jaune, qui contient une poudre blanche, sur laquelle même j'avais écrit: Dangereux! et sais-tu ce qu'il y avait dedans? De l'arsenic! et tu vas toucher à cela! prendre une bassine qui est à côté!

– À côté! s'écria madame Homais en joignant les mains. De l'arsenic? Tu pouvais nous empoisonner tous!

Et les enfants se mirent à pousser des cris, comme s'ils avaient déjà senti dans leurs entrailles d'atroces douleurs. »

TROY. TUESDAY, MAY 13, 1857. 5 PM. APPROX.

IT WAS LOUDON who had broken the news to him. Come to get him. Late last night. What time? His watch unwound. To see the Professor of Geology standing at his door, his cravat loose, his eyes shadowed even in the darkness. I wished for you to know as soon as — he had broken off. Rumor travels swift. I wished to come to you more swiftly. The words Loudon spoke entered him and he sat down hard on the step of the house. His legs would not hold him. The taper he had carried down the stairs fell from his hand and Loudon stepped quickly on the wick. The warm darkness all around. A horn sounding from the river, nighttime travellers, hooves too, sounding on the cobbles, it all went on as it always did, despite this. Two nights ago, Max standing just where Loudon stood now. Washington had raised his hand in farewell and Max had clasped his palm, smiling, smiling. With Loudon before him Washington tried to get up, failed, and felt the professor take both his hands, make a stand for him to rise against. Loudon's bony fingers, the backs of his hands softened by age. Loudon could not tell him much. Not who found him. Perhaps whoever it was wished to keep his name out of it. A physician had been called, but it was no good. A hypodermic needle found, Loudon knew that. *Wenn es Zeit ist zu gehen, wird es Zeit zu gehen*, Max used to say. Washington recalled that once his father had said to him: you must listen to a man who speaks in jest, for he will never be more serious.

He had not listened. He had not wished to hear.

Now, the clear light of a spring afternoon on the Hudson spilled in through the window of Max's room. A mess — his things everywhere, his books and clothes, scattered and rumpled, on table and bed and floor, but that was not unusual. I make my own order, he would say, it is my own system, dear Wash, and it suits me down to the ground. You cannot see the ground for everything you keep piled upon it, Washington would answer, and that became their joke, or one of them, one of many. But he could smell the chamberpot under the bed, heavily sweet and bitter, and that was not like Max, for he was fastidious in that regard, his linen always clean, his collars always fresh.

Still he could not believe that Max would not be coming back. Would not step through the door. Wrinkle his nose at the stench.

Apologize. Embrace him. His height and breadth. His warm and living self.

You should be quick, Loudon had said. Professor Loudon had eyes green as river stones, sharp despite his age. Loudon had no wife, but that was true of many of the men who worked here; men whose passion for science and instruction had — it seemed — permitted them no other.

Why had he come here? What was there here for him? What did he hope to gain? On the table were books and papers, lecture notes, letters, a volume on hydrography, an open bottle of ink. Davies' *Elements of Surveying.* Almost without thinking he lifted the glass stopper and closed the bottle, as if to preserve it for the owner's return. A gesture he had made before. Max, turning over bottles, the ink crusted to a dry and useless rime at the base. *Ach, weh!*

Beside the Davies was the novel, in two volumes, which Max had ordered from Paris; it had arrived just two weeks ago and his friend had pronounced himself immediately engrossed. *Un succès de scandale*, he had said, and one night had begun to read aloud to Washington, who asked him to please desist because he was trying to come to grips with the mining of coal — Williams and Millar's treatise propped up in his lap — but Max would have none of it. His French was good, hardly accented, the language comfortable in his mouth.

— *Vous est-il arrivé parfois, reprit* Léon, de *rencontrer dans un livre une idée vague que l'on a eue, quelque image obscurcie qui revient de loin, et comme l'exposition entière de votre sentiment le plus délié?*

— *Jamais dans un livre sur les mines de charbon,* Washington had replied, and Max had tipped back his head and laughed, showing his white throat, freshly-shaven; his razor had been lying, soaped and stubbled, by his bowl.

At least he had not used the razor, Washington thought. A

shudder passed through his body and it was as if the warm spring air turned suddenly cold, but then was pouring hot again, a flush all up through him, his own blood rising in — shame — he would call it that, he would name it. He must leave here. He did not need Loudon to hurry him along. He could not bear it. The two volumes of the novel were in one hand. The ink bottle in another, for some reason he would never fathom. One door closing behind him, the door to this abandoned room. And another, as he came to the street. The house door, its heavy knocker, slamming shut.

◊

« Alors le souvenir des Bertaux lui arriva. Elle revit la ferme, la mare bourbeuse, son père en blouse sous les pommiers, et elle se revit elle-même, comme autrefois, écrémant avec son doigt les terrines de lait dans la laiterie. Mais, aux fulgurations de l'heure présente, sa vie passée, si nette jusqu'alors, s'évanouissait tout entière, et elle doutait presque de l'avoir vécue. Elle était là; puis autour du bal, il n'y avait plus que de l'ombre, étalée sur tout le reste. Elle mangeait alors une glace au marasquin, qu'elle tenait de la main gauche dans une coquille de vermeil, et fermait à demi les yeux, la cuiller entre les dents. »

BROOKLYN. MONDAY, SEPTEMBER 17, 1877. 11.45 AM.

WITHIN A BLOCK they had come to a cart settled against High Street, men milling around it, their voices loud and then a little quieter when they saw her, her prim worsted, and saw Kingsley too, a little bit of the dandy about him, beneath the street dust his boots always polished, a sheen to his waistcoat, that heavy watch chain, its shining links a semaphore of wealth and power. One man whispered to another, recognized her perhaps, and she did not look away but straight at him, his blackened face, and she smiled, for did she not belong here? If she thought it was so then it would be so. Washington had never said as much but he had shown as much. He trusted her to understand. She would trust herself.

— Mrs Hannigan! Kingsley cried to the woman behind the cart, wide of face, broad of hip, stark white hair pulled severely back and reflecting the sun like a first fall of snow. He moved through the men and Emily followed, he was Moses parting the sea, the men fell away before him and the woman beamed as she saw his approach.

— You can't get enough of me, can you boy? she cried as she pushed her ragged sleeves up over her thick arms. Emily kept behind Kingsley and moved into the fishy, oily penumbra surrounding the woman's stall, as he reached into his waistcoat pocket for coins, exchanging them for two greasy paper bags.

— You know me, Mrs Hannigan, far too well! he said, and then turned quickly, go on, he said to Emily, back out you go, away from this crowd, come on you fellows, let the lady pass! They pooled away like a receding tide at his command, and was that his hand on the small of her back, hastening her away from the cart and the crowd? The briefest of gestures; surely not, and yet her consciousness lingered there for a moment, the fabric just below her waist, considering the layers of material between his palm, his fingers, and her skin. Many layers: gloves, worsted, bone, linen. He was walking beside her now and she saw that he had in fact removed his gloves, they were tucked beneath his arm, and as if it were the most ordinary thing in the world to do, he stepped into an empty lot where a house had been, the one next to it too looking as if it were ready to come down. This was not the wreckage caused by her husband's great work, the families evicted, their homes destroyed in the name of progress: this was the dereliction of time and poverty; dandelion clocks springing up through tumbled brick and splintered wood. Kingsley stepped into the space as if it were his sitting room, and indeed, at the far end of the lot she saw the remains of what must have been a hearth. Enough brick still standing to make a rough seat, and here William Kingsley, general contractor and Vice-President of the New York Bridge Company, settled himself in what was clearly a familiar manner.

— Here. He handed one of the paper bags to her. The grease had now wholly saturated its base. She reached out but then pulled back her hand, and swiftly removed her own gloves, tucking them into her reticule. Quite right, Mrs Roebling, he said. This is just like bridge work. You'll have the knack of it in no time.

— What is this, Mr Kingsley, and where have you led me?

— *This* is one of Mrs Hannigan's soft-shell crabs, Mrs Roebling. I confess myself quite addicted. She makes them fresh every morning, fries them in clean oil, and trundles her cart from the shore to her station. Sometimes, you know, she does not even charge me! I think she has her eye on me. But today I believe she noticed I was in company, so I had to hand over my coin. She may well be the jealous type. Now do sit down, Mrs Roebling, you must enjoy your crab in comfort.

She could do nothing but obey. And yet it did not feel like obedience, but rather equality. He had reached into his bag and brought out a shaggy creature, fried entire, its skinny legs crumbed and brown. He bit; its liquid ran down his fingers and he leaned over, his legs wide to keep the fine cloth of his trousers away from any drips. Impeccable, he muttered with his mouth full. Impeccable.

She could not keep herself from laughing. Settling beside him she drew out her own crustacean, warm and springy in her fingers, and leant over just as he had, or nearly: side-saddle, her knees tucked safely away. The crab was crisp and tender, almost gelatinous inside, its shell-less body yielding softly to her teeth and tongue.

— Oh my, she said when she had swallowed. Well. I thank you, Mr Kingsley. What a fine surprise.

— I am full of surprises, he said.

She did not answer. For a moment they ate contentedly in silence. She had not realized she was hungry. Or how hungry she was.

— You have enjoyed this delicacy before, I think?

She nodded, her mouth full. Swallowed. In Newport, at the cottage General Warren takes. The cook there has a way with them.

— What? Finer than Mrs Hannigan's? He put a look of outrage on his face.

— O, well, she said. Let us say the circumstances are different.

— There is so much to be said for circumstance, Mrs Roebling, do you not think?

— Indeed, Mr Kingsley. That is certainly the case.

The crab was gone. Her fingers were greasy. Without a word he held out a clean square of silk, pulled deftly from his breast pocket. She could smell lavender soap.

— Thank you, she said. She wiped her fingers, held the soft fabric, hesitated.

— May I? Kingsley took it back from her, wiped his own fingers, folded it, tucked it into the pocket of his trousers.

Kate. That was his wife's name. There were three children. Harry, he was the eldest boy — a few years older than John. Harry, like the young man they had encountered in the bridge office. She could remark on this coincidence — though it was not really a coincidence at all, just something she had noticed, and Harry was not such an uncommon name. Kingsley might not appreciate the comparison. She could inquire whether Mrs Kingsley was fond of soft-shell crab. She felt her thoughts running this way and that. She decided to say nothing.

— Ten million dollars, Kingsley said.

— Mr Kingsley?

— You heard me, I am sure, Mrs Roebling. Ten million dollars. How many of Mrs Hannigan's crabs would that buy, do you suppose? I should not like to begin to count.

◊

« Mais, dès qu'elle fut partie, Emma ne tarda pas à émerveiller Bovary par son bon sens pratique. Il allait falloir prendre des informations, vérifier les hypothèques, voir s'il y avait lieu à une licitation ou à une liquidation. Elle citait des termes techniques, au hasard, prononçait les grands mots d'ordre, d'avenir, de prévoyance, et continuellement exagérait les embarras de la succession ; si bien qu'un jour elle lui montra le modèle d'une autorisation générale pour ‹ gérer et administrer ses affaires, faire tous emprunts, signer et endosser tous billets, payer toutes sommes, etc. › Elle avait profité des leçons de Lheureux. »

BROOKLYN. MONDAY, SEPTEMBER 17, 1877. NOON.

IT WAS AS well she had not mentioned his wife or his son. Now they would play a different game. Now she faced another choice: she could pretend not to know to what he referred. But she sensed two things — simultaneously, at least that was how it seemed to her. First, that such a pretence would be of little use. A delay, not a refutation. Second, that this dissembling would not please William Kingsley. And she wished — she discovered — to please him.

She had left the greasy paper bag beside her on the uneven surface on which they sat. She picked it up, crumpled it; no matter that the oil slicked her palm again.

— The work will last rather longer than Mrs Hannigan's luncheon, Mr Kingsley. Or don't you agree?

— Of course I agree, Mrs Roebling. But I wonder whether you would remind your husband that Mr Roebling's bid — I mean his father's bid — was for seven million dollars. That was to be the cost of the work.

— This was the cause of your summons, then, Mr Kingsley? To upbraid me for matters beyond my control?

— I have no wish to upbraid you, Mrs Roebling. Please. Do not think it.

She peered at him. He looked — contrite.

— I have not seen your husband for four years, Mrs Roebling. No one sees the chief engineer. Not even his friend Col. Paine. Only you. I am correct, am I not?

His ungloved hand on hers. His palm dry, rough. Wealth would never smooth a workman's hands. He would feel her wedding ring, the little spray of diamonds on her finger, against his skin.

— Emily, he said.

And she did not pull her hand away. The sun warmed her hair, the back of her neck. A horse clopped by, its hooves echoing hollow.

— You don't rebuke me, he said. She kept silent. Then I will say it again. Emily. I wonder: will you say my name?

— Mr Kingsley. She opened her eyes wide, all innocence.

— Now, then, he said. Both of them smiling.

— William Kingsley. William Charles Kingsley, I think.

— William will do, he said. Listen to me. I must be blunt with you. Your husband believes me to be his enemy. At least, I think he believes that, from the letters I see in your hand; I wish to assure you that this is not the case. I am not entirely sure, however, that I will alter his thinking. And so I must hope to convince you, at least, that we can be friends.

A brief pause. That you and I can be friends. Mrs Roebling. Emily.

He squeezed her fingers. She did not pull away.

— So this is all a stratagem, Mr Kingsley? *William.* Your tactic in this battle-plan to charm me with Mrs Hannigan's soft-shell crabs?

— Strategy and tactics, my dear! How clear it is that there is soldiering in your blood!

My dear. She let that pass.

— You do not answer my question.

— Ruthless as a soldier too, I see. No. It is not a stratagem. You are a woman of discerning taste, I know. Quality can be had at all levels of expense.

Looking at him, she could see the sun catch the golden bristles on his throat where the razor had done its work; into her mind came an intimate image of him, lathered, blade in hand; though surely he would have a barber, some trusty man he went to each morning, hot fragrant water and steaming towels.

— Please do not think I condescend to you, Emily. You do not think that, do you?

— No, she said. Mr Kingsley, I do not.

He raised an eyebrow.

— William, she said. I do not.

— Then attend to me. I will tell you, first, that you have skills that your husband — even were he well — does not. He looked at her. See? he said, smiling. I note you have not defended him; I think this is because you already understand of what it is I speak. You are a person of great intelligence, Mrs Emily Warren Roebling; you have a sharp eye and a keen mind. You are a woman, and so you have had to hold your tongue — have you not? — while the men about you, your illustrious brother, your famous father-in-law, your husband, speak their minds, but you have listened as closely as any man, I believe. I know you understand the deflection of those strands better than I do now.

He turned to her with a questioning look. She did not contradict him. She sat with her hands folded in her lap.

— You know this is not flattery. I am no flatterer, Emily, I am a man of business. Your husband is an engineer — a great one — but he believes that businessmen such as I stand in his way. It is my suspicion that you do not entirely agree, though you may never say those words aloud to him.

— I am listening, she said.

— I have your husband's interests at heart —

She could not keep from a breath of laughter.

— Emily, I do. I have as much wish as he does to see this great work completed. We are at a stiff point now, my dear; the country is in trouble, money is short, and there are men who speak against your husband every day. Already the bridge has cost half again as much as the original estimate. Why should this be? Cannot the costs of stone and steel, men and equipment, be calculated in advance? Some say: the *cheating* engineer. Please — he saw her look; she could not disguise it — I am reporting only what I hear.

Only moments ago she had felt a kind of excitement, delight almost, at this unexpected interlude. It had frightened her and pleased her. It had been a long time, she thought, since she had felt the mixture of those two sensations, as long ago as the time just before and just after her marriage. And yet she had observed, these last few months, some shift in her regard for William Kingsley, an awareness of his presence in a room, the way he listened when she spoke. When his letters arrived, practical and businesslike, she enjoyed the sight of his hand, its loops and dips and dashes.

— How dare they, she said. Last year my husband sold all

of his shares in the Roebling company — after his honor, the company's honor, was — frankly put — impugned. You cannot know what that cost him. Cost his spirit, I mean. The Roebling company made its bid for the wire contract; the wire contract was awarded to Mr Haigh.

— I have heard what your husband thinks of Mr Haigh. Sour grapes, they say.

— *Some* say. *They* say. You hold these mysterious gossips over my head, William Kingsley.

— What do you make of Mr Haigh, I wonder?

— My opinion of Mr Haigh is not required, she said. She did not believe these words, even as she spoke them.

— Well, he said, let me say that is answer enough. He turned his blue eyes to her, held her gaze. But I sense you are dismayed at my manner of doing business. This is the world of men, you know. If you will participate, you must stand up for yourself. And you must value your own opinion as much as all those gossips, as you call them, value theirs. Come, he said, walk with me. We will go to the work. You can assess the deflection.

He stood and held out his hand. Despite herself, she took it in rising; held it, even, just a moment too long. She could feel her own heart beating beneath her plain dress. He turned away from her and they walked again together side by side, as they had from the bridge office, but now she felt the space between them flex as they strode inland, away from the river and towards the great granite bulk of the anchorage, where huge iron eyebars emerged from a sarcophagus of stone, the iron rings catching and holding the strands of spinning cable as she would hold the reins of her horse.

The office here was a low wooden building, sturdily and cleanly built. They had to thread their way through the site, past stacks of wood and piles of brick and stone, clusters of tools, smaller and larger reels of wire. One huge wooden cable drum with the initials BWM — Brooklyn Wire Mills — burned into the pine stood empty by the door of the office, its steel already spooled into the work. He rapped on the door, opened it, poked in his head.

— Mr Young! he called. I am here with Mrs Roebling, as I promised. (What did he promise? And when? How certain was he of her — acquiescence? She could turn on her heel now, and go. She had had enough of his lectures. This was her opinion, which he had told her not a moment ago she should value.)

She heard Young, the foreman, speak to Kingsley, but did not hear what he said. He had a limp, now, Young: he had been badly affected by his work down below, and kept more to this desk in the office than he had in years past. But her husband trusted him absolutely, and so, for that matter, did she. Young and Farrington together kept the machine of the bridgework smoothly oiled.

She turned her back to Kingsley as he spoke to Young; shading her eyes with her hand, she looked for Paine or McNulty. She wished to discuss a small matter regarding the splicing of the wire. Special care had to be taken regarding the abutting ends of each wire as it was cut before being drawn together into what was called a vanishing thread — the splice, correctly made, stronger than the unjoined wire. In her reticule she had a sample splice; she intended to bring back another. She could see neither engineer; she would send a boy to seek one of them out.

The iron staircase tracked back and forth across the face of the anchorage, a zig-zag that looked sturdy at ground level, delicate and lacy as it neared the top of the granite pile. Eight laddered flights of metal steps. Kingsley had stepped inside the office now. She lifted the hem of her skirt and walked towards the stairs.

◊

« Et Emma se mit à rire, d'un rire atroce, frénétique, désespéré, croyant voir la face hideuse du misérable, qui se dressait dans les ténèbres éternelles comme un épouvantement.

Il souffla bien fort ce jour-là, Et le jupon court s'envola!

Une convulsion la rabattit sur le matelas. Tous s'approchèrent. Elle n'existait plus. »

✣ ✣ ✣ ✣ ✣

BROOKLYN. SUNDAY, OCTOBER 7, 1877. 5 PM. APPROX.

THE STORY SPLIT in two and bound in green leather.

Emily in her chamber, settled on the chaise which runs beneath the window on the river side of the house. Her hands tremble as she closes the book. She sent Liza away when she came to light the fire and now she is cold; now she wishes she had let the girl go about her business. If she tried to name what she was feeling it might be — no, she could not find it. As if she had risen up from deep water into air, gasping, yet in that water she had moved like a seal, like a mermaid, as if the novel's atmosphere was home to her. The wonder that ends in horror. Emma Bovary dead.

Charles Bovary dead. Their little girl, Berthe, a pauper, despised.

The shimmer of beginning turned to dust and ruin. Don't be foolish, she tells herself. She rises, looks at herself in the glass, the oil lamp casting shadows which make her look . . . older? Younger? She reaches up, unpins her hair so it falls about her shoulders, runs her fingers through it, drags her nails against her scalp. Wash had written to her from — Petersburg? All these questions, dredged up by an old book! Petersburg, perhaps. A decade ago. More. Yet to this day she recalled his words because she had committed them to memory, so shocking, so thrilling his request. *You draw a picture of our Wedding night as you think it will be, and then I will send you one in return. Will you Pet or don't you think yourself equal to the task. Take a drink before you commence. I wish I had the knack of drawing as you do* — he had signed the letter — adoring —

She had got up early, morning after morning, lit a candle, sat at her little table with her sharpened pencil and the blank page. Quaking, and that queer feeling in her belly that was better than anything but which made it hard to draw. Laughing at herself now, all these years later, far down the road of familiarity and the land that lay beyond familiarity: the terrain of weariness, trouble, danger. Her brother had a book of engravings of Greek statues, she had filched it from the shelves and pored over the pages to guide her work — but nothing was ever right. She had to burn the clumsy drawings in the grate, hiding them away until the fires were lit again.

They had discovered what they wanted together, she and Wash. It is hard to think on, now. Before John's bloody and disastrous birth, before all this. Wash's white body, convulsing, his agony, the slick filth from the caisson dragged through the house, she pushed them away, Paine, McNulty, Liza with her basin of hot water. Emily had torn at his shirt, splashed him with alcohol, brandy, whiskey, whatever they had, rubbed salt on his skin until his flesh rose in welts. Nothing did any good. Only silence and stillness and even that. Even that.

Processions of doctors. Useless. Charles Bovary, setting that boy's leg.

The time *before*. Those first times. The first time. Seeing him across the room before they were even introduced. She had heard Gecky speak of him, what a fine soldier he was, so capable, brave and willing, and somehow the young man with the broad forehead and keen placid gaze could only have been Captain Roebling. His name such a mouthful. You must call me Wash, he had said, almost immediately. The softness of that, on her tongue.

Holding the book now. Wishing for a fire. Unwilling to call the girl. Weighing the two volumes in her hands. Perhaps she would acquire a finer edition from Brentano's. Opening it again, running the pads of her fingers over the foxed page. M. K. A., those initials. And then the memory almost comes to her, of a photograph, a stiff glass plate of two young men, two boys, side by side, arms around each other's necks, held in safety, held in the past, before death, before damage, before the steel wire of their lives bound her, bound them both, to this place, to this moment. The memory almost comes, but it does not, and Emily sits alone in her room in the gathering dark.

◊

« Ils descendirent. Rodolphe attacha les chevaux. Elle allait devant, sur la mousse, entre les ornières.

Mais sa robe trop longue l'embarrassait, bien qu'elle la portât relevée par la queue, et Rodolphe, marchant derrière elle, contemplait entre ce drap noir et la bottine noire, la délicatesse de son bas blanc, qui lui semblait quelque chose de sa nudité.

Elle s'arrêta.

– Je suis fatiguée, dit-elle.

– Allons, essayez encore! reprit-il. Du courage! »

✣ ✣ ✣ ✣ ✣

BROOKLYN. MONDAY, SEPTEMBER, 17, 1877. 12.24 PM.

HE CAUGHT HER at the top. He was a little breathless. The swift, authoritative tap of his boot soles.

— Mrs Roebling!

One of the men had dropped the big iron hammer he had in his hand when she appeared on top of the anchorage. The stairs were no harder to take than the ones in her house, though perhaps a little narrower; how it was she had never climbed them before, she could not say. Kingsley's words seemed to push against her back, propelling her forward. Sour grapes. And her own words. My opinion is not required. On the surface of the anchorage, boards and tools and stone blocks scattered about; a wheelbarrow, a barrel of nails. The man with the hammer reached down to his feet to collect it; when he straightened, he brushed his blackened hand against the rim of his battered hat in a sort of salute; she nodded, then kept her chin up, purposeful, as she knew what her business was here.

— Mrs Roebling!

The grease from the crabs shining on their fingers. The crumbs on her tongue.

The sign stood before the anchor bars; it was new. Last Friday her husband had dictated the letter that contained the text which was now painted, bold and black, upon a wide wooden panel. She had written them in pencil on lined paper before copying them in ink.

Safe for only 25 men at one time. Do not walk close together. Nor run, jump or trot. Break step!

It was signed: W. A. *Roebling, Eng'r in Chief.*

Kingsley had caught up with her. He was hatless; he must have left it on Young's desk in his haste to catch her. The sun lit the red in his hair. A bead of sweat ran past his ear towards his collar.

— I would take the air, Mr Kingsley, she said. My husband says there is too much traffic on this footbridge; all day long Mr Young is pestered by hoi polloi, wanting to test their nerve against the height. Mr Martin has taken his daughters across, I am told; every penny-a-liner will make a daredevil show. And yet the wife of the chief engineer has remained earthbound. Why is that? Because she is in her husband's sick-room, Mr Kingsley, where he toils night and day for the good of this work, for the good of not one city but two, where he fights against men like you. How dare you, William Kingsley. How dare you.

And yet he stood so close to her now. Some vibration in the air, shivering across her; not the breeze which kicked up a stray flag of paper and blew it over the side of the anchorage.

Do not walk close together. And yet when she strode away he followed, just behind her.

— Emily, he said. You must —

What must she? Her whole life. Father, brother, husband. School master, school mistress, whisper of gossip, *must* like a flock of birds around her head, circling carrion.

There were gaps between the boards. Each board about four feet wide, perhaps six inches in width. Perhaps. A run of slender cable left and right. She reached out with one hand and then the other, but then took her reticule off her wrist, slipping it quickly into the pocket beneath her skirt. She looked down; no height here, where the footbridge lifted off from the stone, but ahead — she lifted her glance, and there it was: the tower, its arches, eyes as blue as his, the sky shining through stone portals. Beneath the soles of her boots the walkway flexed and swayed, muscle of wood and wire, and she allowed the movement into her body and stepped forward, beginning to feel the curve towards the tower. She made her own movement bold and firm though there was a fluttering in her throat now as the breeze began to pick up, it seemed, at her every step, running its fingers through her hair and tugging at the pins that bound it to her skull. Gulls wheeled over the river, dipping and crying, and the horn of a ferryboat sounded, rising up towards her. Shouts, cries, the squeal of metal on metal, all the cost of it, ten-million-dollars-worth of work beneath her feet, running through her palms as she held tight to the wire with her kid-gloved hands. She heard him behind her. *Do not walk close together.* And yet they walked upwards, both of them, now over the river itself far below, its silver plate like the back of a photograph, and her whole self gathered here in terror and delight. Upwards. Up and up and up.

◊

« Des moires frissonnaient sur la robe de satin, blanche comme un clair de lune. Emma disparaissait dessous; et il lui semblait que, s'épandant au dehors d'elle-même, elle se perdait confusément dans l'entourage des choses, dans le silence, dans la nuit, dans le vent qui passait, dans les senteurs humides qui montaient. »

BROOKLYN. FRIDAY, SEPTEMBER 8, 1882. 9.45 PM.

IN THE DARKNESS, she held up her hand. A great iron door-knocker. She put her gloved fingers against it but did not lift the ring yet.

The journey had been too long; she was too tired. She knew that her hair was untidy and there was mud on the hem of her black dress. Her mourning coat had been purchased thoughtlessly and in haste, and as the fall weather came in, it was no match for the chill. She had been cold all the way down from Newport. She had chosen to stand on the deck of the steamer and let the wind beat at her, push against the wool of her skirts, run hard through the fur at her throat, slap her cheeks. She had left the cottage almost before dawn, walking the few blocks to the marina to avoid causing a disturbance. The night before her departure she had asked the cook — a brisk, white-haired New Englander whose competent service had been included in their hire of the place — to leave a cold meat sandwich in the ice box for the morning. She had asked the woman quietly, out of her husband's hearing, and Mrs Crewe had given a quick nod of assent. The sandwich, when she went to look for it in the shadowed kitchen fourteen or so hours ago, was neatly wrapped in brown paper. She had liked Mrs Crewe from the start, and then when Gecky died, the cook had quietly ensured that the household ran ever more smoothly. She would place a biscuit on the saucer of Emily's teacup, and not take the cup until the biscuit had gone.

— *What do you think you are doing, Ems?*

She could hear her brother's voice as if he were standing over her, a fine and handsome soldier and she a little girl. *Gecky do it*, he would say, taking up whatever it was she struggled with, using the nickname, the plea, she had put upon him as a baby. On his deathbed he had said it.

Do not think of it now.

Now she did not recall eating the sandwich. The hollow in her vitals was nothing to do with hunger. As the steamboat had drawn towards the pier, she had craned her neck back, looking up into the gathering night, the first faint dapple of stars, looking up at those huge stone towers, their blinded eyes, the cables taut, spun from that thief's wire. Now the whole bridge floor ran shore to shore, it was the thing entire, the great creation.

Yet the great creation incomplete: it was a ferry which brought her from the tip of New York to the Heights of Brooklyn, and once again she had disdained a carriage, walked up alone through the lamplit streets. As the two of them had once walked, so many times together, she and William Kingsley, as her husband lay on one bed or another, stricken, blinded, and she carrying the engine of his mind in her own.

— *What do you think you are doing, Ems?*

O, Gecky. This is not your fight. Tears at the edges of her eyes. It was the cold, that was all. A rill of shiver ran all through her, shaking her shoulders, her hips. She must not stand here any longer. That in itself was a scandal, an affront. The iron in her fist. Lifted the knocker and dropped it once, twice, three times. She could see light at the back of the house. She had sent no card, no message. He might be —

— Miss?

The girl squinted out from the hall. You only recognise what you expect to see.

— Sylvia, she said. It's Mrs Roebling. May I come in?

— O missus! The door swinging wide, the warmth of the hallway a blissful shock. She sighed before she could stop herself.

— Missus, here, let me — the girl reaching up for her coat. You must come in by the fire, the cold comes off you like a rain, missus.

— Sylvia? Who is at the door?

Before the girl could open her mouth, Emily opened hers. The voice had come from the parlour above, and so she called up.

— Mrs Kingsley. It is Emily Roebling. I must apologise to you for appearing on your doorstep in this manner, at such an hour. I assure you I would not —

He stepped out from the room, stood in his carpet slippers at the head of the stairs.

— Emily, he said. There was no question in his voice. No answer, either. His face impassive. She imagined Mrs Kingsley, Kate, by the fire in the parlor, her needlework stilled on her lap.

— I apologise for the intrusion. To say his name? William. She did not. Left the hole for it hanging there, in the air of the staircase. I must speak to you, she said. I did not know what else to do.

— Please, he said, will you come up? Sylvia, fetch Mrs Roebling — what would you like?

— I would like some hot tea, she said. I thank you.

— Bring tea, Sylvia, and perhaps some of that fine fruitcake. A slice or two.

The girl nodded, curtsied, as Emily made her way up the stairs on heavy legs. When she entered the parlor, Mrs Kingsley had risen. She was a tall, elegant woman; not beautiful, but fine-featured, carved. The years had not thickened her narrow waist. She wore watered silk and her silver-blonde hair was in a neat chignon at the nape of her neck.

— Mrs Roebling, she said. You are welcome in this house — at any hour, of course. Her voice as even as her husband's. You will allow me to say, I was terribly grieved to hear of the death of General Warren. The loss of a brother is a sore one.

— I am grateful for your hospitality. Truly I am, Emily said, and grateful too for your sympathy. General Warren's death has indeed been difficult for us all. Especially at such a time.

— Kate, my dear, he said, forgive me, but will you leave us? I have a sense there is some business Mrs Roebling would like to discuss and I would not wish to weary you with such matters.

The glance that passed between husband and wife was so familiar to her she nearly laughed — it would have been a relief to laugh — but she kept her composure.

— Of course, Kate Kingsley said. I will say goodnight then, Mrs Roebling. You must make yourself at home. When Mrs Kingsley left the parlor she kept her gaze straight ahead, and did not take Emily's offered eye.

When they were alone, he gestured toward the settee, and she gratefully sat down.

— Perhaps a little glass of whiskey while we wait for our tea?

— Yes please, she said. Thank you.

He poured two glasses from a crystal decanter and sat across from her. It was a long time since they had been alone in a room together. She observed his familiar gestures: the way he hitched at his trousers before he sat, the little jerk of his chin as he settled. As he handed her one glass, as she sipped the amber fire gratefully, he reached back and picked up a newspaper, laying it between them on the black lacquer table.

— I too, he said, was grieved to hear of your honored brother's death. But I do not think you have come here in mourning dress for my condolence. This explains your visit, I assume.

On the right-hand side of the paper's front page was an interview, given by her husband, to a journalist who had come calling just as she had gone for her morning ride two days before. A *journalist.* So he had claimed to be. Prettyman, he was called, so Col. Roebling said smilingly. What had possessed him? Perhaps he — Col. Roebling, her Wash, who lived not in the world but in closed rooms, whose attention was selective, who kept her as a shield; sometimes it was impossible not to imagine this, impossible not to resent him, Col. Roebling, her Wash — perhaps he had somehow allowed himself to think the worst was over. That he could say what he liked now. That the bridge stood, incomplete but ineradicable, permanent as a pyramid, so what did it matter for him to call into question the morals and motives of the men who paid his salary still?

This is why she had come to see William Kingsley. But despite the warmth of the fire, the cold ran up and down her arms.

— We are 'playing politics', Col. Roebling says. This man, that man, me perhaps, or Mayor Low, we wish to run for governor, we care nothing for the bridge, only for ourselves. We act out of spite and call him an invalid. I think I need not remind you that your husband has called himself an invalid, many times. He looked clear at her. Many times.

— Yes, she said. I know.

She drank her whiskey down. He refilled her glass. Just then there was a bustle at the door, and the maid entered with a tray: a china teapot, teacups of translucent porcelain, fruitcake sliced and buttered. She set the tray down on the table.

— Shall I — ?

— We will pour our own tea, Sylvia, thank you. You may leave us for the night.

A quick curtsey. Her back in its black dress, the same black as Emily's, disappearing out the door, which she closed quietly behind her.

He did not touch the pot.

— You have never asked me for anything, Emily, he said. His face suddenly softened — just a little. You have never had to. His rough hands folded between his knees. Have you?

— No, she said. I have not.

— I have given, he said. Willingly. At every turn. Have I not?

— Of course, William. Of course you have. And you know I am grateful. And that my husband is grateful, though he will not say it.

She watched him sip his whiskey. His trim whiskers grayer than his hair. His eyes as blue as they ever were. All the things she did not know about him crowded around her suddenly: the words she had never heard him speak, the flesh below his collar which she had never seen, his easy stride beside hers in Paris, perhaps, as they stood before a painting, as he admired her in figured damask, fastened a ruby bracelet around her wrist.

— He is always in the room with us. Is he not?

They vanished, the images, everything she did not know, the other, impossible life.

— Yes, she said. I suppose he is. He must be. We would not know each other otherwise, William. Isn't that so?

— Indeed it is, my dear. Indeed it is.

Now he poured the tea and she took her cup. Reached for the fruitcake; the little silver fork and knife on the plate were engraved with the Kingsleys' initials twined together. She cut off a little portion, took a bite.

— Still, he said. Just this once, Emily, I will admit it. I should like to hear you ask. Ask for what you want, from me.

She sat back on the settee. Looked with her eyes into his and now held herself high with him on the swaying footbridge between the towers, the bold wind between its wooden slats, catching at her woollen skirt, how she was glad of the nails in her boot soles then! The gulls wheeled around them and just yards away a bare-chested black-headed young man sat in a canvas cradle sling and worked the wire, easy in himself as if he sat in an armchair by a fire like this one. She had raised her arm, lifted it from the cold metal rope to which she had been clinging, and waved, the movement caught his attention and he waved back, his laughter carried away on the clear air. Then a gust strong enough to shake the footbridge like a hound would worry a rat — and she swung her hand back down to the rope, her heart in her throat, but William Kingsley wrapped his arm around her waist, quickly and firmly, holding her steady against the wind. How she had craved the height. The possibility of falling. The two cities and the blue-black harbour spread out beneath them, all those lives, hearts lungs throats eyes hands feet mouths.

She came back to the present.

— The meeting of the Bridge Company is in three days' time, she said. On Monday. I know what is to be discussed. I know what is to be put to the vote. I know when change is in the wind. Farrington gone, William! Walked off just like that! Who could ever have thought.

— He and Martin don't get along.

— Exactly. Charles Martin, with his gimlet eye on the post of chief engineer.

— My dear, you go too far.

— William. Do not, in this room with me before you, make

me concur with the Colonel in showing yourself to be playing politics. You know I do not go too far. If you wish for honesty then you must offer it back to me yourself.

— How I have always loved to spar with you, Emily.

— And now you are making light of this grave situation, or seeming to! William, I cannot bear it!

She could not help it. Her eyes filled. She cursed herself. But he reached out and took her hand and she was not sorry for that.

— William, my brother is dead, my dear brother and protector, whose courage was questioned, whose name was slandered by men not fit to polish his boots. General Sheridan, calling G. K. Warren, General Warren, a coward. My brother died of a broken heart, William. And the very same kinds of men — she looked straight at him — have slandered my husband at every turn, called him unfit, an imbecile, and worse. And he has borne it, and I have borne it, because what choice do we have? He has no choice for he is his father's son. And I have no choice because I am his wife, William. I have no choice.

William Kingsley looked straight back at her. William Kingsley, general contractor, President of the Board of Trustees of the New York and Brooklyn Bridge, looked back at her and did not give an inch. She pulled her hand out of his clasp.

— Well, then, she said. I will ask. As you demand as I ask. Speak for him, William. I beg you, if begging is what you insist upon. Though I hope you are not so vain as to require me to kneel before you here on your fine English carpet. Should Col. Roebling be replaced as chief engineer? That will be the question put to the vote. And you know as well as I do that Washington has no comfortable margin, and now things are worse than they were before. 'I have a mind to stick', he told Mr Prettyman — as if it were up to him! But you have influence, William. Stranahan, Slocum — they are persuadable men. And you — William — you are persuasive.

— Slocum, you think? He raised an eyebrow, nearly smiled.

— Yes, I know. General Slocum and my husband have not always been of a mind. To say the least. That is how my husband's telling goes. But yet I feel he is a man of honor.

For a little while Kingsley said nothing. He ignored tea, whiskey, fruitcake. They both looked into the fire, which was low now, and he made no move to rebuild it. The little flames hissed, threw weak sparks.

— I will do my best, he said at last. I give you my word. For I too am a man of honor, Emily. I hope you know that.

— Of course I do, William, she said. You know I do.

She stood.

— I must be going, she said. Look at the time. The gold-faced clock on the mantelpiece ticked and ticked again. You will give my best to Mrs Kingsley.

— Of course I shall. Have you a carriage?

— No, she said. It's not far to walk.

— Emily, he said, rising, allow me —

— No, she said. Don't be silly. It's only a few blocks to the house.

— But — is there anyone there? It will be dark and cold and —

— I hope I still know how to build a fire, she said. I have a key to the front door and that is all I require. I'll travel back to Newport by the earliest boat.

Together they left the parlor; he walked ahead of her down the stairs. His hair was thinning, just a little. He unbolted the door and she permitted herself to watch the movement of his hands, the way the delicate bones shifted under his skin. The night air cooled her face.

— Thank you, William, she said.

He did not speak, but gave a quick and courteous bow. She laughed, and then he did too, just very quietly, just a little.

— Good night, my dear, he said. Be careful.

— I will, she said. And then she walked past him, out to the stoop and down its stone steps to the sidewalk, keeping her gaze fixed ahead of her, knowing he stood watching her. She turned towards Columbia Heights, the ring of her shoes on the ground, and listened for the sound of the closing door. It did not come. She kept walking.

WOMEN AND MEN

WASHINGTON, D.C. FEBRUARY, 1864.

HE HAD SEEN her across the hall, her arm looped through the General's accommodating elbow. Her carriage straight right to the crown of her head, where her brown curls were neatly pinned. She was in profile, listening attentively to Major Carter: Carter's habit was to stroke his blond moustaches when he let his opinions fly, and Wash could observe the action now. Her satin dress was a pale sky blue, a gentle echo of her brother's uniform; the shawl around her shoulders, ivory.

In truth, only Emily would recall the color of this dress, its fabric, the softness of the light merino wool warming the nape of her neck. She would correct him, often, in the years to come when he would say he was sure her gown had been green, or mauve, or orange. Orange!

— I am only testing you, dear, he would say. With the suggestion of orange, I mean.

— You will recall the form of a wire splice for decades, she would reply, but not the shade of my attire on the night we met.

— But your brown eyes, he would say. Their shade is indelible to me.

It was like another dance between them, this call and response.

He had wished to make his way across the crowded floor towards her; had smoothed the front of his borrowed coat and run his fingers along the edges of his slicked-back hair, checking for cowlicks. Elvira would never forgive him a cowlick, that he knew. He was feeling almost up-to-the-minute, despite the events of last night. He allowed the thought — briefly — that perhaps they had never even occurred. He had woken with Paine's form stilly sepulchral in the next cot, his own head pounding in time with the notes of the bugle's early call. The sweetness of that sangaree was transformed to sour bile in his mouth; he swiftly shoved aside the recollection of the proffered glass, the shimmer of oyster-flesh, his desire. The crack of his fist against Anson's jaw. Beneath the rough blanket he opened his hand and closed it, then rose quickly into the chill air, to light the stove and begin the day. There was nothing for it.

At the rattle and sputter of the coffee pot, Paine had opened his eyes, sat up, stretched, knelt beside his bed again for morning prayer, swallowed down some bitter boiling brew as he pulled his suspenders up, drew on his boots. They were like an old married couple now, he and Paine. He wondered if Paine observed what he was sure was his own ashy pallor — he had no need to look in a shaving glass to confirm it. But perhaps not. It was his friend's way always to imagine the best. He felt ashamed now, considering that. Another thought to push away.

But the day had revived him. The dance hall he had built was perfectly complete, sprung floor and all. He had laid a weave of thin-cut timber under the boards to make the surface answer to a dancer's step; had set a line of privates to sand the whole thing smooth. There was a supper-room too, with a sheltered kitchen at the side; and something about the swift pleasure of the construction, the sweet scent of the wood, made him recall working on the Trenton house when they had all first moved there, those quiet hours when he was a boy, working side by side with Charles Swan. Throughout the day, officers and men both had passed by and hailed him, admiring proportion and paintwork. There was no better cure for a headache than vanity.

Paine had strolled by in the early afternoon to inspect the work.

— Well, he said. If you won't be a dancing-master, you can supply the necessaries. He gave a little nod: his mark of approval.

— Funny sort of war work, Wash said.

— Better than what was up at Morton's Ford.

— Don't, Wash said. That idiot Butler.

— Now, now. That's court-martialling talk, Roebling. Paine smiled. You be careful with your tongue when you've had a ration or two in your fine construction here. He mimed taking a drink. Paine himself had long ago been conscripted into the Cold Water Army and never touched a drop.

— You'll keep me in line, Will, I'm sure.

— Fraid I won't, Paine said. No pirouetting for me. I've got a map to copy.

— Which map?

— Yours, Captain, Paine said. Your little sketch of the Ford. General Butler wishes to distribute some evidence of the whole mishap. Ours is not to reason why, hey?

Wash's map of the skirmish — he supposed that was the word — had been hastily made. It was not his finest work, but that suited the disordered events of the day.

— I thought General Warren might have mentioned it when he saw you last night, Paine said.

The heat ran up Wash's neck. Paine was not fishing; that was not his way.

— No, Wash said. No mention.

— No doubt he wishes to put the affair behind him. And he is not one to be impolite about a fellow officer.

Neither was this any kind of poke or prod. Plain-talking Paine. He was a rare creature. John Roebling would have use for such a man, Wash knew: if this bloody war ever ended, that is.

— Say, Wash said, and the words were out of his mouth before he could call them back, if you'll be holed up at your desk tonight with your quill and ink pot, I don't suppose I could borrow your coat? I'll polish up the buttons. It'll save me making a fool of myself in hunting around for mine underneath the chairs of the higher-ups.

— Sure, Paine said. Lucky for you I've just mended the elbow.

It had been as easy as that; and so it was Paine's coat that lay over his ribs as he observed the band tuning up, the strings vibrating, the notes of a cornet cutting through the talk. Now she had turned, the General's younger sister, and it seemed as if she was looking straight at him, though most likely she only saw the dancers, for she clapped her gloved hands lightly in time to the music, and he could see her body sway a little, back and forth, keeping time, the hem of her skirt sweeping gently against the floor, the toes of her slippers peeping out beneath, *one and two and three and four.* Warren stood beside her with a new warmth in his sober features; he was close enough to her that very occasionally their shoulders touched, her shawl against his well-cut coat. Wash's own — or rather Paine's — was loose across the back, the sleeves a little long.

And then he was certain: she did look at him. Her gaze lanced through the dancers, their moving bodies, whirling fabric, lamplit heat, landed on him, caught his eyes in her look.

— Like Odysseus's arrow through the axeheads, he would say in the years to come. Straight through. No impediment. Right on target.

— Think how long Odysseus had loved his Penelope, she would say. And you did not know me at all.

— O, he said, but I did. I had loved you a long time. It was just that we had not met.

WIESBADEN. JUNE, 1873.

— I believe, Emily said, that there are letters waiting for me here. She gave her name in her careful German. The clerk nodded his head briskly and turned to the row of dark wooden pigeonholes behind the desk; from the aperture with a stiff, blackletter R beneath he drew a packet of paper tied neatly with cream cotton ribbon.

— *Hier sind Ihre Briefe, Frau Röbling. Der letzte kam gestern an.*

— *Vielen Dank*, she said, nodding briskly in return. Across the panelled lobby of the hotel she could see Frau Weigert, sitting at a table at the edge of the conservatory, smiling at her as she engaged in conversation. The packet of letters in her gloved hand, she walked towards her companion.

— How beautifully you speak, Frau Weigert said. You had intimated that you were — uncertain of your skill in the language. I am most impressed.

— You are too kind, dear Hanna. I might remark that asking for correspondence at a hotel desk may be pulled from a travelers' phrase-book; but I have been making attempts at fluency. And I have been reading, or trying, too. *Goldelse*, by your Fraulein Marlitt. It is most engaging. And clearly, simply written.

Hanna Weigert's eyes, a sweet deep brown, showed her true smile. Romance is always engaging, she said. Especially for us married ladies! She laughed, tilting up her chin to show her smooth white throat. Emily was grateful for Frau Weigert's warmth and ease; though her settled contentment, the seeming simplicity of her life, set off little flickers of . . . envy, or something close to it, in Emily's thoughts. Hanna's husband Friederich was a distant Mühlhausen cousin, now employed as a senior surveyor on the Rhine. When the Roeblings had arrived in Wiesbaden — just three days ago — the young woman had offered her friendship swiftly. Emily had been to dine with them at their modestly elegant home up towards the Neroberg and met their twin boys, pink-cheeked and silent in matching sailor suits.

Emily sipped at the glass of water set before her; there was always water here, salty and severe. I hope you won't mind my remarking, Emily said, that your own English is perfectly turned.

— I can hardly take credit for it, the young woman replied. We had an English nursemaid when I was a girl. I had no choice but to learn if I were to have the treats I desired.

She smoothed her gown against her lap; the dark fabric was simple yet rich. And as to treats, Hanna continued, what are your desires? Shall we take tea here? Or a carriage ride round the Kurpark, or to the Neroberg?

It was a few hours past noon; a fine early summer day. The leaves on the city's trees were bright green, dancing a little in the light breeze. A carriage ride would be fine; Emily felt in her body a craving for movement, the horses at a trot, pulling her along. And it would be polite to accept Hanna Weigert's offer. More than polite — she enjoyed the young woman's liveliness, the way her laughter came easily. In some way — despite the stolid Friedrich, despite her twins — she seemed more a girl than a woman, though she was, surely, not so much younger than Emily herself. She had a way, this young woman, of passing the time with conversation that was neither frivolous nor prying; she knew, obviously, what had brought them to Wiesbaden, how Col. Roebling's health had sent them chasing across Europe so that Washington could sit himself under one waterspout after another. Had it helped? Distance had helped, she believed; distance between her husband and the work that had nearly killed him, not merely the danger, the pressure, the brutal attacks that came at any hour of day or night, but the work he truly loathed — the politics, the persuasion, the work she had discovered, in fact, that she had taken to naturally.

Perhaps — too naturally.

Hanna Weigert sat in expectant silence. The wife of the chief engineer of the East River Bridge might excuse herself, say to her hostess, you must forgive me, dear Frau Weigert, but there are matters to which I must attend, given the state of my husband's health. Last night both Weigerts, husband and wife both, had inquired with great solicitation after Washington; she had explained that he was very comfortable at their lodging — a graceful apartment over the park, with quarters for a maid and a cook — and dining on cold breast of boiled chicken. He could not tolerate company; the traveling had exhausted him; he was here to recuperate in perfect peace and — she was full of gratitude for her hosts' understanding — even the calm atmosphere of the Weigerts' lovely home would have overwhelmed him.

— I wish him the swiftest return to health, Herr Weigert had said, raising his glass of rich yellow wine. His English was heavily accented; not nearly as good as his pretty wife's.

She had not confided in the couple — why would she? — how far her matrimonial duties had stretched as the work took greater and greater toll on Washington. But as his health declined, Col. Roebling would countenance no one's presence but hers; trusted no one but her. She had known his mind from the moment they met at that long-ago ball. It was just after the sinking of the New York caisson that she had begun to go on her own to the Bridge office, to bring messages and retrieve them, initially. Washington had said they should send a boy — Paine would find one — and she had seemed to agree with his proposal but had not spoken of it to Paine, and there were times, now, when Washington was too weak to be aware of how things actually got done. He was never not aware of the work at the site, of the plans, of what actually did get done; that was different — no matter what, the shape of the work remained in the forefront of his mind, however much he suffered.

Emily had allowed her thoughts to drift too far from the table; she chided herself silently. She had tucked the packet of letters into the inside pocket of her neat woollen jacket; she could feel them, distorting the smooth lining ever so slightly, pressing against her ribcage, asking for her attention.

WASHINGTON, D.C. FEBRUARY, 1864.

— Emily, the General said, I have the honor to present to you my aide-de-camp, Captain Roebling.

There was a warmth in Warren's expression that Washington had never observed before. Not that the General was a cold man — far from it — and there were those who thought he had far too much feeling for a soldier; that he was missing the steel, Wash might call it brutality, necessary for battle. Yet in battle he was decisive, with a coolness the younger officer admired and wished to emulate; it seemed to Wash that Warren understood the difference between swiftness and haste. There was a quality of stillness in his face that inspired confidence, yet here, in the lamplit ballroom, his regard was animated as he turned his gaze to his younger sister. Her head came little past his shoulder, and her features were distinctly . . . plumper than her sibling's, but there was a clarity to her brow that showed their familial connection. And the corners of her pretty mouth drew up as Warren's did; Wash found himself smiling in answer.

She made a little curtsey, dropping one knee slightly and inclining her head. He bowed in return, stiffly from the waist.

— Miss Warren, he said. The honor is all mine. I am so pleased you are able to join us here in the capital. I had heard a rumor you might appear — how delightful to discover the truth.

As soon as it was out of his mouth, of course, he knew he had erred. A *rumor.*

The General observed calmly; watched his sister's amused glance. She turned to the young woman beside her — in violet muslin with her blonde hair in tidy ringlets — and put her gloved hand on her friend's wrist.

— Do you hear that, Miss Chase? I am *spoken of in camp.* What more could a lady wish for, I wonder?

— Well, said Miss Chase, so it was for Helen of Troy. You could do worse than take her as a model, surely.

— Miss Warren, Wash said, please, I —

His words halted, like water stoppered up behind a dam.

— Would you like another sally? she asked plainly. She had to tilt her chin to look up at him. I am sure 'pleased to meet you' will do.

— Well then, he said, be assured that I am. Pleased to meet you. That is, of course, what it was my intention to convey.

She offered her gloved hand and he took her fingers lightly. A shared pressure, fleeting.

— I thank you, she said. It is my pleasure too. He got a glimpse of her pearly white teeth. As to rumor, I have heard a deal about you from General Warren. Perhaps if we should become better acquainted I shall reveal whether his opinions veered toward the positive or the negative.

He felt himself color and felt too Warren's eyes on him.

— Emily, the General said. I don't believe it's ladylike to tease.

— You will know my brother's high standards of behavior, Emily said.

— Indeed, said Wash. He always ensures we keep our buttons polished.

— I hear, said the General, that Corporal Boucher volunteered the recipe for his eggnog. If you have not tasted the stuff, I assure you it is very fine. Perhaps, Captain Roebling, you would like to escort Miss Warren towards the punch bowl.

— I do enjoy eggnog, Emily Warren said. I find it is just the thing to fortify one for dancing.

— Well then, said Wash, let us find the Corporal's concoction. He cocked his elbow away from his body and she slipped her arm through as if it were the most natural thing in the world.

The drink was cool and frothy and served in soldiers' tin cups. They toasted General Meade and General Warren.

— And, Emily Warren said, a toast to new acquaintance. Her dark eyes looked keenly into his. It did not seem possible that they had not met before.

— General Warren tells me that you are also an engineer and surveyor, as he is, she went on. He says you are as skilled as any he has ever met or seen, she said.

— I am going to allow myself to count that on the positive side, Wash said. Unless of course you think that might make me dull. I suspect, you know, sometimes, that I might be.

— False modesty is not attractive, Captain, came her brisk reply.

— I assure you, Miss Warren, there is nothing false about it. If you ask my sisters, they will tell you I am ferociously dull. My own brothers too might agree.

— I look forward to the opportunity of addressing this issue with your sisters, Emily Warren said, and quizzing your brothers on the matter too.

She did not move her gaze from his. Her confidence, her familiarity, seemed so natural he could hardly question it. It was as if she saw his sisters, his brothers, ranged around him; as if she already stood beside Elvira, their heads bent close together to share a confidence, and already he knew that by the morning would have written to Elvira to describe his meeting with Emily Warren, the General's vivacious sister.

But he saw too that she was blushing, two spots of color high on her cheeks, right beneath the deep irises of her eyes. She perceived what he had, how with her remark she had inserted herself into his familial life, in just a few words set out a whole scene. It was a scene in a Trenton drawing-room, in a time beyond the grinding machine of the war: a low sun sinking behind the mill and the canal, glasses of schnapps instead of eggnog, firelight, teasing warmth. Into this swift dream suddenly came the figure of his father, standing at the edge of the room, cravat tied tight, hands behind his back — but Wash pushed this figure out of his mind, just as he pushed the girl from last night from his mind too, Violet, *Vye*-let.

And suddenly it seemed to him that he could step forward. She had showed him there was a door. He could choose to step over the threshold. Why should he not?

— It is true that my sister Elvira might defend me, he said. I believe she finds my company tolerable. She is very lively, as you are.

— How do you know I am lively, Captain? You only met me a moment ago.

— Well, he said, it is instantly apparent. It is in your voice. It is in your eye. It is in your manner. I will admit that I observed this liveliness, the liveliness of Miss Emily Warren, from across the length of the dance hall, as I stood over there by the door working up the nerve to walk towards you.

— You are very observant, she said. To see all this in a person, in an instant, from across a crowded room.

— I am a surveyor, Miss Warren, he said. Like your brother. I earn my bread by my observations.

On the other side of the hall, opposite the table where the eggnog and other drinks and small comestibles were set out, he had built a platform for the band. The players were drawn from the musical ranks of various regiments. There was Corporal Loomas on flute, Sergeant Allamon on the piano; McCloy was a mandolin player from Georgia who had left his state to stick with the Union. Washington admired McCloy; he was a neat hand on the strings too. Whetzel on the viola; Rathburn, a private, on cornet. He had listened to them rehearsing as he put the finishing touches on the venue; it was only the bass player who had to be found from the capital's ranks of musicians as no soldier thought it prudent to lug such an instrument from camp to camp.

— And won't you be taking up the fiddle? Paine had asked him earlier in the week. I do miss hearing you.

— A little self-aggrandizing, don't you think? To build a hall and play in it?

— No one plays as well as you, Paine said.

— I treasure such a compliment from a fellow officer, Wash smiled. Truly, I do. But as you know, I've been studying my steps and I won't have a chance to try them out if I'm scraping out tunes all night.

She was smiling up at him. Miss Warren. Emily. He considered what it would be like to hold that name in his mouth, hear it on his tongue. Easy. Informal. His heart was quick.

— The dancing, he said, will shortly begin, I believe. He must attempt to sound less hesitant. I wonder if I might have the honor of turning a reel with you. Or two.

— Two! She laughed. He observed her neat round chin, the stem of her throat. I like a reel, you will not be surprised to hear. On account of my liveliness, no doubt.

— *Esteemed ladies! Bold fellow officers!* The call came from the front of the hall. It was Captain Lupton, the evening's fiddler, his bright sash tied tight at the hip, his hair gleaming with pomade. He and Wash had traded tunes once or twice. His people had come from England just at the time that Wash's own father had crossed the ocean; he had music in his head from the counties of Suffolk and Norfolk, flat places, Lupton's father had told him, where notes carried out far in the long dark nights. *Will you take your places for the Grand March?*

— Will you? Wash asked.

— I surely will, she said, and he discovered he had reached out his hand again to hers, and she accepted his touch, squeezed his fingers with hers. Then took a step back to prepare to join the dance and —

— O! she exclaimed. Her gaze cast down to the floor. As she had moved away from him, her cloud-pale dress had caught on a splinter raised from the boards; it had pierced the fabric of her skirt and rent it so she stood as if she were pinned, not moving lest the damage be even greater.

It would be done in a moment. Please, he said, allow me — and he knelt swiftly, taking the splinter of wood between the finger and thumb of his left hand and pinching away the material of her gown with the other. It was a sliver about the length of his thumb-joint, sharp as a blade. He tucked it away in his sash and attempted to smooth the cloth which had torn, pressing at the little tear to even out the threads as best he could. He stood.

— I am afraid you will need a seamstress, he said. But better the hem of your skirt than the sole of your foot. He almost said: *the sole of your pretty foot*. But he did not.

— Indeed, she said, that is true, in both cases. The seamstress and my foot. She looked at him straight with mirth in her eyes. I blame this shoddy wartime construction, you know.

The blood rose in his cheeks again and already it was a sensation he had started to enjoy, that she could tease him and bring out the feeling he worked hard to keep down.

— I cannot argue with you there, Miss Warren, he said. I happen to know the architect in charge of the job, and he is a shoddy sort of fellow.

— Well then you must bring him into line, she said. Is that not the role of an officer? To ensure his men walk the straight and narrow path?

The lamplight sparked in her dark eyes and the warmth of the room brought a flush to her rounded cheeks. Another person — another man — might not have thought her beautiful. She would never think of herself as such; and he would never be satisfied with any photograph taken of her. The stillness required for making an image did not suit her; the glory of her was all in movement, in glance and action and talk. But the tilt of her nose, the breadth of her brow, the angle of her neck as she regarded him, all these he found immediately and intensely endearing.

Now he did allow himself — just for a moment — to recollect what had transpired the night before. Two young women in such different situations. The previous evening, his temper heated with drink and desire, with confusion and disgust, he had not been able to consider what circumstances had brought Violet (her name a chime in his mind) to Madam Sophia's establishment. He realised now that in the moments in which he had fled, fired by a poisonous admixture of lust and shame, he had despised her, certain she had chosen this life, and chosen indeed to humiliate him. Himself in particular: Captain Roebling, Washington.

He could not have said the presence of another young woman — this young woman in particular, Emily Warren — altered his thinking. If he were to tell Miss Warren of his . . . adventure — which certainly, certainly, he never would! — he was somehow certain that while she would no doubt find his own conduct disgraceful, and swear off his company forever, she would find in her heart forgiveness and compassion for Miss Violet. No one would choose such a life without having walked down the path of dark experience. And in the course of this war, such paths abounded, became inevitable, unavoidable. To the shame of his action now was added, in a flash, another layer of dismay, of judgment on himself.

A clatter of drum; a blast of cornet. Lupton's voice thrown towards the hewn rafters: *Ladies and gentlemen, your places please for the march!* Emily Warren slipped her arm into Captain Roebling's, and together they moved towards the dance.

WIESBADEN. JUNE, 1873.

May 13, 1873 — Brooklyn Heights

My dear Mrs Roebling,
I trust this finds you well. By the time you read this I presume that you and the Colonel will have settled in Wiesbaden. I understand now, from your note dated earlier this month, that I might have found you by letter in Auteuil, but you had remarked, before your departure from these United States, that you did not know how long you might remain in France, or whether the treatments there would be suitable for the Colonel. I hope that they were, and that travel across Europe has not over-fatigued either of you.

She had, in the end, gone for a carriage ride with Frau Weigert, up to the Neroberg and the Russian Church.

— My mother saw the Duchess Lili when she arrived here with the Duke. There was a procession to welcome them, with open carriages. Such a beautiful girl, my mother said. Such a tiny waist! Sashed in scarlet, my mother said, and her hair under a coronet shining, black as mourning silk.

Schwarz wie Trauerseide — Emily had to ask Hanna to repeat the phrase, which she did as the carriage wound slowly up towards the chapel's shining domes.

— You English, pulling your words apart! Hanna Weigert laughed. We Dutch, we like to run them together for economy's sake. "Mourning silk": that is what my mother always said, and told me it was a premonition, that she thought of the phrase, looking at the beautiful, young, new Duchess — and knew a pall was cast over her, that she would die before long. But my mother, you know, was a storyteller. And she liked to be right about things! Hanna laughed again.

The day remained bright, but the sun had begun his descent towards the horizon; the shadows of the trees bluing on the earth. She was just a girl when she died — you'll see! Her tomb is so beautiful. The whole place is a monument to love — more than one to faith — Hanna coloured a little — I hope you will not think me blasphemous for saying so.

— Of course not, my dear, Emily said, and briefly squeezed her companion's gloved hand. I am glad to know your thoughts on such matters, and grateful you feel you may be frank with me.

The chapel sat on a plateau towards the height of the berg; walnut, oak, hornbeam bowed in the shadow of the building's walls. Sunlight caught the edges of the domes' gilding, pulling soft gleams from their swelling surfaces, every aspect of it different from the rough red verticality of the Marktkirche in the center of town. They pulled up just yards from the door; the gray gelding stamped and shook his ears, for he had thought he was on his way home. Hanna Weigert told the coachman they would not be long; he tapped the end of his whip against the low brim of his cap in acknowledgment.

Massed candles; a fog of incense dense as a cloud, though there was no service and no priest. Emily blinked, her eyes stinging, then took the scent into her lungs, tasting it. It was like being inside a jewelery box, Emily thought; she could have believed the pale marble walls were velvet; the stained glass in the windows shone ruby, emerald, sapphire, and everywhere there was gold and silver on candlesticks and crucifixes, a richness distinct from any house of worship she had ever visited before.

At the center of it all was the tomb of the Duchess. Hanna Weigert walked towards it and Emily followed — feeling as if she were being drawn forward, though there was nowhere else to go, really; yet all the same her feet, cold inside her thin boots, seemed to move without her command. Elizabeth's effigy was — like so much of the rest of the building — carved from marble, palest white with casts of gray and lightly veined; the finest marble from Carrara. When Washington had gone to Maine in search of granite for his towers, he had told her on his return of the great quarries in Italy's northern Alps, how he wished to visit them, see this hard, flexible mineral for himself as it was drawn from the earth. Michelangelo's stone. Marble could hold breath, or so it seemed, Wash had said to her once. And so it was here: the Duchess lay on a stone bed, her stone bedding ruched beneath her, lightly covered by a stone blanket which folded neatly over her delicate feet. Her right hand by her side; her left on her belly, just beneath the swell of her modest breasts. The sheened lids of her eyes, closed in a gentle sleep; a crown of flowers in her hair.

Emily could hear her own breath; feel the rise and fall of her own breast beneath linen and lacing and wool. Hanna Weigert, breathing beside her. Both of them looking — expectantly, she would have said — at the glowing tomb, as if waiting for the Duchess to open her marble eyes, for her marble mouth to speak.

— They lived at Biebrich, in the *schloss* there, you know, Hanna said. She kept her voice soft. Not a whisper, but nearly, speaking to the holiness of the place. You would have seen it when you arrived, I think — you came by the river, yes?

— We did, Emily said. Yes. At the bottom of the park. Like an ordinary house, in a way only so very much larger.

— Yes, isn't it! Precisely. One could almost imagine what it would be like to live there. Only, not quite. Hanna shrugged and gave a little smile.

— How did she die? Emily asked.

— In childbirth, Hanna said. A little daughter. Who also died, and is buried here with her mother.

— O, Emily said. How — sad. What an inadequate thing to say. Not that Hanna would remark; no criticism, Emily was sure, would even cross the young woman's mind. Emily knew the strong impression she had made and that Hanna Weigert wished to please and impress her, so had brought her to this place. And in this place Emily felt a sudden rush, it would be wrong to call it a memory: it was a presence, an immediacy, of that close little room in Mühlhausen in which she had nearly bled to death. The metal smell of the soaked sheets. The girl — Sophie, someone's cousin — who had calmly braided her hair as she felt herself emptied, colder and colder as the blood left her body. The baby had stopped moving, she was sure, but voices swirled above her, urging calm, assuring her that all was in hand. Someone started screaming. O! She was screaming. That was her own voice. She fell asleep and had fearful dreams: brutal engines, iron rails, shrieks and dragging.

She must write John another letter. He liked her drawings. She would draw the trees in the Kurpark. She would try to draw a bear: he liked bears and would sometimes pretend to be one, and she would pretend to be afraid as he roared at her before crawling into her lap. The sense of his warm little body against her own. The voices had been right, six years ago in that stifling room. All was in hand. All was well. Or nearly so. Frau Röbling, the Mühlhausen doctor had said, you must be careful. You and Herr Röbling. To have any more children would be — a risk, he had said. I believe a grave risk. Light from the window glinting off his small round spectacles as he spoke. The nursemaid, walking up and down with the baby, little Johann, little John; Wash taking her hand, squeezing her fingers. All was well.

— Frau Röbling?

— Ah, Frau Weigert, you must forgive me. I was in a dream. Thank you for bringing me to this place. It is very striking.

— She looks so peaceful, I always think, Hanna Weigert

said. Somehow it calms me, to see her. Perhaps you think that is — queer.

— I do not, Emily said. We must all find peace where we can. There is little enough of it in this world.

— You must wish for some yourself, now; I have taken you on quite the excursion! Our coachman will drive you to your residence, of course; you won't mind if he leaves me first at Weinbergstrasse? I promised the boys I would be home for their tea and to tell them a story. You must miss your boy, she said.

— I do, Emily said. But he is with my sister; she spoils him, so I am not certain he will be missing me! And I thank you for the carriage. And it is time I returned to the Colonel, as you return to your children.

They had not been so long inside the chapel, yet by the time Emily pushed open the heavy door, the light had taken another turn and the breeze that caught her hair — escaping as ever from the pins that held them — felt cooler, a hint of evening in its breath. A shiver went down her, from her neck to the ends of her fingers and the soles of her feet. How narrow an escape it had been, there on that bed, so very far from anything that felt like home, the blood, the baby, some other world tugging at her and saying, *come, come, when this is over there will be peace.* It had been like a voice, it truly had, calling her — something she had never told Wash, how drawn she had felt to darkness that seemed like light.

Later, some months later, when they were in the house in Brooklyn, on Hicks Street, Wash had shown her the notes his father had taken, his father's strong sloping hand, notes from the spirit gatherings that had become his passion. Old John Roebling, stiff in his chair in a candlelit room, demanding answers from the dead just as he did from the living. *It is taught by most Spirits, who have made communications on the subject, that there are 7 spheres, calling our Earth the 1st. At our last meeting you stated the number as 8. Which is the truth, Seven? Or Eight?* Two years later he would be dead himself. He would know the answers now. Emily was still in wait. She drew her stiff woollen coat tight around her shoulders, walked towards the carriage, saw the coachman hop down from his seat to assist her.

— We will take you home, Hanna said. Emily felt sure her new friend had seen some shadow cross her face. You are tired, I think. Such a long journey you have had! I have hardly left little Wiesbaden myself, I can hardly imagine.

— It is a great privilege to travel, Emily said. But yes, dear Hanna, it is tiring too. I will be glad to be by our fire. And see how my husband does. She had stammered a little, in speaking; had almost said, my poor husband, but then stopped herself. How ill he was, how little hope there seemed to be: it was something they kept to themselves.

— *Bitte zur Wohnung von Frau Röbling*, Hanna said as the door was opened for them. Emily saw now that the coachman was a handsome man, his strong-featured face, dark eyes, seeming to hold some wisdom. The wisdom of patience, perhaps. A man before them, Emily thought, waiting on them, a man with an entire life of which she knew nothing at all.

The two women settled themselves in the carriage. Emily could feel Frau Weigert's warm little shoulder beside hers, and it was a comfort. The carriage rocked and began to move.

WASHINGTON, D.C. FEBRUARY, 1864.

Of course, there had been dances in Saxonburg when he was a boy, dances in Trenton, in Troy. There had been balls in Pennsylvania and Petersburg, along the Rappahannock and even one not far from Antietam Creek, though that astonished him now. The 51st New York had thrown up a tent one night as they marched toward that ground in Maryland — there had been some sort of local alchy, local girls in calico, and that evening he had indeed had his turn at the fiddle. Two nights later most of the soldiers kicking up their heels were wounded or dead. Often the former worse than the latter. But whether at home or in an Army tent, Wash Roebling never felt himself the most elegant dancer: Ferd had a graceful line to his leg, much to his elder brother's chagrin. He was too inclined to keep his eyes on the floor, wary of treading on a dainty toe.

But something was different tonight. Despite the mishap of the splinter — or, he would sometimes think, because of it — in the hall he had built, he felt a sense of permission, granted mysteriously by the deep brown shining gaze of Miss Emily Warren as she took his hands in hers and moved along the floor, her breath coming quick, her steps light and easy. Even as they reeled and moved through the other dancers, she stayed at the edge of his eye, a corner of bright sky always visible, the grace of her movement quite distinct from that of the other young women, somehow. He would often — in their future life, and then, many years later, even after her death — conjure her by her carriage: walking towards him or away, mounting a horse with steadiness and ease, stepping up into a gig or barouche. Her dance-card had been marked by the time they were introduced — yet he had been able to pencil himself in for three dances; he was the only one of her partners so favored, a fact he forbore to remark upon but which he held high in his awakening heart. And so they dipped and turned to the gay music of the band, grinning as they skirled under a parade of raised arms, *right hand through, left hand through, do-si-do, head partners down and back*, and if they had eyes for anything but each other, they might have seen General Warren smiling at them from beneath his pomaded moustache.

They clapped for the band at the end of the reel, and then danced a quadrille and a polka too. He did once not look down at his feet!

— Captain Roebling, she said, as they stood once more by the punch-bowl, my brother failed to tell me that you were such an . . . able terpsichorist. Her smile. The tip of her tongue, just visible, behind her teeth.

— 'Terpsichorist'! He laughed, observing the light sheen of moisture at her collarbone. Aren't you the light-footed scholar!

— We had Greek at school, she said. I can name all the Nine Muses for you.

— Well, he said, as to that, I thank you for your compliment, but it is you, Miss Warren, who are tonight possessed by the spirit of Terpsichore.

— Do you know, Captain Roebling — seeing as we have just danced two reels — *and* a polka — I believe I would not object if you were to call me Emily. I believe my brother would not object either, I will add.

Emily. He would say it, in just a moment. But not yet.

— You believe, he said. But perhaps, Miss Warren, I should wish for a little more certainty.

He was not entirely in jest. There was a little silence between them as the band continued to play; a Nine Pin dance, punctuated by laughter as one officer or another was left standing bereft of a partner. The silence was a little bubble, holding them apart from the hubbub, the heat, the movement. The scent, too, of bodies partaking of pleasurable exertion, the perspiration of the dance of an entirely different character than the sweat of terror so pervasive and unrelenting. Yet relenting in this moment. And even within this moment, just the two of them, one woman and one man, each the other's only companion now.

— Washington Roebling. I would like you to call me Emily. And I should like to call you Wash. I think that's what they call you. I heard Lieutenant Granger — she gestured toward Granger, who was now standing near Miss Chase — call you so between, I believe, the lancier and the reel.

— More belief, he smiled. But let's allow for conviction. Wash is what they call me. Not such a mouthful as all the rest.

— Wash, she said. The movement of her lips in saying it, the pink in her cheeks. She glanced down at the sanded floor and as she did so began, idly it seemed, to pull at the fingertips of her gloves and soon her ringless hands were bare. She looked up at him again and —

— Roebling!

He felt himself start, the whole room had vanished except for this square of floor that held them both, and he had no awareness of the body that had appeared by his shoulder, the rough voice, the black gaze.

— Congratulations are in order, Captain Roebling! Your . . . strength and skill are only to be admired, they are the talk of the ball, comrade! We all dance beneath your sturdy roof! But I hope — that I do not interrupt?

— Captain Anson, he said, turning to face him as he spoke. His own voice kept quiet and even as he could make it. But his heart beat in his chest as it had not on Little Round Top, for Anson stood before him grinning, Wash's own coat slung over one arm — and on the other, Violet, a closed-mouth smile set prim on her china-doll face.

He saw Anson take it all in. Wash's own intent. Emily Warren's fingers. The shimmering gap of air between them, full of life as two magnets that might be drawn together in an instant.

— How do you do, said Emily. She spoke directly at Violet; her look was open and warm. Somehow she had slipped her gloves back on; she held her hand out to the young woman opposite her, bobbed a little curtsey; Violet bobbed right back. I am Miss Emily Warren, she said.

— The sister of the general! Violet exclaimed. Truly, she said, it is an honor to make your acquaintance. I am Miss Violet Fairchild.

It had crossed Washington's mind to wonder during last night's shameful escapade, whether 'Violet' was the name this girl was born with; now he was in no doubt that it was not. She was in mauve silk tonight, still high-necked and modest, but with teardrop pearls dangling from her delicate earlobes.

— Well! exclaimed Anson, the sister of the general, come all the way from West Point for our revels! We are indeed in a state of grace, he said. Good Captain R, I hope you will see fit to introduce me to your partner in that last reel?

There was nothing for it but to do as Anson asked. Bile rose in Wash's throat. There was still a mark on Anson's jaw beneath the shadow of his beard; how he would have wished to set his fist there again! But he felt himself prisoned, a hostage. The sly looks of Anson and *Miss Violet Fairchild* held him as fast as if his arms had been pinned to his sides. Captain — he had to hunt for his fellow officer's first name — Raymond Anson, he said, may I present Miss Emily Warren.

A curtsey, a little bow from Anson, who then looked Emily up and down in such an insolent manner it was positively an invitation to strike. But if Miss Warren was discomfited, she did not show it.

— An honor, Anson said. And I hope, Miss Warren, you will convey my personal admiration — and the gratitude of the whole Army, of course — to your esteemed brother. He gave an oily grin. But my dear Roebling, he went on, I believe you and Miss Fairchild may already be acquainted?

Wash's heart made a dash for the soles of his boots and it was only by main force of will that he was able to keep the air moving in and out of his lungs and his face — as he fervently, fervently hoped — expressionless. He could feel Emily's eyes on him, well-disposed and expectant. He himself had no inkling, in that instant, what he might say or what action he might take. It was disgraceful even to draw the comparison, he knew, but it was very like the moment he had learned to understand far too well, the moment before a battle, before the first cannon was fired, before the first shell exploded, when the men all around had loaded their rifles and held them steady but the air was suddenly filled with a terrible silence, no sound of breath or motion.

He looked at Miss Fairchild. Violet. *Vye-let.* She made no acknowledgement of Anson's observation — but met Wash's eyes for the briefest instant and then cast her eyes down. Anson, he saw, held her elbow tightly, his dun gloves digging into the silk of her gown and creasing it beneath the pressure of his grip. So, this is how it was.

— I — fear I do not recall, he managed at last.

— Really, Captain R, Anson said. The lady will take offence. And Miss Warren — well, who knows what conclusion she will draw regarding your manners.

And, as in a battle, there was no retreat, there was only plunging forward, ignorant of what the cost might be.

— That cannot be helped, Washington said. He was filled with shame and confusion. It was a pressure against his temples, against the bridge of his nose. The ruination of his life opened like a chasm, unbridgeable, and his errors and failings ranged before him, from his boyhood to the present moment. The fear of his father's rage that had made him the liar he was, unable to summon whatever noble gesture was now required; the efforts he'd made over the years to save his own skin. Yet what choice had there been? What choice? And just then it seemed it appeared he was certain he saw the dark head of a tall man in civilian dress stroll across the room, perhaps ten yards from where they stood in this quartet of awkwardness; the stranger moved more slowly, more gracefully, than the men and women who surrounded him, and it seemed to Washington that when the strolling man turned to look in their direction he looked with the bright bold eyes of Max Andermann. Wash shook his head. It was not so. A ghost. Only a ghost.

He and Anson stood facing each other. He turned to the girl. You must accept my apologies, he said. I have — a bad mind for faces.

— Even such a pretty one as this? Anson said. His gloved finger briefly stroked the girl's cheek; Wash saw her flinch, and he knew that Emily did too. Something shifted then, in the air. Violet appeared to soften; she smiled at Emily in return. For the first time Washington saw what she really looked like. He saw some kitchen, not very long ago and not so very far from here, he saw a woman at a stove, a woman not unlike his own mother, a woman with floured hands and a tired face, and this pretty girl, her child. Patched dresses, broken shoes.

— I do accept it, she said. It makes no never mind to me. You must not put yourself in a-fluster about it.

— You are gracious, Wash said, and I am appreciative. And appreciative too, Captain Anson, that you have retrieved my coat from the General's headquarters where I left it last night.

As he spoke, Max came into his mind again, the way his friend would recount the glories of his sabre-work, his strong arms imitating the action he described: how suddenly in a bout there would be an opening, a sense that somehow your opponent was allowing you entry, that it was not even his being unable to resist you but positively inviting you in to vanquish him. So it was in this moment. And he saw in Anson's face the calculation that here was Captain Roebling with the General's sister on his arm, though the possibility of that calculation had not occurred to Wash himself. Beside him was not 'the General's sister' but Emily, his Emily, and in that moment too he understood that from her he would draw strength for the rest of his life.

Anson thrust the coat towards him and Wash took it. Why, it is my pleasure Captain, Anson said. You know I am always willing to assist a fellow soldier.

— Indeed I do, Captain, and I commend you for your thoughtfulness and courtesy. But look — he jerked his chin in the direction of the band — is that not Major Willard waving for you? I am sure it is. He looks most anxious to be in your company.

Anson did not turn to look. If he knew it was a lie — another one — he did not show it.

— Miss Warren, he said, it has been a pleasure to make your acquaintance. I trust you will enjoy the remainder of the evening's hospitality, and I wish you safe passage back to New York.

— I thank you, Emily said. And I promise I will convey your regards to the General. She gave another little dip of a curtsey and extended her hand to Violet Fairchild. I hope we find each other again in kindness, Miss Fairchild; kindness is what we must wish for in all this conflict.

— Truly that is so, Violet said. She did not look at Washington again. Anson no longer held her by the elbow, yet she walked with him after he saluted and turned away and they moved across the smooth — smooth-enough — surface of the sprung floor.

Emily and Washington together watched the pair enter the crowd. Then Emily glanced at the bundled cloth in Wash's arms.

— You came to dance in a borrowed coat?

— It seemed tiresome to retrieve it, he said, which was true. I knew I should return to the General's office before very long, and my bunkmate was happy to lend his. (One falsehood, one truth. A reasonable balance. Or at least, so he must consider in the circumstances.)

— It is a good friend who will lend his coat to another, she said. He had no wish to dance himself?

— He is a good friend, Wash said. Another truth. Captain Paine. He had a map to draw. No peace for the wicked, as the book says. Though Captain Paine in truth is as good a fellow as you could find. The lightness of his remark returned Wash's contrition to him; he hoped it did not show in his face.

— My brother has spoken of him, I am sure, Emily said. Captain Paine. She looked thoughtful, her brow furrowing ever so slightly so a fine line appeared above the bridge of her nose. The sight brought on a flood of adoration, the gates of his heart opening wide. *William*, she said, recalling what she had sought. Captain William Paine.

— Indeed, Wash answered. She did not seem to object — wonder of wonders — as he allowed his regard to rest upon her fully, to take in her strong little chin and roundy nose, her bright dark eyes, the angle of her shoulder and the pale skin of her wrist. I hope you will come to know Captain Paine as I do, and admire him as I do.

Ten years later — almost precisely to the day, although the alignment never came to his mind — he would listen as Emily and Will Paine stood close together in a fire-lit sickroom, the air full of a sickroom's stenches, his own stenches, hear their lowered voices in close and urgent consultation. They believed him to be asleep, or comatose.

— And what if he dies, Colonel Paine? What then?

— You must not say such things, Mrs Roebling. He will not die.

— You and he were soldiers together, Will. You know when death stands just outside the door. You know there must be ranks of men behind to step in when others have fallen.

— I come to believe that you know the work as well as any, Mrs Roebling. I would say you have been a soldier yourself.

It gave him peace to hear them. He thought he would never know peace again. He thought his bones would explode. His blood ran like hot lead.

— You know, Will, that is not the way the world works. And that is not my work. My work is with Cruse and Kingsley and the others. It will be you or Martin.

— Martin, Will said. If it comes to it. But Mrs Roebling — how I ardently hope it will not. I am your husband's man.

That was Will Paine. Now and ever.

Now, this February evening of 1864, all that was in the unimaginable future. Just a few days beyond the present moment, the President would write a brief note to the Senate, nominating General Grant to be Lieutenant General of the Army; a couple of months beyond the present moment, Captain Anson would fall at Saunders Field in a brutal enfilade; Washington would be tasked with writing to his widow, that task his first intelligence that Anson had been married. He would imagine — he knew not why — a girl with a fall of long dark hair and gold-flecked eyes, her hands busy with needlework. The address was not so far from the capital. *He fell bravely*, Washington wrote, *fighting to the last.* Although he did not witness the captain's death, he did not doubt that his words were true.

But now — now Will Paine sat some few hundred yards away in a cold bunk, scratching away with pen and ink by the light of a guttering oil lamp. Now — Washington Roebling crooked his elbow out, and as if it were the most natural thing in the world, Emily Warren linked her arm with his.

— Perhaps we might take a little air, Emily said. I wouldn't mind a breath, after all this excitement.

— Certainly, he said, though I should not like you to catch a chill on my account.

— Well then, she replied, isn't it fortunate that you have me on one arm and a spare coat on the other?

He laughed as he settled it around her shoulders; there was a peculiar intimacy to the gesture, he thought, as if they had already agreed something between them, a duty of care. Several of his fellow soldiers, and all of the ladies they passed, smiled at them as they aimed for the door: it led out onto a narrow sheltered porch, which he had constructed — surely — just for this purpose. There was no one else outside, though beyond the hall the camp went about its nightly business. There was other distant music in the cold air from fiddles and banjos played in tents and barracks; the combination between those faint sounds and the band's sprightly tunes made a pleasing cacophony.

The air was brittle with chill; the sky a black span pricked with points of light. They stood, a pair, side by side; Emily drew his coat more closely around her body and the gesture pleased him more than he could ever have expressed.

— A very pretty young woman, Miss Violet Fairchild, Emily said.

That squeeze in his belly again, that falling. He gazed out across the camp.

— I suppose so, he said. Yes.

— You suppose? I thought you men were always very certain of such matters, she said. I imagine you are being polite, for my sake.

She shifted slightly, rocking on her heels; the cloth of her coat — his coat — brushed against his arm.

— Well, he said. Well. Perhaps. I hope you will forgive me.

— There is little to forgive where good manners are concerned, surely, she said. Only — I would hope that between you and I there would be frankness as well as courtesy. She gave a light laugh. 'Between you and me', that is the proper grammar I believe. Isn't it strange how it sounds wrong?

— Nothing you say sounds wrong, he ventured.

— Well, Wash, she said, I imagine that if we spend a deal more time in each other's company you may revise that opinion somewhat. But I hope, I will confess, that you do have the opportunity to discover my true nature.

— I hope so too, he said, sincerely. And I cannot be franker than that. He could, of course, have been franker than that. Could reveal — well, he would. He was certain there would come a moment. In the future. Near or far. It was not cowardice — he told himself — that now was not the moment to share his every flaw. She would learn. She might — somehow, he was certain — forgive. That word again. He would truly discover its necessity, in the decades to come.

He turned to look at her then, the moon-soft contours of her face in shadow, but shining all the same; the starlight catching her glance, her curls. The silence between them was easy and plain. His shame receded. A new leaf. A new life. From this very moment. He knew it.

— Will you object, he asked, if I have a pull on my cigar? He patted at the pockets of the coat he wore.

— I will not object, she said. I have witnessed a fellow smoking before, you know. My brother is fond of a cigar.

— He gave me the ones I have, Wash said, only —

— What?

— Well, he said, you know, I have just realized — you, dear Emily, are in possession of my tobacco. Tucked into the inside pocket there you'll find my necessaries.

She dipped her hand in above the buttons she'd fastened to keep out the chill and extracted his worn leather cigar case; a little tin match-safe followed.

— My friend Paine will not sully his lungs with the stuff, Wash said. He struck a light on the sole of his shoe and set the quick yellow flame to the end of his smoke. I started this one upon the completion of the hall, he said. I can finish the celebration now I've seen it in use.

The sweet smoke he exhaled hovered near them; she watched him draw on the cigar, take in its vapour, expel it. The night was so still it made little clouds alongside the steam of their breath before drifting slowly away and dissipating into the dark. Soon, he knew, they should re-enter the chamber, re-join the company. They would be looked for. He wished for no gossip. At least not yet. And then he felt it again, the pressure of her body against his as she leaned — ever so lightly — against him.

— You shall have to tell me what other bad habits you have, Captain Roebling, she said. I have a feeling I'm going to need to make myself accustomed to them.

WIESBADEN. JUNE, 1873.

The house was silent when she entered, the upstairs windows dark. *Home* didn't seem the right word for this place, or at least not yet, though the three-story building, tucked behind an iron gate on the slope of a hill, was comfortable, spacious, warm. From her upstairs room she could see the trees in the park nodding their heads, the rich cluster of their crowns; if she were to open the window she would see the evening sun glinting off the surface of the sleek lake, the play of the fountain. Water, water everywhere.

A knock on the door of her room.

— *Guten Abend, Frau Röbling.* I wish to inform you that Colonel Roebling is resting.

The girl made a curtsey of sorts. She had come highly recommended; a younger brother, Emily had been told, had been very ill for years, and the girl — Ewelina — had nursed him. The brother was dead now. The girl was free to care for others. Emily was grateful for her hard life.

— The Colonel ate something before retiring? she asked. Colonel was *Oberst*. She always struggled to call it to mind, even having heard it a moment before.

— Yes, the girl said, nodding firmly. She made an effort to speak clearly and slowly, so Emily could understand. He had eaten the last of the boiled chicken, and some broth; Ewelina had given him his injection. She had never used a hypodermic before but had been a quick student when Emily demonstrated how to deliver the tincture into the vein. Wash sat very still, his arm outstretched with a length of yellow silk — where had that come from? She could not recall acquiring the fabric, so perhaps the girl had discovered it in the house — tied as a tourniquet above his elbow, his gray eyes level, inscrutable.

— Thank you, Emily said. It was good to take the air. And you may rest now; I will tend to Colonel Roebling when he wakes in the night.

— It is no trouble to look after the Colonel, the girl said. He is — a most interesting man.

Strictly speaking, this remark was an impertinence. But the girl's face, which always carried an expression of sadness, seemed a little brighter. Yes, her husband was an interesting man. It was striking that he had felt able to converse with the girl. She was glad. That part of herself which had become caretaker, nursemaid, secretary — and increasingly, she felt, engineer — registered this coolly. That part of her which was wife, Washington's wife, seemed at a remove. Far from her. From this room, this girl, her sleeping husband. The letters from Kingsley pushed against her ribs.

— What did you speak of, with the Colonel? I trust you don't mind that I enquire.

Perhaps she sounded imperious. It was not always possible to judge quite how one sounded, speaking in a language that was not one's own. And the girl colored a little at her question, shuffled her feet on the carpet.

— He asked me what I knew of the waters here. My native waters, he called them. *Meine Heimatgewässer.*

— It sounds very fine, put that way. And what do you know?

— A little. Because of my brother. Of course, Emily thought. I said that I do not like the taste, the girl said.

— I don't imagine anyone likes the taste, Emily replied. Certainly the Colonel does not, though he dutifully drinks his draughts!

They stood there for another moment. The silence, like the coming darkness, thickened. As if some boundary had been crossed and no retreat was now possible. They were two women in a room who might speak of anything at all. Emily suddenly, urgently, wanted this servant-girl out of her way.

— That will be all, she said. Thank you. You may go. The last as emphasis. The girl nodded, turned, and fled. She had moved so quickly that her black skirt swished behind her like a tail.

At last, at last. Emily was alone.

The girl had lit the lamps and there was a fire in the grate, coal that burned low and warm. If she had not scared the poor thing off, Ewelina would have drawn the curtains, but in truth Emily liked the violet dusk brushing against the glass like a cat wishing to be stroked. She liked the air here. It was soft and clean; so unlike Brooklyn, Trenton, New York. A little like Cold Spring — not far from woodland, from a broad river far enough from a city's harbor to seem unsullied by commerce. Unspanned by bridges of any description. She would feel at peace here, or at least — she could. If things were different. If everything, perhaps, were different. This longing for things to be not as they were seemed sometimes to have poisoned her. It coursed through her now, the longing, and sometimes was so powerful that she felt like a wire, a steel wire, pulled tight to snapping, fracturing.

She stood by the fire a moment, reached out her palms towards the glow. The gold of her wedding ring caught the light. She removed her jacket and reached into its inner pocket to extract the letters, the smooth satin lining where the bundled words nestled. Untying the ribbon again. Counting. Seven letters. A letter a week. Too few? Too many? She could not judge. It seemed measured, one letter every week. Cautious. She wished for something other than caution, sometimes. Tension, compression. Every sum calculated, every weight of stone and angle of wire. No room for incaution here.

William Kingsley's handwriting reminded Emily of her late father-in-law's. It was strong, bold, sloping confidently towards the future. She could see where, every line or so, he had dipped his pen into his inkwell: the lettering thinned and then thickened in rhythm, like the waves of the ocean the missive had crossed. There were no blots. Her husband's handwriting was more contained, a little neater; a five-page letter from William Kingsley would take much less time to read than a five-page letter from Washington Roebling. In the days when Washington Roebling wrote letters, of course. Now she took his dictation. The words were his; the handwriting, hers. Sometimes there were blots. Oftentimes his eyes were too bad even to look over her work; but when he was able to take in the fast slant of her writing she could tell — she believed — that he bit his lip, forbearing to criticize.

> *You will have had your regular reports from Paine; I know he will have informed you that the work progresses apace. I think in this letter to tell you of my visit to the South Brooklyn Steam-engine Works yesterday; the second of the great anchor plates was successfully cast. As you know I can call myself a jaded man when it comes to the work that goes on in this world, yet I could not but be impressed by what I witnessed there, the skill, the immensity of the result. The iron for the plate had been placed in two huge vats, each encased in fire-brick; by the time I arrived late afternoon the fire had been burning for six hours. I assure you I kept at a safe distance as the liquid iron was transferred to a tank by means of enormous ladles — the men wielding these ladles, in their great leather aprons and fire-masks, seeming like soup-cooks from the darkest regions of Hades itself.*

Emily smiled at the image. William Kingsley was not given to poetic language; he must have been very struck indeed by the ladling of the molten iron.

This tank was further heated by a charcoal fire — the soup kept to simmer, as it were — and then the plug was withdrawn from the base of the tank. Within a moment or two all the great mass of fluid metal was transferred to a huge mold made of baked loam, the loam formed into the spider-shape of the plate; and so in this manner the casting was successfully accomplished. The escape of gas from the vent-pipe while the molten iron was running out resembled the rumbling of distant thunder; the floor beneath our feet trembled as the iron flowed towards its desired shape — twenty-three tons of iron, sixteen by seventeen feet, three feet thick. As I am sure you will recall, the cost for this plate alone is $3,200; that is, however, precisely the sum forecast, so perhaps we can hope for fewer grumbles from the cities of New York and Brooklyn. I believe you saw the first anchor plate laid in state in Brooklyn, so you will understand what a feat this is. Mr Cobb (that is the name of the foreman) and his crew are to be commended.

Emily closed her eyes; allowed herself, for a moment, to imagine she stood beside William Kingsley at the South Brooklyn Steam-engine Works. The foundry was at Red Hook; beyond, the Buttermilk Channel and Governors Island. She recalled her husband's correspondence with the owner — a Mr Elijah Bluether — and the specifications for the plate. She was no longer astonished at how much her mind retained; sitting at her husband's side hour upon hour, day upon day, week upon week, month upon month, as his health worsened and his task grew more urgent, her increasing comprehension of the work created a framework in which, it seemed, almost infinite amounts of information could be stored. A vision of the great splayed anchor-plate led her to Elijah Bleuther; the thought of Bleuther and the anchor plates led her to the anchor bars and her correspondence with the companies that would manufacture them: the Keystone Bridge Company, the Edge Moor Iron Company, the Phoenix Iron Company: Mr Thomas Garrabrant, Messrs Hull and Loomas, Mr Joad Springer, respectively. Messrs Hull and Loomas, in their letters, had ceased to refer to the Colonel and now wrote directly to her.

She draped her jacket over the back of the chair where she now sat, in front of the light claw-footed table before the window which she had made her desk. She was hungry. She would call the girl back, ask for something simple: soup, black bread and butter. She liked the dark bread here, dense and moist, thick with little buds of grain.

Emily set Kingsley's letters out on the table. She had peeked into two of them in the carriage; now she cracked the seals on the rest. She glanced through them, taking in their scope. A discussion of the awarding of the contract for the Brooklyn anchorage: O'Brien, the lowest bidder, had threatened to *kick up a stink*, those were Kingsley's words, when he learned the work had gone elsewhere. Emily had met Mr O'Brien and was unsurprised by this news. The most recent letter included some description of the latest meeting of the Board; again, little that was surprising. Kingsley always wrote the name of the Company's secretary out in full: Mr Orestes Penthilus Quintard. She should not have found his name amusing, but she did; and somehow — her mind retained so very much, but this she did not recollect — William Kingsley had come to know she was amused and always wrote out the three words in full in his descriptions of the Board's gatherings. Indeed, he always took pains to mention the secretary even when no mention, strictly speaking, would have been necessary.

She must call for that soup and bread. Yet her hunger had abated; the flutter of nerves beneath the lacing of her bodice had pushed it aside. She read through the letters more carefully now — and then felt herself blush (here alone, her husband drugged and asleep in the room above) to acknowledge that what she sought she would not find, apart from that glancing reference to the Company secretary's orotund appellation. He would not refer to Kate, his wife, or to his children; he wrote of business, of the challenges and obstacles of construction and how they might be overcome. *One mind can in a few hours think out enough work to keep a thousand men employed for years,* her husband had been wont to say: and so it was. What his — her husband's — mind had conceived had sent not a thousand men but many more than that to stone yards and ironworks and mills, to the edge of the river and far down beneath its surface. What he had designed sent men to their deaths, and had almost cost him his own life. And in amongst those thousand and more, there was William Kingsley's life, and her life too.

Nothing was as she had imagined it would be. A decade ago — or nearly — in the months before her marriage, she had written her own letters to her fiancé, confessing her fears that her fate as the wife of an engineer would echo that of his own mother's, prisoned (for so it seemed) in the domestic sphere, a passel of children yanking at her draggled skirts while her husband traveled the country on man's business, a fine silk hat on his head and a cigar in his pocket. His reply, as clear in her mind now as the day she received it, had been both sting and comfort, reprimand and reassurance. Did she feel ashamed now, of that ancient inquiry, sent to a soldier in the thick of battle, her words insisting attention be paid to her own cares? She had been but a girl — would she console that girl now, or commiserate? Certainly, she had been at her husband's side, but had never believed he would be —

Before they set sail for Europe, she had been down near the Bridge office. Hardly anyone remarked on her presence now, she had become such a familiar sight. And she must indeed have been invisible to the two workmen who smoked as they headed in the direction of the bridge — *The chief engineer is a wreck*, one of them said to the other, and his companion nodded. The breeze picked up, the rest of their conversation became inaudible. The word had stayed with her. A *wreck*.

Her eyes grew hot. She opened them wide to forestall tears. Sometimes, she could barely admit to herself, she was, almost, glad of what she had gained. Increasing knowledge. Increasing confidence. Skill of eye, ear, understanding, judgment. To look over accounts and see what was amiss; to understand a question of measurement or stress upon the instant. The chief engineer's word was law, but she knew now how to shape what she brought to him, how to answer with his own intelligence. It had permeated her sensibility to such a degree that she could feel they were one person — though that one person was so very different from anyone she might have considered becoming back before that evening, so long ago, when he had taken her hands and they had danced, and the dreadful war had receded for an hour, that cold night warmed by their two hearts.

It was not that her husband had grown cold.

It was not that.

Kingsley too was bound — nearly as much as she was, as her husband was — by the bridge work. He was a man of vision — broader than her husband's, there was no getting around it. She knew very well what he did not write of in his letters, the talk that swirled around him, of cash carried in leather satchels across the cities of Brooklyn and New York in order to expedite some great work or other, including the work of the bridge. Such rumors were not her concern; they were gossip, and quite beneath her. She knew Kingsley was glad of her silence on the subject, and so between them — Emily Roebling and William Kingsley — there had arisen what she could only call an intimacy, fostered by their joint commitment and resolute focus on the work. A man might wish to be wealthy and also have principles, that was Emily's private conviction. She admired his comprehensive understanding of metropolitan progress, his involvement in various works. The first time she had visited the Central Park she had driven up as far as the Engineers' Gate and stood with her hand on the warm brown stone wall which stretched, she knew, for nearly five miles around the circumference. She knew the circumference because Kingsley had described it; and done so because he himself had built those walls. No, not with his own hands — but she was glad, in truth, that he had preserved his health as Washington had not. Had not been able to.

It was not that her husband had grown cold.

It was not that.

She searched through the letters. He wrote also to her husband, and she read those letters aloud to him. These, however, were addressed to her. Her heart swayed like a ship rocking on the ocean. Beat fast like a girl's. How glad she was to be treated as equal; and yet there was something she missed. Something she wished for that she could not — should not, or must not — name. The truth was that she felt easy in his company; could speak her mind. He was glad of it, she knew. And he appreciated her mind, and had done so from their very first interactions, which could not be said (at the very least!) of every man she met.

Here was the penultimate letter, written on paper from the Astor House. As it happened — his words pertained to the very place she had just called into her mind.

My dear Mrs Roebling — I thought of you

she read

I thought of you, and the Colonel

she did not sigh as she read

I thought of you, and the Colonel as I stood on the fine Italian terrace of the Central Park three days ago. I was in attendance at the dedication of the new statue that has been placed above the fountain there; 'the Angel of the Waters', the piece is called, and is intended to beckon to the visitor's mind the curative pool of Bethesda of which John's gospel speaks; of course you seek those healing waters too, so very far from New York City.

He considered her, then, as he stood in the Park. listening to speeches, observing the crowd, the dignitaries, with his keen gaze.

And further, perhaps, to your interest — the sculptress is a Miss Stebbins, who studied in Rome. You, Mrs Roebling, may not think it remarkable that a woman should carve a statue placed absolutely in the center of New York City, but I can assure you that most of the assembled company — and the scribblers who write for the papers, the Eagle included — are absolutely agog at the thought, and I am quite certain that some of the criticism of this new addition to our great municipal park springs simply from this fact. 'Like a servant girl executing a polka in the privacy of the back kitchen,' I read somewhere. I will not enclose a clipping. I, however, admired the Angel's bronze form, stepping lightly forward as I observed, her spread wings gentle — yet emphatic too, almost fierce. She carries lilies in her left hand; the assembled company was reminded in several speeches (none by me, I am pleased to say) that lilies are the symbol of purity. Miss Stebbins did not speak, but watched over all with a steady gaze not unlike that of her creation.

She read the paragraph over. And again. She did think it remarkable — admirable — that a woman should make her mark this way on the city. She would choose to interpret Mr Kingsley's words as a compliment; she guessed he made some alignment between Miss Stebbins's achievement and what she must now call her own work on the East River Bridge. *Miss* Stebbins. She was not married, then. Emily had always wished to visit Rome. She wondered, now, if she ever would.

There was a little more about the ceremony; a mention that in the next letter information on the board would be forthcoming. As it had been. Kingsley was a man who kept his promises. *Yours respectfully, William C. Kingsley.*

It rose in her then, an — agonized feeling, what other words were there for it? A tightness in her breast, a corset of emotion drawn in sharply, constricting her ribs, her heart. Frau Weigert would be at her home and hearth, now, tending to her boys, her husband both caring and heedless. As husbands were. As Kingsley would be, were she to perceive him so, in the daily manner of a wife. She felt herself flush, the room too hot now. She set the letters down on her table — too hard, the thud of her palm, her fingers smudging William Kingsley's confident hand, the serpentine S of a *Stebbins* now slumped, blurred.

Emily turned up the two small lamps on the table; saw that her hand shook as she did so. She listened, stilling her own quick breath, trying to judge if the noise she had made — or the force of her own feeling — had woken her husband from his medicinal sleep. She could hear nothing but the bark of a dog in the distance, the little soft crackle of the coal in the grate. She took one deep breath, and then another, and then one more. She would fold the letters neatly and put them away. In a moment, that is what she would do.

EXPLOSIVE

A more brilliant illumination within a restricted area has never been witnessed in the city.

— Brooklyn Daily Eagle, *May 25, 1883.*

✣ ✣ ✣ ✣ ✣

BROOKLYN. 1870.

THE WEIGHT OF the pistol was heavy in his hand. Years since he had held one. Five years.

— All right?

Paine nodded, a group of men huddling behind him. In the half light, their faces gleamed with sweat; Washington's own shirt was soaked beneath his waistcoat.

He cocked the pistol and fired it, pointing the barrel down towards the iron shoe of the caisson; even though the gun was in his own hand, the crack made him jump, his wrist twitching, his eyes closing, his heart beating even faster than it normally did down here.

— Nothing, Paine said. Fine.

Another charge, heavier, and nothing in the caisson was affected. For two weeks they had hardly been able to get the thing to sink at all: great boulders underneath the edges of the chamber stopped all progress, and picks and shovels were no good against them. Craggy surfaces of crystalline traprock, gneiss and rotten quartz. This rate of progress was useless. No caisson; no tower. No tower; no bridge. We must blast the boulders away, Washington had said to Paine last week. I fear it will be the only way. Are you sure? Paine had asked, as they stood in the twilight, both of them weary from a day's nearly fruitless work. The effect of any blast might be —

— I know, Washington said. I know. But what else is there to do?

The concussion of the blasts might damage the men — deafen them — might wreck the caisson itself. The whole experiment could be fatal.

We must try, Washington said. We can start small.

The pistol was the trial. And soon enough, they were blasting all day, drilling holes in the base of the boulders, some of them fourteen feet across, so they would shoot bodily into the caisson where the men would break them up with pickaxes. The rifle powder made clouds of black smoke that darkened the chamber; the men were slicked with the sulphur-smelling dust.

Emily made him go down the scullery to remove his clothes at the end of the day and told the maid to have hot water and towels ready for his return. That return was unpredictable, and often the water was cold by the time he was able to use it. He kept even longer hours than he had before, prowling around the caisson as the blasting went on; he was afraid of the pine roof catching fire — it would not be long before he discovered how justified were his fears. There were days he didn't see the light: down before sunrise, back up after sunset. He saw his little boy only when he slept.

And one day he noticed Paine watching him as the men finished drilling a boulder before laying in the powder charge; only then did he realize that he was standing with his hand clamped over his mouth, his shoulders tight, his stomach in a knot. The concussion of the blast carrying those visions of cannon and shell — he must not think of it —

He bent over, vomited. Spattering his boots. No one cared. It happened all the time down here. Paine still watching him when he managed to straighten himself, and he nodded so that Paine would see that he was fine, just fine. The compressed air thick in his chest. That was the beginning. That was the first time.

GETTYSBURG. 1863.

The boy had appeared at breakfast. Sitting on a rock, staring at him as he dipped his cracker in his coffee to soften it, wide eyes in a dirty face, his uniform ragged and his boots too big, the skin around his ankles chafed raw above the leather. The boy's jacket was buttoned right up; Washington couldn't see a shirt beneath it. He took a bite of biscuit, chewed, made the effort to swallow. The boy's gaze didn't move.

— You eaten? he said to the boy.

— Nuh-uh, the boy answered.

— Who are you with? Washington couldn't see any badge on the boy's coat; he wasn't wearing a cap. All around them were the sounds of the camp in the morning, the chorus of lung-tearing coughs that drowned out the songs of any birds foolish enough to linger in this place; the rattle of pans and tin plates, rammers shoved down into musket barrels, swearing, coarse laughter. Smoke rose up from their fires and mingled with the dawn mist.

The boy gave no answer, but kept staring at Washington's breakfast, such as it was; and so Washington handed him the coffee and the cracker and watched as the boy wolfed it down, or tried to. There weren't many teeth left in his mouth; he had to bite and gulp like a dog, turning his head to the side to soften the biscuit, which was nearly hard as wood.

— Go a little slower, Washington said. You'll make yourself sick.

There was another tin cup on the ground by the tent flap; Washington reached in and poured himself another cup from the pot. It tasted awful, burned and thin, but it was hot. He gave the boy two more crackers and a piece of salt pork, the last he had. The boy didn't look much more than thirteen or fourteen. When Washington asked his name, his regiment, he got no answer. Even in the summer's heat the boy shook, his hands trembling so the coffee nearly spilled from the cup,

Washington supposed he'd have to figure out what to do about the boy. Paine was still asleep inside the tent; he'd be sure to have a good idea when he woke. Maybe it didn't matter, anyhow. He thought of himself at that age, hungry and lost. But at least there hadn't been a war. At least there hadn't been this.

A few tents along Washington heard the sound of a scuffle; the dull crack of a fist on bone.

— *I'll shit wherever I fuckin well want! You stay out of my shittin way! I'll shit all over you, all over you and your mother, too!*

He smiled at the boy, because what else was there to do? The boy smiled back.

And then there was another crack, and where the boy's nose and mouth had been there was a blossom of brilliant red, a gray-pink cloud that hovered around the boy's head, and a noise from the boy's throat and lungs, a gurgling shriek and then a sigh of breath, and the boy's eyes, bright as sunlight shining through spring leaves, opened even wider, blinked once as if affronted at the sight of Washington spitting out his coffee, throwing the tin cup aside to catch the boy before he fell on his face, what was left of his face, in the dirt. The pale shards of his teeth, what was left of them, in that awful crater.

And then the major riding by, spraying up the earth on the boy, over them both, his fine black horse in a sweat for all it wasn't yet eight o'clock.

— *Come on, boys,* he yelled, *come on! We're gunna give 'em hell today!*

BROOKLYN. 1883.

Her two quick raps on the door. He could sense her hand, hovering, waiting to see whether she should knock again. He might let her: pretend to be asleep. He could keep pretending, even after that. She would not try three times. He smiled at the plaster ceiling: there was a hairline crack running out from the chandelier's rose. How had he not noticed it before? She would wish to have it seen to. Don't worry, little crack, he thought to himself. I won't give you up to her.

— Come in, he said.

The click of the latch; a pair of straw-coloured kid gloves in her hand, her hair tied in a knot at her neck. He could see a little gray in there now, at her temples; she pretended not to mind.

She had that look around her mouth. The corners turned down, just slightly; a stranger might think she was frowning. He knew she was not.

— Have you rested? Her hand still lightly on the doorknob. Standing in the space between entry and exit. Assessing the quality of her welcome.

— My dear. As you see, he said. Come, sit. You must be weary from your exertions.

— Exertions? she said. Why do you presume I have been exerting myself? Perhaps I have only been to the dressmaker's, or to tea with Mrs Gordon.

— I think either would be exertion enough, at least for me, he said. Certainly, I should be weary if I had been to the dressmaker's. If I'd had tea with Mrs Gordon, I might turn into Rip van Winkle and not wake for a hundred years.

— Oh, now, she said. Mrs Gordon is ever so fond of you.

— I wish I had a dollar for all the ladies you say are fond of me. I should be a wealthy man.

Her eyebrow raised, just a fraction. At her throat she was wearing the black opal he had given her — what? A decade ago? A Mr O'Brien had written from Queensland, with a description of the stone. So many thousands of miles away. He had asked for it to be set in a plain gold bezel with a sturdy pin; whatever colour she wore the stone would spark an echo, blazing a rainbow in sunlight.

— In any case, he said. I think you have been to the dressmaker's. Do I know that frock?

— I am sure you do, she said. It is not new. I have not been to the dressmaker's. I took the carriage to the park. Such a glorious day.

— And yet, he said, I am not sure it is of those glories you wish to speak.

— Well, no, she said. Dearest. I passed by the office, you know, and —

— Dearest, he said. He took her hand. It was warm in his own. You need not, he said. Anymore. They are doing just fine without us, now.

Sometimes she would simply choose not to listen. He could not blame her.

— Mr Detwiller was there, she said, with his proposal.

The clock in the hall downstairs, ticking. A ferry horn, on the river, the boat coming in to dock, or leaving. The looping call of a red cardinal.

— I think what he suggests will make a very fine sight, she continued. A very fine sight indeed.

— You know my thoughts on Mr Detwiller's *proposal*, he said. You know *them* very well indeed.

He pulled himself up from the chaise. There was a pain under his ribs, and a pain that circled the back of his head, from ear to ear; sitting up made it worse. Sunlight flashed off the surface of the river and through the window's wide panes, making him squint; he put a hand over his eyes.

— Shall I draw the blind? she asked. Her voice was cool.

— Yes, he said. Please.

Her skirt rustled as she moved across the room. At the window she took hold of the cord to the blind, but then stood, for just a moment, gazing outward; he watched her as she looked at the structure now spanning the water from shore to shore. He could not see it from where he sat: her expression, as she gazed at the bridge, did not change. She pulled the blind closed and the room fell into shadow.

— There is a danger of fire, he said. I have said this time and again. And — beyond the fire — how will the bridge be cleared? Mayor Low will not wish to be rushed from this structure of which he claims to be so proud. Who will harry him from the promenade? The police? Mr Kingsley? The President of the United States? Mr Detwiller's proposal may seem attractive to those who wish to trumpet an achievement which is not, in fact, theirs — but it is not attractive to me. I will not allow it. There will be no fireworks on the bridge. No bombs. No rockets. No roman candles. The very idea is asinine. That is the end of it.

His breath came short, now. The walls of the room closed in tight around him. The edges of his vision blurred. He gripped the chaise with both his hands, digging his nails into the velvet.

— Washington, she said, in that low voice.

— Don't, he said. Do. Not.

— Washington, she said. Husband.

— That is the end of it, I said.

He did not look at her. His eyes on the Turkey carpet under his slippers; and then to the shaded window, the blind glowing ochre against the afternoon sun.

— I do not imagine it is, she said gently, the end of it. In any case, you must rest now. I shall leave you be.

— I am sorry, he said, and turned to her. She touched his shoulder with her small strong hand; she bent, and kissed him lightly on the forehead.

— Are you? she asked. I'm not so sure of that.

GETTYSBURG. 1863.

He had observed Paine holding a notebook and pencil in his left hand as he rode along, the reins looped around the pommel of his saddle so that it was a simple matter to write on horseback, never pausing to fumble for the book in his pocket or pull the writing instrument out from behind his ear. Paine could write at a trot, and Washington had seen him draw a map this way, the horse's back rising and falling beneath him, Paine seeming never to move, no matter how rough the ground, his eyes flicking from the landscape to his work, his pencil moving as lightly and carefully as if he had been seated at a desk in library.

And so when Butterfield had ordered, *Roebling, you must observe the line and report on the strength of our divisions*, Washington had thought only of how he would hold his notebook and pencil; that was far better than considering how many Reb shooters there would be along that distance, happy to see a lone Union man touring this place as if these Pennsylvania fields were a park and he was out for his morning ride. There had been the boy at breakfast, just yesterday, shot where they sat. Butterfield's aide had shaken Washington's shoulder at dawn, told him to go immediately to the general, who had hardly met his eye as he issued his instruction. Butterfield's father was a businessman, they said; he had the air of one who expected to find his shoes shined and lined up by his bed every morning.

Now, away from camp, he could hear the birds singing. For these birds, he thought, this is an ordinary morning. Orioles, chickadees, the sharp shouts of jays; they would scatter in time and be silenced. He saw them flit from tree to tree, trees still standing tall or trees blasted to pieces; they would peck seeds off the ground, not an inch away from the corpses strewn everywhere, the bodies through which he had to find a path. He looked outward, not down, or at least this is what he tried to do, but if he did not look down he would hear the crack of bone when his mount stepped on the body of a fallen man, the blue and gray uniforms indistinguishable in the mud.

Everything was sensation. The trickle of sweat through his hair and down his collar as the sun rose higher and fixed its gaze on his back; the rough leather of the reins against his palm; the sounds of the camps, little groups of men rising, eating, pissing, groaning, shrieking. He tried to hear the birdsong, not the noises made by the men: he tried to listen out for the distant rustle that would mean a Reb and his weapon laying down in the brush, closing one eye before he squeezed the trigger. He made his notes in his little book: sometimes he could see a flag fixed into the ground that would identify a brigade, sometimes he had to canter up, dismount, poke his head into a tent: *We're the 1st Rhode Island Light*, said a boy with bare, filthy feet; *the 5th Michigan here*, said a man old enough to be his father, gray hair gathered in a tail down his back. General Meade wanted to stitch them all back together just so, into an orderly quilt of war, as if there were any such thing.

Crack! — and his horse shied up, rearing on her hind legs, the ball was that close. A little loosening in his bowels: there was nothing like a rifle shot to open the sphincter. He breathed in deep, taking in the morning air to calm himself — with his left hand still holding his little notebook tight, he stroked his horse's neck, Sally, someone had named her. Sally, he said. Good girl. Three miles of this, the sun getting hotter until he had to fan himself with his hat. Three more rifle shots, and before the last one came he felt the hairs rise on the back of his neck as if he knew what was coming. Peculiar. Holding on tight with his knees to Sally's flanks so she hardly shuddered as the ball passed by. A man can get used to anything.

Back at camp he stood before Butterfield, tore pages out of his book and handed over his notes. Neat writing, Butterfield said. Good. Washington did not reply, as no remark seemed to be called for. Butterfield looked like the kind of man who would think he ought to be foreman at the wire mill, but wouldn't last: the kind of man the others talked about behind his back, who got his lunchpail stolen or his shoelaces snatched. But he wore a cloak of money so he would never have to work at a mill. Washington saluted and set out to find some breakfast, but Paine found him before he could.

— General wants us to look at some maps, he said. Meade, he meant.

— Wish I could get something to eat, you know. Riding all morning.

— I heard. Along the line?

— Indeed. All helter-skelter. No one knows where anyone else is.

Paine shook his head. And so it goes, he said. He patted his pockets. Thought I had a spare biscuit in there for you, Wash, he said, but no. Fear you'd get just crumbs and lint.

— I'm not yet ready to eat the lining of your pockets, Will. We'll see if it comes to that. But thanks.

Meade was in a two-room log-built house that served as his headquarters. It was old and had been poorly-made: broken shingles littered the ground all around and the spaces between the logs let in as much light as the crooked windows. The general's coat was stained and his eyes were tired; he looked like he could have done without the task of running the army, but like all the rest of them, he had no choice.

— Good morning, gentlemen, he said to them. He looked at Washington. You the surveyor?

— I've been along the line this morning, sir, Washington said. But Captain Paine here is your surveyor.

— Come look at these maps, then, Meade said. There was a table in the middle of the room; maps that looked like they'd been dragged through the mud were unrolled on its surface, the corners held down with rocks on one side, tin cups on the other. How Washington wished for coffee. His stomach growled. We got them from a land-agent, Meade went on. I can't say how reliable they are.

Just then there was a rumble, like thunder in the distance, though the sky this morning was a clean clear blue. Paine stood on one side of the table, Washington and the general on the other, and later on Washington would recall how Paine reached out to hold onto the edges of the table to steady himself, or so it seemed, bracing his feet apart like a man on a ship in a storm. The tin cups shook a little, and now Washington saw that one of them was full of cold coffee, he could have drunk that right down, but it slopped out onto the map when the cup tipped over from the force of the thunder that was now roaring above them and around them as the Confederate cannon began blasting all together, a roaring chorus of artillery, hundreds of pieces — it must have been — firing all at once.

A man can get used to anything, he had thought only an hour ago, but this was something else, as if the noise was a wall he was being thrown against, and for a moment he felt his father's hands on his collar, the force of his father's wiry arms just before he threw him across a room or out a door, but this was not his father's rage, it was something larger and more awful even than that, and immediately the rough-hewn logs of the little building began to splinter, the exploding shells hacking like axes against the wood. Paine stared at him and he stared at Paine and by this time the general and his aide-de-camp — what was the man's name? — had hurled themselves to the ground, and the door was still open, and through the open door he saw the horses tethered outside bucking and rearing and screaming, and then one of them, a bay with a bright white blaze down its nose, cut clean in half by a shell, the two halves dropping to the earth suddenly but silently, or rather, the sound the body would have made was drowned out, drowned out completely by the bombardment that was everywhere.

He thought the drums of his ears would burst. And now he too threw himself to the ground, and when he did he felt that spilled cup of coffee drip down on his neck from the table, the liquid slid along his cheek and down along towards his lip, and even in this moment when the coffee touched his tongue Washington thought, that was fine coffee, I wish I'd had a cup of coffee, and ever after he would consider this to be extraordinary, that in a moment of mortal fear he could still taste that coffee. Now Paine was on the floor too, the dirt of the ground in his whiskers — he always kept his whiskers neat — and then Paine reached out his ungloved hand, and Washington took it in his own, because at a moment like this what else was there to do.

BROOKLYN. 1883.

The papers were on the table at his bedside, beside the water-jug, the glass, and the saucer where the syringe rested. A telegram confirming that the promenade of the bridge would be thoroughly soaked with water; the chief engineer had wished to know how many thousands of gallons would be used, for a plain assurance was not enough. The soaking must be performed by the Fire Department, not by Mr Detwiller and his men. It was not Mr Detwiller who would be called to put a conflagration out, therefore we cannot be assured that Mr Detwiller will pay sufficient attention to the task. Mr Detwiller, indeed, is the man to ensure a conflagration begins, is he not?

— Washington, she had said, when he dictated his orders to her, this is not the best way to go about this.

How many times. How many times had she said these words to him. He said nothing.

— O Wash, she said. You must be reconciled. There is no choice.

She hardly ever called him that anymore, Wash. She would say, the Colonel, if there were others in the room; Husband, she might say to him, or the three long syllables of his name. He had not been Wash in years. And yet, just now, it had come round again.

— You have ensured there is no choice, Em, he said. That I have no choice here is a deed of your own making.

And yet she saw he was smiling. Perhaps that too was rare, these days. Too rare.

— No one will ever forget this occasion, my dear, she said. I promise.

He shook his head. Two days to go and already he could hear the servants traipsing through the house, dusting, polishing, standing on chairs to tie bows of white ribbon to the banisters and light fixtures, arranging sprays of bay laurel and moving chairs and tables from this room to that, a whole commotion of preparation for the opening of the bridge; commotion not confined to the bridge itself but marching right into their home, where there would be exclaiming, and handshaking, and oyster-eating and champagne-drinking.

— I will have a glass of plain hock, he said, changing the subject, at least somewhat. I do not enjoy champagne.

— You used to say it made you sneeze, she said. She laid her palm over the back of his hand and their eyes met. Hers were so dark. Had he ever really seen her thoughts?

— Did I? I suppose I did. A long time ago. I must not sneeze all over Mayor Low. How unfortunate that would be.

— Indeed, she said, most unfortunate.

He lifted her hand to his mouth; kissed it.

— The Fire Department, he said. That is all I will say on the matter, now.

And so the Fire Department had offered their confirmation, and here was the telegram to prove it, right beside him. The house was quiet now, at last. The servants were moving the chairs and tables back to their rightful places, untying the white ribbons from the banisters and light fixtures, disposing of broken glasses, mopping up the melting ice which had cradled those platters of oysters. How he had survived the evening, he hardly knew. I will stay here, he told Emily, on this settee by the stairs. If there's anyone I must speak to, you can bring them to me. She had agreed; and for the most part, in fact, he had been left in peace. For a while he had smoked a cigar; mostly he had been able to observe the men in their frock-coats, the women in their bright spring dresses; and while sometimes he could hear them exclaiming at the wonder of the bridge, marveling at the extraordinary procession which had just crossed it — crossed it as if it had always been there — for the most part they spoke of whatever it is people in society speak of, and in that he had not much interest at all. At one point Emily had brought over a beaming, portly gentleman with muttonchop whiskers and a heavy gold watchchain.

— Colonel, she said. The President of the United States.

Washington moved to stand, but the gentleman put out his hand, urging Washington to say in his seat. Arthur, that was the President's name. Washington did not think much of him, but smiled and nodded as the President recited platitudes regarding progress, improvement, growth — there was something in there too about the fellowship of man. Yes.

He had been about to go upstairs when Paine came over, slipping neatly through the throng. He held a glass of beer in his hand.

— Where did you get that? Washington asked.

— Oh, there's beer, Paine said. Would you like some?

— No, thank you, Washington answered. But I see she has catered for all tastes. Come, he said to Paine, sit down a moment.

And so Paine sat down beside him on the settee, and they looked out together at the finery, the drifting cigar smoke, the sugar model of the bridge on the long table.

— Impressive that lasted this long, Paine said, gesturing at the confection.

— I wouldn't like to tell you the price of that, Washington said. I think I shall get myself into the sweetmeat trade.

Paine touched his hand to Washington's shoulder. Well, he said, I imagine you'll want to rest. I should be going. Yet he did not rise, not yet, and they sat in silence for a moment or two, before Paine got to his feet.

— Good to see you, Colonel, Washington said. I'm glad you came to find me.

— And very good to see you too, Colonel, Paine said. You look after yourself.

He made a little salute, and Washington returned it. Paine turned his back, walked purposefully through the crowd and disappeared into it.

It had cheered him to see Paine, he thought now as he lay in his bed. He was not, in fact, especially tired, but they had all expected him to want to go to bed. Emily had followed the last guest out to attend yet another celebration. The small clock over the mantlepiece ticked. Five minutes to eight. He closed his eyes and lay still, the pillows against his neck, the weight of the coverlet over his lap and arms. He opened his eyes and looked at the syringe, and then back at the clock. Tick, tick, tick, tick.

From the shore, from the Heights, there was a constant roaring sound, the noise of the crowd pressing against the barriers, calling, shouting, a blurred cacophony of humanity, and from the river itself the sound of ships' horns and boats' whistles of every description, hooting, blaring, just as they had the day they brought the first rope across — he had been told — but now he could hear it for himself. The noise swallowed the hiss of the first rockets (young Miss Detwiller, apparently, lighting the fuze) as they rose from the centre of the span, but heard them, all fifty of them, when they exploded high over the bridge.

He stared at the ceiling. He laced his fingers together over his chest and felt his heart beat against his palms. He had asked for an inventory from the pyrotechnicist — so he called himself — who had happily provided one: six thousand four-pound skyrockets, four hundred bombshells, one hundred and twenty-five fountains of colored lights. Zinc bombshells, ten inches in diameter, to be fired five hundred feet in the air from mortars arranged along the bridge: each bombshell to hold six hundred stars of various colors. Balloons would be launched, discharging 'stars and meteors', he had been told; to each balloon a postal card was attached and the finder of the balloon was to notify the pyrotechnicists when and where it was found. This is calculated to keep up the excitement over the opening of the bridge, Detwiller had written; when Washington had made to tear up the letter, Emily had snatched it from his hands.

He had not drawn the blinds — he should have — he could not rise now from his bed — the light against his eyelids was pink and gold and green. The thunder of the explosions, rattling the glass, shaking the house, volley after volley of manufactured radiance, and he could hear the screams of the crowd, the shrieking of the multitude, and he could feel against his cheek the dirt floor of that cabin in Pennsylvania, see the entrails of that fine bay horse; he could taste the bitter coffee he'd drunk with that nameless boy. Where was Paine. Ah, Paine had gone. And Emily, out there amidst the blasting stars. He must wait, that was all. It would be over soon. Wait.

EPILOGUE: PEACE

I have long been of the opinion that a graduate should not work with his father — at least such a father as I had — When I ventured to have a different opinion on some professional problem I was called a fool — my teacher was a damned fool . . . If I still dared to hold an opinion then a storm of vituperation followed by a hurricane of personal abuse and attacks on my life. In his frenzied rage, the spit would fly, his arms clove the air, he jumped & swore and cursed with horribly distorted features — any man with more spunk than I had would have killed him.

— WASHINGTON A. ROEBLING

✣ ✣ ✣ ✣ ✣

From *Chief Engineer: Washington A. Roebling, The Man Who Built the Brooklyn Bridge*

IT WAS DURING his travels through Germany that Washington encountered the invention of one Eugen Langen, a German engineer four years older than himself. 'A smart, ingenious, shrewd and able man,' he called Langen in a letter to his father. Langen had been working on a small engine, powered by gas rather than coal; Washington believed there might be a future in Langen's work. After their encounter in Frankfurt he wrote: 'This little engine supplies a want, which has long been felt in Germany, and to some extent in America also, that of a cheap & economical motor for small mechanics who cannot afford to have a steam engine or whose work is too intermittent to require the steady use of one.' A close description of nearly six pages followed. A steam engine, with its external boiler, is a cumbersome machine; coal is an inefficient fuel, but liquid fuel — kerosene — had been developed in the 1850s. A few days later, however, he went further in describing to his father what he had seen: 'The motive power of the machine depends upon the principle that 95% of air mixed with 5% of common coal gas (by volume) produces an explosive mixture of considerable power . . . His idea is that a company should be formed to buy his patent and then manufacture the machines under the patent in the United States . . . Langan [sic] has put the refusal of the thing at my disposal for a certain length of time. It is an entirely new thing and I have not the slightest doubt will take well in the U.S.'

The letter to his father was cautious, especially as regards his own involvement in this new technology. And yet he was thinking of what awaited him back in the States. At 30, he believed — married, more independent after his trip — that he might have a choice about what he would do with his life. He'd written to his brother Ferdinand about an idea for a business using scrap metal from the wire mill in Trenton: 'I will have to go to work at something as soon as I get back and may as well do that.' But when he had announced his engagement to Emily to his father, John Roebling had made his feelings clear regarding the future of the family business. No 'strangers' for John Roebling: Washington was 'expected to step in & help forwarding the interests of the family as well as yours individually.'

Washington saw the gas engine — small, flexible, portable — as an even better bet than scrap metal. In mid-September

Washington wrote to Charles Swan — his letters to Swan are always more open and informal than those he wrote to his father. 'Suppose you mention that Gas Machine to Charley Carr and see what he thinks of it . . . If I were only home now I think I could make the thing go and make something of it.' And to Ferdinand back in Trenton he proposed a real business plan — one that had nothing to do with building bridges or manufacturing wire. This was a bid for whole new life. 'I want to make you a proposition in regard to the Gas Machine. You say they want $100,000 for the patent, which with gold at 40% perm & Exchange 10% would bring it up to $150,000. The thing would then be to form a company to buy the patent for $200,000 which would leave $25,000 for each of us without spending anything. The Co. could then either dispose of the rights to make money out of it or by making a small assessment of the stockholders start the manufacturing of the engines. There could be no better time than now to start such a thing. There have been so many boiler explosions all over the country for the past year (averaging about one a day with more or less loss of life) that the news papers are taking up the matter very generally,' he wrote. This was the moment to be seized, and Washington knew it. But money — a lot of money — would be required for the initial investment, and the one rich man they knew didn't think much of the whole idea. 'Father says he won't have anything to do with it, if he had I should want to be out. He does not seem to care much how we get along and the sooner we can be independent of all others the better it will be for us.... I wish you would write to me as soon as you get this letter and let me know what you think...'

This letter was written on the 12th of November, 1867. It crossed with a letter from his father, written from Trenton two days previously. John had been speaking to his in-laws about Washington's ideas. John's older sister, Frederike Amalia — of whom he was extremely fond, by Washington's account — had married a prosperous Mühlhausen merchant called Meissner; the family had gradually all relocated to the United States, following the Roeblings. John Roebling wrote in very plain language to his son: 'The Meissners enquired what I was doing about Langens [sic] Machine. I told them I had nothing whatever to do with it, and at the same time informed them that Langen did not want to have anything to do with their firm. They feel sore about [it] and I wish you had never concerned yourself about it. There is no money in it, I am satisfied.'

There would be no more discussion of engines. If John Roebling thought there was no money to be made in bringing Langen's new-fangled invention to the United States, then there was no arguing the case. He reminded his son of the bad luck the Swedish engineer John Ericsson — who had designed the *Monitor* for Lincoln during the war, and also developed the screw propellor — had with his 'caloric engine', which used hot air to move pistons, rather than high-pressure steam. The innovation never caught on, and the ship that bore his name, the *Ericsson*, sank in a storm off New York in 1854.

John Roebling was mistaken regarding the future of the gas engine. By the time Washington encountered Langen, the latter had already joined forces with Nikolaus August Otto, whose four-stroke engine would make the modern automobile possible; their company, N. A. Otto & Cie, in Cologne, was the world's first engine factory. Together they had won a gold medal at the Paris Exhibition; in later years the company — which still exists today as Deutz AG — would employ Gottlieb Daimler and Wilhelm Maybach. There would be money in gas engines, for sure, but it would not be Washington Roebling who made it. We don't know what he would have said to Emily when his father's letter arrived, or indeed, whether he would have said anything at all. Perhaps his resignation was wholly private. In the Union Army he had followed orders. Now he was his father's lieutenant, and that was where his work, and the path of his life, lay. His father's wealth was not available to him, he knew that much.

In later years, when the automobile came into wide use — Henry Ford's Model T appeared in 1908 — it was always said that Washington Roebling disliked them. He refused ever to ride in one, preferring the Trenton trolley cars, even when he was a very old man.

ENGINE

PARIS. JUNE, 1867.

— *S'IL VOUS PLAIT.* Please, the dapper Frenchman said. He held his hand out to Emily. *Il n'y a aucune raison d'avoir peur, je vous promets.* I promise you there is nothing to fear!

Washington followed close behind as a smiling Emily ascended the wooden steps set up close against the sturdy wicker basket; with her left hand she held her skirts, her right she put in the Frenchman's offered palm, steadying herself as she climbed.

— That's it, that's it, he said, switching to heavily-accented English. Very good, mademoiselle, very good!

She laughed. You are too charming, M. Nadar, she said. You know it is *madame*, but I thank you. As she spoke she put a hand on the little swell of her belly, though the fullness of her dress nearly concealed what was as yet hidden there. Her face was bright in the Paris summer sunshine; the baby seemed not to sap her strength but rather added fuel to her always vivid fire.

— And now you, monsieur, he said. O, and my apologies to you too — Colonel! He spoke all the syllables: col-on-el. Yesterday they had visited his studio in the Boulevard des Capucines; the photographer's name — a replica of his flamboyant signature — was displayed in enormous, illuminated letters across the facade of the building. Neither Washington nor Emily had ever seen the like, and Emily had been most impressed.

— Perhaps your father will tell the trustees of the Bridge

Company that he would like such a sign across his bridge, she had whispered to Wash. She had been most taken by the naturalness of Nadar's work, and stood for a long time before a portrait of Sarah Bernhardt — the Divine Sarah! — with her curls spilling down her back, a velvet cloak loose about her bared shoulders. Emily would have wished for a portrait with her husband: the last had been taken before their marriage, two years ago, a stiff affair captured by a Trenton photographer who had somehow ensured the couple looked as if they would rather be anywhere else than in a frame together.

— There is not enough time to do you justice, Nadar had said. If I had known you were coming —

They had simply walked in off the street. But when the great photographer had learned what had brought the handsome couple to Europe, he was most intrigued. *Bien sûr*, he had said, of course I know the name of Roebling! *Votre père est un grand homme*, he had said to Washington. To draw a locomotive across Niagara Falls! That is an achievement indeed.

Sometimes Washington thought he would be glad if he never heard the words *Niagara Falls* again. But of course, the young engineer simply nodded, acknowledging the compliment, allowing the shadow of it to fall upon himself. And Nadar, he thought, had a little something of John Roebling about him, his father's force, energy, curiosity. Nadar was blunt and thick where his father was slender, and his hair was rust-red, shot with gray. He was, Washington supposed, in between John Roebling's age and his own; there was something established about him, in his expensive but ill-cared for clothes; the heavy gold watch chain that was missing several links and had been mended with leather twine.

And so, in lieu of a photograph in his studio, Nadar had invited young Roebling and his pretty, pregnant wife to visit him instead on the Champ de Mars, where — to celebrate and document the Exposition Universelle — he was making photographic images from a captive balloon. A smooth-faced boy — nicely dressed but with broken shoes — had met them at their pension and led them to the Seine, where they climbed into one of the riverboats dedicated to taking visitors from the city to the site of the Exposition Universelle. At the Pont d'Iena — Lamandé's handsome, five-arched bridge — they had disembarked and walked a little farther along the riverbank, through crowds whose dress showed that rich and poor both mingled here among the wonders of the world. The day was a little overcast but the sky hinted blue; Emily took Wash's arm and both of them sniffed the air, which was, Wash thought, enticing and revolting all at once; the scent of the press of bodies, of hot chocolate, of smoked meat, of cigars, mingling all together into an indescribable brew.

They passed through a gate — a mustachio'd man in a fanciful uniform, all velvet and gold braid, waved them through — which led to a vast enclosure, its wooden walls leaning back as if in awe of its centerpiece: a great balloon, its apex perhaps as tall as a seven-story building, tethered to the ground by cables — of both hemp and wire, as far as Wash could tell. There was a light breeze, and the huge orb bobbed and dipped as the wind buffeted its smooth surface, which was the color of red india rubber.

— Are you sure, my dearest Em, you wouldn't rather stay on the ground?

He knew, of course, what the answer would be; her eyes were shining with eagerness. As for himself — well, it had been four years since Wash had contemplated any aerial effort, and that last had been above a battlefield. Those still Virginia dawns, himself in a little woven basket hardly bigger than the circumference of his waist, the ropes held fast by strong-armed, sturdy-legged privates whose names somehow stuck fast in his head. Stevenson, O'Callaghan, Bjornholm — a huge, Lutheran Swede from Minnesota who was fanatical in his hatred of slavery and had traveled across the continent to enlist — Lapierre, a New Yorker through and through, a thug from the Five Points who would always share a cigar. Washington would save the cigar for after his descent, knowing that as he floated hundreds of feet above the deceptively peaceful greenery, his attention must be kept on his sketchbook and notes, not on the taste and scent of tobacco, however pleasing it was to imagine enjoying a celestial smoke. And so it was that one morning he had seen Lee's men moving towards a field in Pennsylvania — he shook the recollection away. Yet the war pulled along his veins as he followed his brisk-footed wife up the ladder; the echo of old battles in the quick beat of his heart.

There were about a dozen others already in the basket of the balloon, which had been fitted with benches, and a little stove for making coffee and tea; there were bottles of wine and champagne. Nadar's photographic apparatus took up some feet of the circumference, and was fixed to the sides of the basket with iron clamps. Now Wash was close enough to some of the cable that held the balloon in place to examine it; he took off his glove and ran a palm along the metal wire.

— Johnson and Nephew, said a voice in his ear. From Manchester. We French don't like to admit when the English have the upper hand, but with this wire, no one can argue.

— No indeed, Wash said. We Americans don't like to admit when the English have the upper hand either, but this is superior stuff.

— Quite the compliment, coming from you, Colonel Roebling. The fellow put out his hand and Wash shook it; he too said 'colon-el' in the French way. I am Henri Giffard, and I am pleased to welcome you aboard my aerostat.

— An honor, M. Giffard. And please — he gestured to Emily, who was peering at the labels on the bottles of champagne — may I introduce my wife, Mrs Roebling. We are delighted to be aboard today.

Giffard, handsome and dark-eyed, bowed, took Emily's hand and kissed it.

— Thrilled, I should say, Emily offered. I have heard something of ballooning from the Colonel, but have never experienced the wonder myself. I am in love with your beautiful city already and to see it from the air will be an extraordinary privilege.

— She is in love with your beautiful city's dressmakers, certainly, Washington said.

— Colonel! she scolded. Her cheeks had flushed pink. A clumsy miscalculation on his part.

— But of course you are, Giffard said smoothly. Who can blame you? If I must admit how fine is English wire, I must be pleased to hear that we French still stand superior in some matters. But Colonel: you have ascended before?

— During the late American war, Washington replied. We used balloons to observe the enemy's movements. It was most effective. And — pleasant, strangely enough.

— Yes, it is pleasant to be in the air; I would like to think of airships as machines of peace, but I fear it will not be so, *à la future.*

— Anything a man can make in peace can be used in war, Washington said.

— That is the pity, Emily said. And a subject for proper discussion. But I confess I should like to return, just now, to what is, as my husband says, pleasant.

— So we shall, *chère madame.* But, you will excuse me, I must prepare for the ascent. I wish to be especially certain that it is smooth and calm for you. *C'est un beau matin.* We have a lovely morning for you. Up we go! *En haut! Allons-y!*

Emily and Wash braced themselves as the aeronaut turned to his work, his clipped French brisk and commanding as he ordered his small crew to take to the cables and pulleys that held the balloon — filled with coal gas, Washington had learned — tethered closely to the ground. Nadar had ducked under a black cloth, in communion with his photographic apparatus.

— O my, Emily said. Here we go!

They began to rise, slowly, majestically. There was none of the jerkiness Washington had experienced as a soldier back in Virginia; the weight of the basket and passengers, the skill of Giffard and his men, made the ascent easy; there was an air of inevitability about the whole thing. The men and women standing at the basket's rim smiled at each other, involuntarily it seemed; it was impossible not to feel that they were all in some sort of delightful conspiracy to leave the weighty matters of the Earth behind. And indeed, to his surprise — and amusement — Washington began to feel his cares drop away; he wondered whether his expression was as awestruck as that of his fellows. He had been waiting for a letter from Belgrand, Haussmann's water-engineer; his father had tasked him most particularly with contacting the architect of Paris's efficient sewers, believing the information he might offer, digging techniques and suchlike, would be of use in the sinking of the caissons. Washington himself did not believe that Belgrand's techniques — while no doubt brilliant — would be of much use in Brooklyn and New York, given the differences in depth, in geology, in purpose.

In truth, Washington rather suspected that John Roebling was as drawn to Belgrand's passion for pure water as he was to his skill as an engineer. *He believes that all men and women, all the people of Paris, should have free access to the freshest and sweetest springs*, the elder Roebling had written in a letter received two days ago. *I will be very glad to hear your report of the water's taste as it comes direct from one of the city's fountains; you will recall that* taste *is a complex matter, and includes acidity or alkalinity, temperature and minerality.*

Washington did indeed recall; needed no prompt to do so. But now, as the ground dropped away beneath them, a new lightness suffused him, as if a new nearness to the sun's light melted away his cloak of strife and obligation. He and Emily and all their fellow passengers were lifted towards the shell-blue sky with its feathery wisps of cloud. The whispers of the breeze replaced the hubbub of the crowds; the rope and cables that tethered their craft creaked sturdily. Washington and Emily leaned against the basket's edge, pressed close together; Washington slipped his arm around Emily's waist.

— Harder and harder to reach, he said, smiling.

— O you! she said.

— You look beautiful, he said simply. Paris is beautiful, but you are more so.

— Why, Wash, she said, leaning close to him. I do believe this place makes you sentimental. Look at it! What riches!

They could see the sweep of the silver river now, glittering in sunlight: the narrow Seine, so easily bridged. There were the great pavilions of the Exposition all along the Champ de Mars; even as they rose, the clanking and hissing of the machinery followed them; they would have had to be as high as the clouds to escape that. They were facing east, towards the obelisk of the Place de la Concorde; the opera house, still cloaked in scaffolding; the new spire of Nôtre Dame. The grand boulevards remaking the ancient city. Warrens of antique buildings torn down, their inhabitants — scattered, like so much dust, like bricks broken and carted off. Warrens of buildings, shacks and shanties, down on the shores of Brooklyn and New York, ready to suffer the same fate. Progress. Well. It was like a war. There was nothing for it.

— Must we leave Tuesday? Emily asked.

— You know we must, Wash said. Manchester awaits. To see, as it happens — he gestured towards a cable, thrumming with tension — Mr Johnson's wire.

— And his nephew's wire, Emily said. Don't forget him. I suppose he had no son.

— Well, there were sons, I believe, some generations ago. They were making wire long before any Roeblings thought of the idea.

— I am glad they did, she said, think of the idea. Those Roeblings. Otherwise I should not have had my trip to Paris. I hope we can come back.

— Of course we can come back.

She turned to look at him, frowning, two neat little lines drawn down between her brows.

— Don't speak so, she said.

— What? What have I said? I said that we could come back. I thought that is what you wished me to say.

— *Precisely*, she said. You thought it was what I wished you to say. So you spoke as a husband speaks when he wants to pacify his wife. You were not *listening*. You were not considering the question.

Washington opened his mouth to speak, then closed it again before any words could emerge. She was not incorrect.

— Your father will be the chief engineer of the East River Bridge, Emily said. But he will attempt, as he did in Cincinnati, to bind you to the work with — and now she jutted her neat round chin out at the balloon's cables — ropes of iron. You will do all the work and have none of the glory. That is the danger. You must see that.

— I will advance by working at his side, Wash said. Dearest Em. This will be a work like no other. No other ever in the world. Far beyond anything we built over the Ohio.

— I do understand that, she said. But you must also have the freedom to build your own life as your father would build his bridge. Your German and French are perfect. Your Italian is not bad. There is so much work to do in the world. Could not some of it be done away from the East River? What a rich life it would be, to travel and see the world. I have been a good companion to you, I hope?

— My darling, he said, I could hope for no better. You are — intrepid. You are an aeronaut! You are both aeronauts, you and our little one, both. He squeezed her hand. Even if the price of that intrepidity must be paid in silk, he said.

She pulled her hand out of his, sharply. I love you, Wash, she said. But I weary sometimes of this. Your harping on about money.

— I harp on about it because we do not have much, Wash said, an edge to his voice now. John A. Roebling's Sons Company is a stringent employer. What there is doesn't stretch far here. I am weary too, of explaining this to you. On this matter it appears that *you* refuse to listen to *me*.

— Well, she said. You might also consider that there are, in this wide world, other opportunities than those provided by John A. Roebling's Sons Company. Or indeed, by John A. Roebling himself. I know these are not my thoughts alone, Wash. I have heard you speak of them. Do not deny it.

An older couple standing near them — he with a full gray beard and a high silk hat, she with great ropes of pearls draped over her silken bosom — shuffled a little further away and turned their backs in an attempt to give Washington and Emily at least the illusion of privacy. The woman lifted her lorgnette to peer at the city sinking and stretching away beneath them; they rose higher and higher, the stays that held the balloon straining and whining as they went.

Once again Washington opened his mouth to speak and thought better of the attempt; so often, she read his thoughts, or at least was willing to say what — in him — refused to come to the surface. The color had risen in her cheeks and she had put one hand on the little swell of her belly again, this time it seemed as if — to protect it? From him? Surely not, but the thought struck him like a blow.

— O Em, he said. Emily. I will not. Deny it. I am sorry. And look at us — look at me — how ridiculous, for us to speak this way, lifted these hundreds of feet above the earth! Will you forgive me? He reached for her hand again, and she took it.

— I will forgive you above the Earth or on it. Mostly I am glad we are of a mind, Wash. That there are other possibilities. Look how they stretch out all around!

The balloon was at its apex; just then, Nadar called out.

— Col-on-el! He called. *Venez ici!* I am about to make an image!

The walked towards the bright-faced Nadar and his apparatus; Giffard stood close by with a glass in his hand.

— A glass of wine? The delicate vessels were nestled in straw, as they might have been on a ship at sea; the aeronaut extracted two of them, poured — champagne — and raised a toast.

— To taking flight, he said. To building bridges. Between our nations, with our industry and our good will.

— I will drink to that, Wash Roebling said.

Nadar's glass stood clipped to his table while he scuffled and fussed beneath a thick velvet cloth. His pinstriped rear protruded; Giffard and the Roeblings forbore to stare, but turned their eyes again to the city spread beneath them.

— I imagine you are going there, Giffard said, gesturing at the pavilions of the Exposition. That outer ring — can you see? La Galerie des Machines. All the iron and steel of all the world is there, he said.

— That is indeed our destination. We hope to meet with the Messrs Krupp, before we visit them in Essen.

— *O là là*, exclaimed the Frenchman, the Krupps with their terrible gigantic gun! You see? This is why I speak so much of peace, Colonel. Peace must have a loud voice to contend with — *le tonnere des canons*. The thunder of the guns. But may I give you some advice?

— Of course, Washington said. I have come to learn, and I am sure there is much to learn from a man who can fly.

Giffard made a little bow. The mention of Krupp recalls it to me, he said; for I met a young German there the other day who reminds me a little of you. You Germans, you all have such an energy — but this young man, he had a spark like yours. I can see it.

— I suppose I might argue that I am an American, not least because I fought a war for the United States, but I must allow I am a Dutchman through and through, and a Frenchman will always see it, Wash said, smiling. He is an engineer, this fellow with the spark?

— Quite so, Giffard said. Precisely, in fact, for that is what he has made. An engine. I think it is quite unique, and I believe you should seek him out. Langen, that is his name. I think he will win a medal. I won't say more. You should see for yourself.

Just then, Nadar emerged from under his black cloth.

— *Le moment est arrivé!* he exclaimed. The boy with the broken shoes stood nearby, watching avidly. Wash recalled himself as a boy then, wondered what he would have felt, suspended high above a great city as if it were nothing at all. He recollected a photographer's studio by a wide silver river, an image captured when he was hardly more than a boy. He slipped his arm once more around his sweet wife's waist — their child growing there, contained and nourished by her dear self — and felt his breath expand out towards the city stretching out so far below, ancient, modern, miraculous. Nadar pressed the shutter, and the image was made.

COLOGNE. AUGUST, 1867.

— Just turn that little cock, Langen said. Wash was crouched close to the ground, his heels lifted from the clean-swept shop floor, balanced on the balls of his feet. The familiar smells of manufacture — hot metal, grease, the working bodies of men — filled the warm air; added to that, the stink of the coal gas, sulphurous and thick. A key-shaped lever ran into the india rubber gas pipe that fed the engine; just as he had in the grand display hall in Paris, Wash twisted it open and the gas began to flow. It ran across the tiny blue flame that awaited its arrival and immediately there was a burst of sound as the gas in the cylinder exploded: Langen reached out a hand and gave the wheel of the engine a little push to set it on its way. In truth — as Wash already knew — no assistance was needed, for instantly the piston in the cylinder began to rise and fall, sucked up and down by the vacuum of the blast. In the aftermath of each bang came the steady racking noise of the gears as they pushed the piston which drove the wheel.

Wash stood, brushed off his hands, which only served to smear the oil on his fingers into his skin. No matter. Outside — beyond the machine shop's grimy panes of glass — the sky was blue and bright and there were birds; as he had walked from the Rheinischer Hof, it had seemed he was followed by a chaffinch, its insistent bright rill hastening his steps. Now the drumming of the machine drowned out nature's work: he let the rhythm ring in his ears.

— I have yet to congratulate you on your medal, Langen, Wash said, raising his voice to be heard over the ruckus. Paris was a triumph for you and Herr Otto.

— Ah well, Langen said, I must admit Otto and I were

gratified. The gold medal of the Exposition Universelle! Too much pride is unsuitable in a man, but when one has worked hard —

— I am with you on the dangers of a prideful nature, Wash replied, but I assure you, from what I saw in Paris, and what I see here, it is entirely justified in this instance, Herr Langen.

They spoke in German, though could have conversed easily enough in English. Langen spoke French too, as good as a native; he had the urbane, confident nature of a man who had always understood what his capabilities were. A few years older than Wash, his dark hair had begun to recede from his round forehead, but he was handsome nonetheless, his dark gaze quick and his smile ready. Washington Roebling had never been so glad of a piece of advice as for that he'd received from Giffard as they floated over the Parisian rooftops and spires. When he had met Eugen Langen and his partner Otto in Paris, he had sensed a shift in himself, a possibility; it had seemed more than natural when Langen invited him to see his new works here in Cologne and well worth the diversion.

— I will be perfectly safe in Mühlhausen, Emily had said when he had proposed the excursion. I am treated like a queen by all your cousins! Even if the baby comes — her calico was stretched tight now over her belly and she held herself as she spoke — what use would *you* be, darling Wash?

Langen's works were not far from the sugar refinery, which was the family business. Langen had always been fascinated, even as a boy, by the machinery that ran the works, he had told Washington. How could it be made to run more smoothly, more quickly, at every stage of the process?

— Steam power requires so much machinery in and of itself, he said as they drank glasses of cold beer. It had been brought to them by a young man whose sole job it was to drive a cart around the works, sugar-works and engine-works both, delivering a twice-daily libation; it had been just the same at the great Krupp works in Essen, only the barrels of beer and the cart had been rather larger. A great machine to drive a machine! Langen exclaimed. It was this I wanted to simplify. To make — practical. Power is not a luxury, here in the 19th century, he said. Power must be available to all. Only a man who is already wealthy — or at least has access to capital — can run a steam engine, a monster with a vast boiler and endless deliveries of coal, an engineer to run the thing and sweltering men to do the shovelling. How can a man invest in his business if he must invest in such a behemoth first?

Washington nodded and took a draw of the beer, which was hoppy and perfectly bitter. It was weak — brewed to quench the thirst of laborers — yet he felt slightly lightheaded. He burped, the air escaping his stomach and mouth before he could suppress it or make any polite gesture to disguise the sound. Langen grinned.

— It's good stuff, isn't it?

— Delicious, Wash said. They stood in silence for a moment. 'Silence', of course, the wrong word, for the engine huffed and clanked, perfectly rhythmic, self-contained, requiring nothing of either man. In the shop adjacent — behind a well-made wooden door — another machine drove lathes, a drill, small planers; the well-made door itself had been cut and smoothed with power from Langen's engine. The same gas that powered the city's streetlights powered the machine; the only trouble in the German states, Langen said, was that not enough towns were, as yet, lit by gas. Wash knew there would be no such issue in New York or Brooklyn, or Pittsburgh or Boston. His own country stretched out westwards, farther every day; the American mania for whatever was novel ensured that progress was relentless, and came whatever the cost. In Paris, when the two had first met, Wash had found himself telling Langen, with whom he felt an instant sympathy, about his adventures in Iowa as a very young man; the land John Roebling had bought there in the years before, and even during the war. Something in my father always believes that a real gentleman is farmer, Wash had said. Now, here in Cologne, Iowa came to his mind again, the men and women he had seen near their settlement, wrapped in woollen blankets, men and women — children with them, sometimes, huddled by their feet — with deep-set eyes that looked blankly at the land that had once been theirs. Sioux, Sac, Fox, he had been told. His father, he knew, felt sorry for them. Yet had bought the land all the same. Warren, his brother-in-law, out in the Dakota territory a decade before the war, had expressed pity for the slaughter he had seen, but expressed too his belief in its necessity.

What did Washington himself think? He thought of himself. As so many did. Of his wife, of his child about to be born. He thought of freedom. He thought that the march of history was relentless. He had no control of these events so very much larger than himself. But this, this in front of his eyes, this oily contraption with its sulphurous stink, was something he could put his hand on, something he could explain and pursue. Those bridges he had built during the war, thrown hastily across rivers — Rappahannock, Shenandoah — and blown up not long after, any achievement of his splintered and sunk. Victory had come for his country, but it seemed to him as divided as it ever was. The President assassinated. His father taking that woman for his wife, at long last, yet sitting around a table with spirit-talkers summoning up the spirit of Wash's poor dead mother. The broiling sun on his back in Cincinnati as he climbed up and down the towers of the Ohio bridge — Emily was right, it was nearly all his work and would never be his monument.

Stone towers on the banks of the Ohio, not so different than the ones his father had drawn for the shores of New York and Brooklyn. Monumental, the images themselves the size of a long mahogany table, the roadway rising up through arches that would not have been out of place in some ancient cathedral. The stone, Wash knew, spoke of strength and stability; to those who believed that it was not possible to build a bridge over the East River — that such a structure would inevitably collapse under its own weight, that no cables could be made strong enough to support it — those towers offered a resonant image stretching back in a line to old Cheops' Pyramid.

But here — here was the future, in this light little machine. The caissons of the East River Bridge would be sunk deep into the earth, immovable, permanent. Here, in swift strokes of forged iron, a piston and a flying wheel, in the slick scent of coal gas, was action, forward motion, all that was to come — surely — visible to him in this workshop in Cologne. If it were not so absolutely real, he might think it a vision, a dream. But here was Langen, with his tightly-laced shoes, his comfortable well-made clothes, the little spray of whiskers his razor had missed above his beard, standing beside him with a glass of beer in his hand; here were windowpanes and a factory floor. A couple of hundred miles away, his clever, beautiful wife paced in an upstairs room, or drank a cup of raspberry-leaf tea prepared by cousin Amalie and served in the family porcelain pattered with bluebells. A little boy or a little girl coming to join them. He longed for fatherhood and was trepidatious, both at once; he feared the appearance of his own father's fury in his soul, that what he worked to keep buried might emerge into light as his child, his children, grew, and he would be helpless against it.

He wished for anything but that. Surely the secret was to break the pattern, to shift for himself in the world. It took a moment for him to recognize the queer feeling in his breast: the feeling of wanting, of refusing to ask himself in which direction his duty lay, but seeing plainly the path of his own desire.

— There is a light in your eye, Langen said, glancing at him frankly. You see it, don't you. What I see.

— Absolutely, Wash said. Absolutely. We must start

with — well, I will buy one from you certainly, to ship back to Trenton. Thankfully all our funds were not exhausted in Paris, and as our family looks after us now in Mühlhausen, we can run our household more cheaply. I would like my father to see this, of course. But particularly Mr Swan.

— Mr Swan?

— He manages the mill for my father. Much more than that. I trust him more than any other. I have known him since I was a boy. He has a head for business. He will know what is best to do.

— I can tell you what is best to do, Langen said. How Washington admired this plain-speaking! To see the path and simply strike out for it. I am going to sell the patent in France, shortly, Langen said. I have an offer of 300,000 francs for the rights.

Another man might have inflated the sum for self-aggrandizing or greedy purposes; Washington, however, was certain that Langen spoke truly. He calculated quickly in his head: $70,000 or thereabouts. Fifteen years of his salary as assistant engineer. He kept his expression neutral.

— We could agree on a lower initial outlay if you were to return a greater portion of the profits, of course. It depends on how you are fixed for capital, Langen said. But I am sure you do not doubt the certainty of success.

— Ah, so it still all comes down to capital, Washington said. He smiled; he knew Langen would take his remark with good humor.

— How fortunate, then, that you are not such a one as those we hope to sell these engines to, Langen said, smiling. John A. Roebling Sons' Company can run its own steam engines and sell its wire around the world. Like me, Roebling, you are an engineer and a manufacturer. We are lucky men.

— The capital is not my own, I should reiterate, Washington said. It is my father's.

— John A. Roebling *Sons'* Company, Langen replied with emphasis.

— Well, yes, Washington said. But all the same, it is my father to whom I must fully explain your — our — proposition, who will —

Who will have the final say. He did not need the speak the words but felt them hang in the air. His glass of beer had warmed. He would have to step away from Langen to set it down somewhere. He did not move.

Langen nodded. I see, he said. And as you remarked, there is your Mr Swan. Will he too be at work on this great bridge?

— No, Washington said. Someone must run the mill while bridges are built, and that is Mr Swan's affair. Which is why I so wish for his opinion on your engine. It is his particular area of expertise.

— And what is your particular area of expertise, Colonel Roebling? You have come to Europe in order to prepare for this work over the East River; what you see in my little workshop here is, perhaps, a diversion. I am a man of serious intent, Colonel. I know what lies ahead. I wish to collaborate with those who see the road ahead as I do.

Washington sensed a pulling-back, a formality, in the use of his military rank, in Langen's tone. Of course Langen was cautious, cautious because he was correct — Washington's own road had been laid out before him long ago, but it was only now that he saw how he might step on to another, one he would forge for himself. He had had a glimpse of it in Paris at the Exposition; here in Cologne it was perfectly clear to him. He must not stumble now. He must be as plain with this plain-speaking German as he could. All he could offer — right now — was his honesty.

— I am not a man of business, Langen, Washington said. That is the truth. You say I am a manufacturer, but I am not, or not yet. Perhaps I should have been if the war had not intervened; I had to go off a-soldiering, and my younger brother stayed at the mill and learned that work. I have no capital, that's the truth. What I have I get from my father, though I expect a salary from the Bridge Company soon enough. But you must believe me when I tell you that I understand what I see here. What could be made of it. What I wish to make. And I will tell you too that I understand there is more to life than bridge-building. What man does not want to carve something out for himself? You have done so, Eugen, done your time at sugar-manufacture and now you have this, your own endeavor. Which will be, I know, a triumph. It is not just the gold medal you will win. Of that I am certain. I wish to be a part of this endeavor. All I can tell you now is that I will work as hard as I can to find the money to ask for — that you deserve. We will find a way to go forward together.

When had Washington last spoken with such passion? With Emily, perhaps, in the dark, lying side by side, the soft sweet curves of her dear body close to his — it was so changed now, that body, belonging as it did to another, their child who was to come. She was shy these days, afraid he would find her less beautiful, but he yearned to kiss the veins that ran like rivers across the white surfaces of her swollen breasts, to caress her taut flank that contained more power within it even than this engine, the power of life itself, of generation. How he would breathe his dreams to her. And — it seemed in another life, before the war, before Emily — to Max, his friend who glittered with river-water and hope, who took his own life when he could not bear the weight of it. The weight of love. Shining Max. Passion must be stepped into, not refused. It had so many shapes. Washington would not step back now. He wanted his own future, not his father's.

— I believe you are sincere, Colonel Roebling. I believe you are the ideal partner for me, and for Otto, in this venture. I know you comprehend this project. Its possibilities. I know you believe in it, and will work hard to for its success. Things will change,

Colonel Roebling. We will be the men to change them.

Now, the rank did not cut, but seemed a mark of respect. Langen raised his glass, smiling. *Prost*! he said, and Washington returned the toast. Langen nodded. A decision had been made.

— Let us find you a fresh glass of beer, Langen said. You must be refreshed when you sit down at my desk to write to your Mr Swan.

COLOGNE. AUGUST, 1867.

My dear Mr Swan —

I notice that things seem to be jogging along slowly at home; I am afraid you don't pray hard enough for the good time that is to come. If the wire rope business is going to die you had better go into the Gas machine business; nothing pays as well as *Gas*.

Suppose you mention the Gas machine to Charley Carr and see what he thinks of it. The little one which I bought will be shipped about October 1, and will get there before I will.

Mr Langen has raised his demands again already which may put it too high. He now wants for his patent in the US $100,000 or else $50,000 + 25% per machine that is manufactured; he has most extraordinary notions about the US & thinks a patent is worth more there than in England.

There is lots of money in the concern however; when the engine is once introduced you will see them applied in every warehouse for hoisting, because they need no engineer, no dangerous boilers, and need not be consuming gas except just at the time when hoisting is going on. There are any quantity of country towns where they have gas but no waterworks, where they will answer for pumping water up for hotels etc.

I don't think it would be a difficult matter to get up a company, even in Trenton, for the manufacture of these machines, there will be no trouble about the demand with judicious advertising; it would be an easy matter to turn a machine a day in a good size shop, and at the rate of profit this makes, one year would suffice to pay for the whole patent. First of all it is necessary to have a machine out there; the sight of a machine actually working is worth more than any number of diagrams or explanations. Another way of disposing of the patents would be by selling state rights, as is usually done; it is still a question with me by which way the most money could be made, for Langen has put the refusal of the thing at my disposal for a certain length of time. It is an entirely new thing and I have not the slightest doubt will take well in the US.

If such people as Bennett & Doherty or Sellers & Co or anybody else with a large machine should know of it, they would secure the thing at once, and then either manufacture for the whole US or else sell the separate state rights and secure the right to manufacture for one state. If I were only home now I think I could make the thing go and make something of it.

When the little engine comes, just set it agoing by running a little india rubber pipe to it from any gas burner; set the fire first to the small burner at the bottom and fill the hollow jacket around the cylinder with water; then start the fly wheel by hand and the thing will run.

Another way to make anything by the patent would be to raise a company with capital of say $125,000, which would have $25,000 for extras, and then sell rights to any manufacturer whatever, charging a royalty for every machine that he makes. It strikes me that that would be the simplest and least risky way in which to make money by it.

The trouble with me is that I have no money of my own to do anything in the matter myself —

Yours affect. — W. A. Roebling

SANTA MONICA, CALIFORNIA. SEPTEMBER, 1876.

The sound of her, just behind him. Something about the quality of her movement, the little brush of her hand as it smoothed her skirt — was that what he heard? Surely not, with the surf rising and falling on the sand stretched out ahead, the Pacific rolling all the way out to the bright horizon — and yet it seemed he could hear, her every gesture apparent to his mind's eye as she set the pins tighter in her hair, folded her shawl, unlaced her little button boots. His feet were already bare, his toes digging into the sand. He felt soothed by the sensation of Emily just behind him, tried to let himself be lulled by the ocean's rhythmic roar. Everything he needed, everything he had ever wanted, was right here. That was the truth of it. He must not forget that.

When she came and sat beside him, she was wearing the broad-brimmed straw hat she had acquired when they first arrived in San Francisco. It had become a little ravelled at the edges, golden threads poking out from the brim at odd angles; yet she had grown attached to it, keeping its violet ribbon — tied now neatly under her chin — clean and pressed. She was not sentimental — neither of them were — yet he felt she wore it as, perhaps, he had once worn his campaign cap, a marker to keep his place in the world. Her place in the world. Wide brim and all, it had not prevented the California sunshine from bringing out the freckles across her nose; those dismayed her, he knew — though Wash himself thought them adorable.

In her hand she held a brown glass bottle; she handed it to him to untwist the wire and pull out the cork. He grinned.

— Whatever would they think at the Visitation convent, dearest?

She laughed. The evening sun caught the tendrils of her hair and gilded them. She looked not a day older than when they had met a dozen years ago — except, perhaps, that she looked more *herself*.

— You won't write and tell them, I trust, she said.

— 'My dear Reverend Mother' — he began, striking a recitative pose.

— O, you! she exclaimed, shoving her gingham-clad shoulder against his. Through his shirt he felt the warmth of her, the give of her skin. Do your work, she insisted. Open our bottle.

He had only got as far as the wire, distracted by their banter. Now he drew the cork out with a satisfying pop and sniffed at the brown glass neck, the little gaseous plume that emanated from their treat. Ah! he exclaimed. Brekle's finest. I would know it anywhere, now.

— Thank goodness for all the Germans brewing beer all across the land, she said. I believe you would be quite bereft, otherwise.

— I am never bereft with you at my side, darling Em, he said. I would, however, be thirsty. He put his mouth to the bottle and took a long pull before passing it back to her to drink. He watched her Adam's apple bob as she swallowed, her lovely throat.

— 'I fear to tell you, Reverend Mother, that Miss Warren has fallen so far that she no longer even requires a vessel from which to drink — drink her *lager*, I might add — '

She sputtered, pointed the neck of the bottle at him fiercely. You said you'd stop, Colonel! Now I must command you! I remind you that I am — well, at least the sister of a General.

He leaned in and kissed her, tasting beer. She did not object — rested the bottle in her lap. How fortunate he was for the ease between them, the mutual accommodation that was — he had discovered — possible when two people truly loved each other and wished to fare forward into the world side by side. His poor mother. He had, and Emily had, what she had never known. Well, his father didn't have it either. But Wash imagined such a thought would never have crossed old John Roebling's mind.

— He seems another fellow entirely, that bashful soldier you courted. But then he found something to believe in.

— How inspired you were when you first saw Mr Langen's engine! That was quite a day in Paris, wasn't it? First a balloon-ride — and then such a fateful meeting.

— Sweet one, he said. I was attempting to pay you a compliment. I should not have believed in Mr Langen's engine if I had not first believed in you — well, in truth, if I had not first felt your belief in me.

— O, Wash, she said.

— I will never tire of hearing you say O, *Wash*, I promise you that. He kissed her again. We should find a good dinner to celebrate yesterday's sale, he said.

For sales were good. They rode right up to places, smelling the creosote of new fencing, seeing buildings that had been thrown up fast — but not too fast. You couldn't sell a gas engine to a fly-by-night sod-breaker, and hornswogglers and soaplocks were to be keenly avoided. Washington looked for a certain sturdiness in buildings built in what would soon no longer be a wilderness at all; as an engineer he could understand, by the mere sight of a construction, what ambition, what vision, the owner possessed. He was rarely wrong. They made three of these trips a year now, criss-crossing the country; Emily would not hear of his travelling alone and she was more than an indomitable companion — their customers were charmed by a woman who could speak of the percentages of coal gas and the horsepower of a piston. O, if a woman can do it, they see how simple it must be! she had said to Wash, laughing, as their journeys began. In the evenings — in boarding houses and small hotels — they kept the accounting of their sales, sending receipts, orders, bank drafts back to Phineas Swan — Charles' industrious nephew — back in Trenton. Washington had ordered a special case for forms, leaflets, stationery: it was battered from use now, but still sturdy enough. Emily's fingers were permanently stained with ink. W. A. *Roebling, Gas Engine & Power Supply Co.* each bill was headed, the typeface both flourishing and direct. When work was finished, they both composed notes for little John and baby Elvira; Washington drew in the margins of these notes, telegraph poles, cactuses, the vistas of the Rocky Mountains.

— Do you suppose there is a good dinner here? Emily asked.

— Colonel Baker assures me there is, Wash said. At Rancho Banderas. A walk from our boarding house.

— Where our wagon is safely kept?

— So too I am assured. Of its safety, I mean.

— You have made me an adventuress, she said. She took his hand and held it. I should never have expected this life.

— I have not made you anything, Wash said. I could not do so if I tried. You were not content to be left back east, Miss Warren, if you recall.

— No, she said. I could not have borne it. And yet —

She did not have to finish her sentence. A wave crashed against the shore, greater than the eight or ten that had preceded it; there was no ship in the distance, nothing but shining ocean stretching out towards the horizon and either side up and down the coast, north and south as far as the eye could see. What power was here, in the depths, what mystery; far greater than his engine, the power of the Earth itself. Another wave broke, lesser than the last. Recession, ascension. Now that he had left off bridge-building, the world seemed more visible to him. He could not explain it, but it was true.

— I know how you miss them, he said.

— As do you, I know.

— Another two weeks, he said. And then we'll be back in Trenton for the winter. Mr Kingsley will wish to hear how his investment fares.

— We have written to him, Emily said. I have, that is.

— You know how he likes the personal touch, Wash said. And he has always been particularly charmed by Emily Warren Roebling.

He pulled her close again, kissed her again, his lips touching her forehead, salty with her sweat and with the Pacific breeze. It pulled her hair beneath the brim of her hat and curling chestnut tendrils brushed against her neck and ears.

— Do you think your father will ever invest? His recalcitrance is — surprising.

— Yes, it is, Washington said evenly. He changes the subject when I raise it, or ignores it altogether, when I write. Perhaps he will alter his thinking when he hears of the work Daimler is doing, and this new fellow Benz; my father may call himself an American, but as far as business goes, the more Dutchmen pile in, the better! He is, in any case, wealthy enough.

— What is it? Emily asked. She was like — a wind-harp, that was the image he wanted, so sensitive to his moods that she sometimes saw the shift in him before he himself perceived it. Is there news from Brooklyn?

— None from Brooklyn, he said, nor likely there will be. He spoke more sharply than he had meant. Emily listened quietly, her palms wrapped around the bottle of beer as if it were a precious object. My father sends me a note from Pennsylvania. Oil City, the place is called — at least that shows us we're in the right business, though it's hardly poetic. Little brother Charles is getting on well. There will be another suspension bridge over the Allegheny River ere long. Charles's vigor is as relentless as that of his sire.

— He is well?

— My father?

Emily said nothing. He knew that was what she had meant, in any case.

— He is always well. Always ill and always well. Always regaling me with some digestive complaint to be cured by the imbibing of coal tar and the application of a freezing stream of water with a fire hose. Always inquiring about my bowels. Yours too, for that matter! He will not say in so many words, but he is proud of Charles and his work; trusts him to take over the mill too. He tells me that business thrives, wire is in high demand as these telegraph poles make their march across the nation — you know my father. Failure is never his favourite topic. Phineas Swan tells me Adams may take over the Brooklyn work, if it is ever to be revived.

— I thought Julius Adams was a railroad engineer.

— Miss Emily Warren, is there nothing they did not ask you to study at the Convent of the Visitation?

— You don't answer my question.

— An accomplished railroad engineer, yes. But more's the point: an accomplished politician. They need a man to restore confidence in the project, and Adams just might be the man for the job. I believe father thinks the collapsed caisson could be restored, but I am fairly certain that's a hopeless case. A new foundation would need to be dug upriver or down — an immense task. My father is too old for such work now, at any rate.

In speaking these words Wash kept his own expression as neutral as he could. He closed his eyes, briefly, and tugged at a tuft of dune grass. Was it desolate here, in this place, or hopeful? Scoured empty or ready to be filled? Both could be true at once, of course.

Emily dug the beer bottle a little into the sand and set her small palm over the back of his hand. For a little while they did not speak but let the afternoon turn itself toward evening, slowly, slowly.

— I like California, she said at last.

— You are changing the subject.

— I opened the subject, she said. I believe that gives me the prerogative to change it.

— What is it you like so much?

— So much seems possible, she said. I don't know quite what I mean. But I know I believe it. And we are far from — all that.

— Yes, he said. It does. Seem possible. And we are. Far from *all that.*

— Perhaps there is no need to go back to Trenton for the winter. The children could stay here with us. We could — we could buy a plot of land. Begin again. Truly.

The sun was sinking now, its warm western rays sprawling out red and gold, showering the ocean's surface with the last brilliance of the day.

— O my America, he said. My new-found-land.

It was good to speak these ancient lines into the bold air, his wife's sweet body at his side.

— Do you know why they call it Santa Monica?

She shook her head. I have never thought to enquire.

— Well now — I'm not sure what the Reverend Mother would think of that omission, he said, but we'll let it pass for the present, I think.

— You will consent to enlighten me? That tilt of her chin he loved so much.

— There are springs here, he said. Fresh clear water. I have refrained from telling Father, fearing he would cross the continent to visit them, but that's another matter — in any case, the people who lived here, they thought them holy. Then the Spanish came. We know the rest, eh? But there was a priest, one of the Spaniards, who thought the spring waters were like the tears of Santa Monica as she wept for her son, the prodigal Augustine.

She furrowed her brow. I thought Augustine was a great father of the church, she said.

— More demerits from the Reverend Mother, I see. Yes, dear

Em, he was, but not at first. I gather there was some sowing of wild oats before he saw the light. So there we are: Santa Monica, named, if you like, thanks to tears shed for an undutiful son.

She turned her head to look at him then, so her brown eyes met his directly.

— Is that what you believe?

— What do you mean? Believe what?

— Believe that you are an undutiful son.

The words, spoken just like that, struck him like a blow. He knew she would have had no such intent; only that she had a plainness about her sometimes — a plainness he welcomed — which meant that she understood when it was no longer possible to turn one's back on the matter in hand. It had been more than five years since fire had ruined the Brooklyn caisson and thereby ruined hopes for a bridge across the East River, at least one built by John A. Roebling. A workman's candle — one moment's inattention — for want of a nail, as the old saw went.

— A man must make his own life, he said. You said it yourself. That when I saw Langen's work, I knew. I understood.

— Yes, she said. You did. As did I. Together, we both did. So there need be no tears for Augustine, Augustus. And there will be a bridge someday. What needs to be made is always made, in the end.

They sat again, quietly, alone on this stretch of beach. The afternoon's warmth was in retreat, but still the air held a welcoming softness.

— Shall we dip our toes in before the sun sinks away?

— O yes, she said. A swim. By all means.

She drew off her hat and shrugged off the shawl from her shoulders, tucked it down carefully among the rough grass. Her calico dress she unbuttoned so she wore only her white shift; there was no one here to see, no one for whom modesty must be preserved, and they were husband and wife. Washington unfastened his collar, removed it; undid his own buttons and pulled his loose shirt over his head, the cooling air against his skin. He stepped out of his trousers, folded them — the sturdy wool was muddy at the hems from days of visiting the local farms and they must be laundered soon — and set them atop Emily's dress and shawl.

They held hands, walking down the dunes and then along the sand, which was soft at first, turning their ankles, their toes grasping for purchase; as they neared the ocean it grew firmer, colder, coiled with the casts of lugworms, with the shells of razor clams and scallops. Their steps were perfectly matched as the sea began to lap against their feet; the water was warm and inviting and their strides lengthened as they moved deeper, to ankle, to knee, to thigh. Emily stumbled as a wave struck her belly and Washington reached for her, held her, and then pulled her right into the water, their laughter rising to meet the cries of the gulls and oystercatchers that wheeled in the wind, swooping, hovering in lift and drag. Washington and Emily swam into the darker, colder green, keeping their eyes on the shore but feeling the pull of vast distance and depth.

He swam up to her, kissed her as she bobbed up and down, white cotton floating away from her shoulders and breasts. The ocean's salt on her sweet lips. A hangnail moon had lifted into the violet sky, the evening star alongside.

— I'm hungry, she said. I hope you're right about that dinner, Colonel Roebling. She rested her wet palm on his wet cheek, pulled a thread of seaweed from his beard.

— Climb aboard, he said. I'll float you home, sweet Em.

She paddled up behind him, twined her arms around his neck, settled her form against him. He moved through the warm deep ocean water, lifting his shoulders, straining only a little with the new weight of Emily on his back; as he did, salt spray splashed up, made him blink, his eyes tear. His face to the shore he wiped the back of his hand across his brow, and as he did so he opened his eyes again and saw that if they had stayed on the sand they would not have been alone — for there was a dark-haired figure, hands in pockets, walking along the beach. A tall, broad man with an open, eager stride. For just a moment, less than a moment, he felt himself flounder, felt a quick tightening of Emily's arm around his neck, her cheek pressed to his.

He blinked again. He had been mistaken. The beach was quite empty, and he and Emily were alone.

Yet there were lights along the shore now, just a few, from the scattered dwellings there, the glimmer of welcome. Santa Monica, the drop-off edge, the beginning and the end. He had got as far away as he possibly could. He had done it. He kicked his legs against the pull of the tide and swam.

AFTERWORD

I WAS SIXTEEN years old when I first walked across the Brooklyn Bridge on a bright, cold December day. I had found *my place* — and I had found too *my person*, a man who died decades before I was born but who spoke clearly to me, a man whose life I knew I understood and could inhabit.

At first, the task seemed — if not simple, then straightforward. No one had written his biography and so I set out, finally, to do so: in 2017 *Chief Engineer: Washington Roebling, The Man Who Built the Brooklyn Bridge* was published.

Decades between that first encounter and my biography. Why so long? The answer, at least in part, is in your hands now. Washington Roebling was not the subject of my interest: he was my second self. As a young woman, looking at images of his handsome face, listening to the wry, laconic and brilliant voice I encountered in letters, in documents, in the public record, I thought I was in love with him. Plenty of folks eventually pointed me in the direction of the Tumblr site, 'My Daguerreotype Boyfriend', 'where early photography meets extreme hotness'.

But that wasn't quite it.

A shudder in the archive. Time opens, closes, is not lived chronologically. So much written in pencil, so much that could have been erased, so many openings for alternate interpretations. Yes, I strove to make *Chief Engineer* as accurate as I possibly could, tracking its protagonist's movements from his boyhood, schooling, service in the Civil War, his marriage to the remarkable Emily Warren, his work on the Brooklyn Bridge and the afterlife that followed — and yet I was always aware of the impossibility of biography.

To believe that a person may be known — truly known — from what is left in written words, in grey cardboard boxes, on microfilm, is plain foolishness, though an edifice of publishing and historical discourse rests on this assumption. I cannot dismiss the endeavour — and yet. We are breath and blood and the tracks we leave are fossils only. If you have ever written a letter (email, text, whatever) and changed your mind later about what you said — and that is every single one of us — you'll know what I mean.

This is before we come to those whose lives are absent from archives entirely. That is most of us.

In *Wash*, my fictional Emily Roebling finds herself reading Flaubert's *Madame Bovary* — as true an account of a life as was ever created. If you abjure "he must have thought" and "she might have wondered" in writing what is called non-fiction (as I believe you should) then it is in the novel or the story that emotion finds its only form.

I have lived with Wash Roebling for forty years and thought about his life, felt it. In fiction the reader scents the battlefield: gunpowder, blood, shit, spring breeze. In fiction the reader experiences the compressed air of a caisson deep below the bed of East River, the heat of a deadly and mysterious fire burning without flame in that strange atmosphere, feels her own throat constrict. In fiction the complex love between husband and wife, or between two friends who hardly know themselves, never mind each other, can be explored so that it resonates in the reader's heart.

Here, in *Wash*, is Washington's truth, told in a sequence of narratives that move forward and back in time, a structure reflective of the way in which — I believe — narrative order is itself a fiction. The soul's time is not the clock's time. Pushing against the whole narrative is the pressure of the choices that could have been made, the life that could have been lived. For Wash, for

Emily, for Max — as I have called him, for no one knows this young man's name, though he did indeed exist — and for those whose lives they touched.

✣ ✣ ✣ ✣ ✣

ACKNOWLEDGEMENTS

EVERY BOOK IS a labour of love. Some feel more so than others: like obsessions, perhaps. This is one of those.

Paddy Crewe first understood what I wanted to do with Wash's life; he saw there was another book hiding inside *Chief Engineer*. He provided support, encouragement, comradeship and sangaree. As in turn did Ruth Newton-Crewe, and I'm sure Ted Newton-Crewe will in his time.

Robin Weigert knows what a debt I owe her for her belief in this work — and her imagination saw an ending I might well have missed. I am lucky enough to be part of a writers' group she hosts with immense skill and sensitivity: as I wrote, I shared chapters of this novel with our crew, that ranges from Los Angeles to London, from New York to Rome: I hope you all know that I couldn't have done it without you, and you know who you are. Joe Spano, Jim Beaver, Garrett Dillahunt, Billy Crudup, Zachary Quinto: you read my work aloud in the most extraordinary way, and your interpretations were vital to my craft.

Francis Gilbert and Theo Wagner, my beloved family. You always knew I could do this: you always knew who I was. I love you.

'Delaware & Raritan' appeared in Blackbird: an online journal of literature and the arts published by Virginia Commonwealth University: thanks to Katherine Mooney Brooks, Lead Associate Editor.

Jenifer Monger at RPI has been a dear and stalwart friend and companion in the archives for a long time now; and thanks to RPI for my cover. Lindsey Hobbs and Kenneth Cobb at the New York City Municipal Archives, thank you too for images.

And finally — in memory of Don Sayenga, who called me Betty, and who always understood. You are much missed, Al.

This book has been typeset by
SALT PUBLISHING LIMITED
using Neacademia, a font designed by Sergei Egorov for the Rosetta Type Foundry in Czechia. It has been manufactured using Holmen Book Cream 65gsm paper, and printed and bound by Clays Limited in Bungay, Suffolk, Great Britain.

CROMER
GREAT BRITAIN
MMXXVI